Road
To a
Shootout

by

Chuck Fair

Literary works:
Novels:
We Are Guerillas
Toil & Time
Time's Collage
Words & Wraps
This Bridge Tells No Tales Road
to a Shootout
Detective from a Golden Age
Right Into Wrong
My Mother Was A Mountain
Being What I'm Not
Atotarho and the French
Bonjour Men of France
Messieurs et Mesdames Permit Me
the Honor to Introduce Myself
Adieu Men of France
A Freedom Fighter in a time
of Misadventure The
Percolators
Deviants Dance
Damnation Days of the Duck Doctrine
<u>Novellas</u>: *A Town of Plenty*
<u>Screenplays</u>:
Retribution,
Steven Sockeye Salmon

2

Contact the author at cfairbooks@gmail.com

Online editions are also available for this title.
For more information, please visit

www.amazon.com/authors/chuckfair

Printed in the United States of America

Road to a Shootout

"John Henry Summerfield!"

"Who are you?" Not used to having a visitor knock at his door, the lone occupant of the hotel room wondered who in the hell was this old woman looking like death warmed over, sitting in a wheelchair and brandishing a cane.

"I'm the wife you deserted, you lousy bastard!"

"Benevolence?"

"You're goddamned right. it is me. I'm that beautiful young bride you took to those godforsaken plains and deserted to a cold-ass wind howling up my skirt and half-naked savages stealing my chickens. My mother said I'd turn out poorly if I took up with you, and she was right. Look at me and look at you."

He thought *she could have torn off my boots with her teeth, if she had any, before I would have known her.* The beautiful girl he married long ago sat in a wheelchair before him, old, gray, and wizen. The sweet-talking young thing he worshiped so long ago in western Virginia possessed a mouth as foul as a two-bit whore.

"What happened to you?"

"Life happened to me. You would know if you stayed put instead of lying low like a devious rodent in this flophouse." She referred to his disappearance for the last twenty years. He wondered how in the hell she knew what he had been doing and where he hid out. Had she been keeping tabs on him?

A coughing fit seized the frail woman. She needed some water, but all he kept in the room was a half-empty beer. He waited for what seemed an eternity until her coughing subsided.

Benevolence took a four-inch smoky-glassed bottle from t and drank a mouthful of the contents. Laudanum, he guessed.

"What are you doing here, and how did you find me?"

"Smoker brought me here. I sold my house to pay a Pinkerton agent to find you."

The last thing Summerfield needed was a Pinkerton agent to know his whereabouts. "Where is Smoker?"

"Hiding in the hallway."

"Tell him to show his face."

"He's afraid."

He stepped past Benevolence and received a jab in his ribs from her cane. "Get in here, Smoker." John Henry knew Smoker, christened George Grimes, since the man worked for him on a scrubby Kansas farm, 160 acres of windblown prairie supporting a sod house. Homesteading the farm took place before Summerfield joined the North for the war against the South. Back then, Smoker, when a strapping boy, could barely say his name, shy as he was. He earned the name "Smoker" not because he smoked cigars like Benevolence, but because he earned extra money smoking hog parts. Epilepsy plagued Smoker, and Summerfield figured that was why he hung around Benevolence most of his life. She, not appalled by his madman fits—"storms in the head," as she called them—cared for him during his seizures. Now Summerfield saw arthritis bent Smoker's wiry frame, but that crooked, winning smile was still there. Dressed in an eastern-dandy suit, tie, and hat, Smoker stood in the doorway, building up his nerve to enter the room. "You bring her here?"

"She forced me to bring her here, John. You know how persuasive she can be."

John Henry turned his attention to his ex-wife, not knowing what to do with her. During his time in the war with the rebels, she took up with another man and moved his girl baby from Kansas to Minnesota while he was starving in a Richmond, Virginia, rebel prison. In all fairness to Benevolence, she thought him killed in the disastrous battle at Manassas when the Yankees turned tail—three thousand bluecoats died, and almost eighteen hundred gray jackets fell. Newspapers called it "Bull Run," but he knew it as the battle at the Manassas rail line, the one the army called the first. The second battle would come later. The hellish fight saw him separated from his unit, ending up in a rebel hellhole, a large tobacco warehouse named Liggot & Company, for two years. During a rare prisoner exchange—officers, not enlisted men—he escaped. His time of enlistment over, he did not reenlist, having no stomach to fight a war where one more dead body—his—did not influence the outcome. Having experienced enough of the Union Army, wherein a man's life owned no more value than a wheat stalk cut down in the field, he returned to Kansas and his wife. The Presbyterian minister at Wichita told him his wife thought him dead, remarried, and left for Minnesota with her new husband. Feeling betrayed after learning she remarried and carried another man's child, he did not follow Benevolence. A year later, he heard Dakota Sioux killed her husband after he opened a trading post along the Minnesota River.

Starving Sioux warriors massacred thirty-eight men in Mankato, Minnesota for denying them proper food rations. After the savages slaughtered her husband, they came upon Benevolence, who tended to Smoker during one of his epileptic fits. The sight of a grown man writhing on the floor, frothing at the mouth in a mad fit, spooked the savages. Benevolence, throwing Smoker over a wagon horse, gathered her two girls—his three-year-old daughter, Jane, and her new baby, Clara, by the man that took his place—out of the fruit cellar and escaped before the Sioux gathered their senses. He never looked her up. Instead, he took a civilian job working for the army in Kansas.

"After me, how many times have you been married Benevolence?"

"Four times, John," Smoker answered for Benevolence.

"No one asked you, you bent-over rat." She directed her attention to her ex-husband. "None of your goddamned business."

"Every one of them, except you, dead as a doorknob," the once shy Smoker said, building up the courage after realizing John Henry would not pistol-whip him.

As frail as she was, Benevolence put a nasty whack on Smoker with her cane. "You say another goddamned word, Smoker, and I will ram this cane so far up your ass you'll have to guzzle the rotgut you swill when you think I'm not looking through the top of your head."

"What are you doing here?" John Henry asked for the second time.

The fire left his ex-wife's eyes, and her frail body, no more than seventy-five pounds, sagged in the wheelchair. Even though it must have been eighty degrees in the room, she pulled her shawl tight around her shoulders. Her voice began to crack. "Our daughter, Jane, and my second daughter, Clara, and Clara's two small girls have been stolen by a gang of murderers. A bloodthirsty killer shot Clara's husband dead in his tracks after forcing Claude into a shootout while his wife and children looked on. After the murderers stripped the house clean of cash and what valuables there be had, they left Clara's mother-in-law, ol' Granny, to roast alive as the robbers burned Clara's house to the ground with Granny in it. They trampled crops and shot the livestock. a gang of lowlife criminals hog-tied and carried off our Jane, my Clara, and Clara's kids.

He only saw his daughter, Jane, once since he returned to Kansas from the war. At that time, she was about eight years old and coming out of a church in Wichita with her mom, half-sister, and her mom's husband—what number of husbands, he did not know. Working as a scout for the U.S. Army, passing through town, he used his responsibility to the army as an excuse not to interfere in their lives.

"You find my girls and grand girls if they are still alive, and bring them back. Shoot down the mangy bastards who stole them and murdered everyone in sight like you did those seven rebel cow drivers in Fort Hays City. Don't spare any of those lowlife dogs; blow every goddamn one of them apart until their guts pour out." Another coughing fit took hold of Benevolence. He gave her the warm beer to drink, but she brushed it away. "I want you to shoot them down one by one, and while their guts spill on the street.

7

They you declare over those dead, mangy dogs: Benevolence Summerfield sends her regards." The ex-husband noted she still used his surname even after being married to four other men.

"Jesus, Benevolence—I haven't handled a pistol in five years." He told the truth, having not done any pistol shooting since leaving Canada.

"John Henry, do you remember what you promised me that first night in our wedding bed? You on top of me and your head full of hot intent, pawing me like some pussy-hungry polecat?"

"Jesus, Benevolence!" Feeling his face flush, John Henry turned and gazed out the window.

"You said you would grant me one wish, no matter what it was. Did I collect on that wish?"

"No."

"I am collecting now, John Henry. Give me that Bible, Smoker. Swear on this good book ."

Preferring to stick his hand into a fire rather than on the 'good Book, John Henry put his hand on the Bible and repeated her words: "I, John Henry Summerfield, swear I will avenge Benevolence Summerfield, or else I deserve to burn in hell."

Benevolence paused and stared at him; the rage in her eyes became banshees escaping hell. "That's not strong enough. Repeat after me: *Or else I deserve to burn in hell until my skin blackens and my bones become brittle and crumble to dust.*"

"Jesus, Benevolence!" He repeated her words.

Another coughing fit seized her. She managed to get the laudanum from her skirt and quaff half of it. The whiskey and opium put her to sleep within minutes. John Henry sank into a chair, overwhelmed by what he promised the dying woman. He wanted to ignore Benevolence's demand, but he couldn't ignore the fact that he deserted her to hard farm life on the Kansas plains to fight a war. leaving only Smoker to defend her—not because he wanted to free slaves or destroy the wealthy plantation owners who worked black men to death, but because farm life bored him, and he sought adventure. For that reason, he felt he owed his ex-wife.

He truly loved her and never took up with another woman, whores excluded.

"She have a place to stay?" he asked the bent man who once worked for him.

"She paid for three months at some hospital-like rooming house near a train station called San Gabriel, not far from here. But I am afraid she can't make it that long, John."

"You stay with her until her time comes, Smoker. Sit on that cot and fill me in on the last twenty years."

Smoker gave the ex-gunslinger an accounting of Benevolence's life during the last twenty years and how she kept tabs on John Henry up through the time of the shootout at Fort Hayes City until his disappearance into thin air. "

Will you be coming after me for bringing her here, John? If'n you do, I won't be hard to find. My smoking hog parts business is doing pretty good. I now supply half the restaurants in Santa Fe."

"Reckon, you are pretty far down on my list, Smoker."

Smoker, given a reprieve, evaluated the shabby hotel room. "I got money now, John if you be needing any."

John Henry ignored his ex-farmhand. "Take her to her care home, Smoker, and you stay with her until she dies. Now get her out of here and leave me alone."

*

"The die has been cast," he said to himself. John Henry didn't put much store in religion, but he would not risk going against his word sworn on the Bible as he just did. He took his leather grip from the closet and stared at the Colt Navy revolver that stayed unused for years. His suit jacket hid the Sharps derringer, a four-barrel .32-caliber pistol he risked carrying when law enforcement forbade gun carrying. It was 1885, after all, and even in a sleepy town like Los Angeles, danger reared its ugly head everywhere.

He threw his shirts, an extra set of denims, and one set of clean socks and underwear on top of the pistol and closed the grip.

He paid the rent to the end of the month, so there was no need to notify anyone of his sudden departure.

Not wanting it to go to waste, he drank the remainder of the beer. Living on short wages taught him not to be wasteful. He didn't have much to show for a lifetime—a few books he studied, teaching himself to read better, pictures of Abraham Lincoln and Ulysses S. Grant, a tin coffee cup, a few chipped plates, and a used ice chest to cool his beer.

Collecting the bicycle leaning against the wall, he put on his derby and descended from the third floor to the street. He took one last look at the sun-scorched tenement house located at Fifth Street and Broadway in Los Angeles, about as far as he could get from bloody Kansas. The tenement house served as his home for the last five years. He kept his life simple, avoiding bars and fights that always broke out in such places. He enjoyed going to the burlesque theater on the weekend and playing mah-jongg in the Chinese section of town once a week after work. He played there because the docile Chinese were less likely to shoot it out over a game. He wore drab secondhand clothing so few would focus their attention on him.

John Henry rode his bicycle over hot, dusty, pedestrian-packed streets to the train depot where he worked twelve hours a day tossing bums off freight cars before he sealed the doors. The Southern Pacific Railway paid him lowlife wages, but until now, it was all he needed. Ever since the shootout on the streets of Fort Hays City, Kansas, where he saw the ring and pinky fingers of his right hand shot off, he ran from revenge seekers. He felt obliged to notify his boss at the railroad yard, an old, tough-as-nails Irishman, that he would not be working today or any day after that.

John Henry spotted a ragamuffin selling newspapers for a penny a copy outside the train station. The kid's scuffed clodhoppers were run down at the heels, and his pants patched. His shirt, too big for him, was a hand-me-down. The kid reminded him of his youth in the western part of Virginia, hustling the streets, shining shoes for a penny, poor as a church mouse's offspring. He gave the kid his bicycle, a new one he'd purchased last year for twenty dollars, plus his lock and chain. The Atchison, Topeka, Santa Fe Railway, and the Southern Pacific Railroad turned around their trains at the depot. After buying a ticket, he waited for the next train connecting to the Mormon haunt known as Salt Lake City.

Around 1861, Samuel Colt manufactured the outdated Navy Colt revolver he carried in his grip; the out-of-date pistol was difficult and slow to reload. He figured a new Colt .45, a smaller and more streamlined one a shooter loaded with cartridges instead of powder, cotton wad, and lead balls. The weapon would cost him $50, a holster $10, a new Remington rifle about $30, and a decent horse and saddle somewhere in a neighborhood of $150; added to this sum would be $40 for a mule. He owned only $32.50 in his pocket. While pedaling his bicycle to the train station, he devised a sketchy plan to raise six hundred dollars. Smoker offered him a loan, but it's hard for a man to take money from a fieldhand who once worked for him. He figured little chance existed to outlive the insane pursuit he swore on the Bible to undertake, so the hermit-like, safe lifestyle he observed in Los Angeles, he planned to throw to the wind.

*

The tall man stood a shade over six feet. He carried his 175 pounds on an angular, lean frame; every frontiersman, rancher, and farmer he saw carried a lean, hard body; he thought them to be a product of their time. At one time, John Henry, with his luminous eyes and well-proportioned face, could have been described as good-looking, but events of past decades—namely, years spent running from death turned him into a hard-looking man, his chiseled face lined and weatherworn. Mustaches were much in fashion, but John Henry remained clean-shaven. Short, cropped brown hair covered his head, and he gazed at the world through hazel eyes set in slanted sockets. He derived from English/Scottish stock with centuries of bloodletting in his genes. He never dressed in a flashy manner or carried a fancy pistol, because that would draw attention, especially in the last ten years, when he avoided attention. Los Angeles seemed tame compared to the volatile plains he left in 1875, where ex-rebel and Yankee soldiers searching for a livelihood lived by the gun; they shot each other at the drop of a hat, usually when liquored up. Rarely did the shooters stand face-to-face; ambush, and backshooting being the common practice.

His world of 1875 claim saw claim jumpers killing prospectors outside of mining towns, cattle rustlers cutting out small herds on the trails from Texas, swindlers cheating laborers out of their paychecks in railroad camps, gamblers fleecing cowboys in saloons, possies hunting down evildoers and hanging them on the spot. Gangs robbed stagecoaches, trains, and anyone unlucky enough to cross their paths. Vigilantes hung cattle rustlers and horse thieves from the nearest tree or telegraph pole.

Criminals fortunate to live long enough to go to trial were locked away in tubercular jails and, if not pulled out into the street and lynched, they died a lingering death. Jail could be a dangerous place for those foul of the law. Adding to the region's instability, corrupt government officials pawned off blankets diseased by smallpox and delivered underfed cattle in business dealings with savages, setting them on the warpath slaughtering settlers.

Until John Henry sat on the train's hard bench and watched Los Angeles disappear through the window, he didn't realize how much Benevolence's terminal illness spooked him. She was the central part of his beginning, and her mortality reminded him of his own. They were both born in 1839, reaching forty-six years of age in 1885. They grew up on the Ohio River, downriver from Pittsburgh. Benevolence's dad worked as a clerk for an iron foundry; her mother cooked for the town saloon. John Henry's dad barely survived as an off-and-on-again carpenter and handyman; his mother worked in the hospital laundry. He and Benevolence met during a Saturday church-sponsored dance. She finished ten years of schooling, which he thought exceptional for a girl of that time; he only finished eight years of schooling before taking a job unloading freight at the train depot, earning thirty cents for twelve hours' work. Wanting more out of life than to be a laborer, or at best, an iron foundry worker or coal miner, John Henry responded after the federal government enacted the Kansas– Nebraska Act and gave away plots of 160 acres to anyone willing to settle there. The stakes of resettlement were high for the country: If more Northern families than Southern ones settled in Kansas, the territory would become a free state; if a larger number of Southerners settled the territory, Kansas would become a slave state. The Drew Scott ruling was observed after the Missouri Compromise and split the North and South into anti-slavery and pro-slavery states.

With bells ringing, he and Benevolence married outside the altar at her Catholic church because he was a Protestant. They spent their savings on steamboat passage to St. Louis. A plow horse pulled a secondhand wagon for which they paid an extravagant price in one of the river towns along the Missouri river, making a fortune off of gullible settlers. A milk cow trailed behind them as they followed the settlers' trail west. Greenhorns that they were, they carried no more than twenty dollars and a smoothbore musket and settled on a desolate plain in Kansas in 1859.

The train John Henry boarded in Los Angeles pulled into Sacramento, the state capital, and he transferred to one leaving for Salt Lake City. He bought a beef sandwich from a street vendor and a pint of whiskey at a nearby general store to handle the long trip to the Mormon town.

Smoker gave him an accounting of Benevolence's life during the last twenty years. The ex-husband found no comfort in her inability to choose a proper husband. He felt he became the first improper one. A gambler shot her third husband, a traveling salesman, over a disputed five-card stud hand. Her fifth husband—the most stable of all, who promised to take her back to her home in newborn West Virginia—worked as a freight driver out of Las Vegas, New Mexico. A wagon overturned on him, crushing him to death. Benevolence ended up living near the trading post town situated on the Santa Fe Trail. From what Smoker related, John Henry's daughter, Jane, Benevolence's second daughter, Clara and Clara's husband, Claude, and Benevolence's grandchildren lived on a respectable ranch outside of Las Vegas with Claude's mother; they farmed a few acres and grazed ten cattle, before outlaws murdered Clara's husband and mother-in-law. John Henry realized he would do the abducted women and children no good if he rushed after them unprepared. Therefore, he planned to take a roundabout road to Las Vegas.

*

The enterprising Mormons, children of Joseph Smith and wards of Brigham Young, built a railroad spur they called the Utah Central; it ran from Promontory Point to Salt Lake City. There, John Henry made his final transfer south to the Mormon capital, though he did not intend to stay long. He knew enough about the God-fearing, hardworking Mormons who turned a godforsaken patch of salt flats into a town to be admired and possessed no desire to linger in the stern town of milk and honey.

In the distance, majestic mountains displaying white peaks rimmed the desolate alkali flats. Disembarking the train, John Henry saw the Mormons were putting up new buildings everywhere. One particular unfinished building, a colossal structure with six half-built spires stabbing the heavens, destined to be the Mormons' temple, rose to four stories. No saloons or houses of ill repute existed in the straitlaced town; no trash blew about the streets.

John Henry walked over wood-plank sidewalks beside wide, well-maintained streets to the Wells Fargo Overland Stage depot wedged between a mercantile store and a blacksmith's shop. The railroad held sway in the untamed land, but the stage line still serviced small towns along the Mormon and Overland Trails. The Union Pacific train took all night to reach Salt Lake City, and he arrived at an early morning hour with enough time to buy breakfast across the street from the Wells Fargo depot, though coffee, being shunned by Mormons, was unavailable. A pretty young woman half his age served him a platter filled with eggs, potatoes, and ham. Blonde hair adorned her porcelain complexion, the purest complexion he ever saw. Her crystal blue eyes seemed to have no depth. He imagined Mormons plucked her off London streets and brought back to health by these far-reaching proselytizers. She

14

reminded him of how young and fresh a flower Benevolence appeared at her age. Regardless of Benevolence and where the girl hailed from, she stirred something in him, a desire denied him since Kansas, telling him he still possessed woman feelings.

John Henry planned to make it east into Wyoming, where he knew small horse ranches existed. And then on to the nearest town, Green River or Rock Springs, where he could replace his obsolete Navy Colt with the latest pistol. Whatever game one played, be it the newly fashionable baseball or the revenge game, a man needed the best equipment to compete with the best. But to buy the best equipment he needed obtain more money than what jingled in his pockets.

John Henry sat on a bench outside the restaurant, occasionally lifting his derby hat to pay respects to strolling women; he observed the six-horse team being hitched to the Wells Fargo stagecoach by the driver and his sidekick, a Negro guard carrying a shotgun. The six horses looked like Canadian Big Browns, bred to pull a load. He walked across the smooth dirt street already watered down by the town's maintenance men and into the Wells Fargo office. Inside he made a pretense of studying the fares to eastward towns, careful that the stagecoach driver saw a defeated look on his face. When the strongbox and the passengers' luggage, including a cowboy's saddle, were loaded atop the stagecoach and the three passengers boarded, he approached the driver, a short, wiry man with a crooked nose and grizzled beard under a sizeable western hat. He carried an older Smith & Wesson .44-caliber revolver on his right hip. John Henry asked, "How much would it cost to ride atop the stagecoach?"—implying he lacked the money to purchase a ticket.

"Best you prepare yourself for a long walk unless you buy a ticket inside 'cause the company don't give discounts."

"I have a five-dollar silver coin I'm prepared to offer for your spending."

The driver removed his wide-brimmed hat, wiped his forehead with his sleeve, spat tobacco juice into the dirt, and swatted at the flies buzzing the horses. His red-rimmed eyes studied John Henry, a derby-wearing man with two fingers blown off his right hand, dressed in a frayed suit jacket and tattered denims and not carrying a weapon. "That small amount of money will buy you a flophouse room for a night or two, but not a stagecoach ride east."

"Name your price, up to ten dollars."

"If you got ten dollars, I'll take it."

"Make it eight dollars, and you have a rider on top."

"Won't get you farther than the other side of the mountain pass."

"I'm thinking it should get me as far as Rock Springs."

The stage driver wiped his forehead again, checked the stagecoach doors were closed tight, spat in the dirt, and climbed atop the stagecoach. He cast a wary glance at John Henry. "You're a hard-dealing man. Meet me on the far side of town where the road takes a bend. I'll slow the horses to a walk so you can climb onto the boot."

Not wanting to draw attention, John Henry half walked and half trotted eastward to the edge of town. From the time he rousted transients off freight cars in the Los Angeles rail yard, he knew that the eastbound road leaving Salt Lake City presented a steep climb, thus the need for six sturdy horses. He chose this route and this particular stagecoach line to pick up the six hundred dollars he needed to fulfill his promise to Benevolence.

Another reason this particular stagecoach appealed to him came from his sense that the Mormons, being God-fearing business people were not inclined to lose one plug nickel and were not the material for a posse. and they likely would not pursue him after he relieved the strongbox of six hundred dollars. They would leave pursuit up to a Pinkerton agent, and he knew no Pinkerton agent operated in Salt Lake City. The agent would have to depart from Denver, or better yet Chicago, giving him time to escape south to New Mexico Territory. True to his word, the stagecoach driver slowed the horses east of town, allowing John Henry to jump on the boot with his grip tied to his back. He climbed atop the stagecoach and sat behind the driver, tapping him on the shoulder to make his presence known. The shotgun-carrying guard, a large and by his manner a congenial Negro, smiled at John Henry, acknowledging his presence. John Henry sized up the armed guard, most likely a freed slave Joseph Smith's brethren brought west and given a helping hand. He gave the driver eight dollars in coins and then observed the man give three dollars to the Negro guard. Slaves won their freedom, yet, according to the stagecoach driver, they failed to win equality.

The stagecoach began its long, slow climb out of the alkali flats on a seemingly endless switchback road. John Henry sat on his grip to ease the stagecoach's constant jarring over the rough road. A hot day prevailed, causing him to sweat inside his suit jacket. Yet he did not remove the jacket because the Sharps derringer was holstered in his right breast pocket. Fifteen years ago, when he was up to his ears in adventure, he designed and ordered a special suede lining, stiffened by leather strips stitched into the breast pocket so the derringer could slip smoothly from his jacket. He taught himself to draw the derringer left-handed with quickness. Marksmanship with the derringer did not matter as much as it did with a Navy Colt, because in explosive situations when he stood within a few feet of his target, the Navy Colt's usage was hindered and the derringer's muzzle could almost touch whoever threatened him. Hard for him to miss at that range.

The hot day and the stagecoach's slow pace caused the driver to swear a stream of profanity. He complained to John Henry: "I told the Wells Fargo boss oxen were needed to pull this steep road, but the bastard wouldn't listen to a word I said. Said oxen on a Wells Fargo stagecoach would hurt their reputation for speedy passenger and cargo delivery." The driver complained about living in a Mormon town, where a man could not find a good drink of whiskey or a friendly female to spend the night with. He spat a brown splatter into the dust and added that his shotgun-carrying Negro cohort was quite ready to settle down among those straitlaced, hairy-faced, churchgoing devils, as the Mormons searched the streets of New York City for a good, God-fearing Negro woman to marry him. After bringing the woman west, they

17

instructed the freed slave to save money and buy godforsaken land in the Mormon desert, where Ute savages still scalped a body. The driver saw no sense in his cohort's hook-up because why settle down with one woman when on a good Saturday night, you could have your choice of a half dozen in any respectable house of ill repute? "Course, that'd be in Cheyenne, not among God's crazy people."

John Henry expressed his agreement about houses of ill repute being proper to a Saturday night, not from personal choice but from life's choice. This answer made the driver congenial, and he wanted to know what happened to John Henry's hand, if the war caused his fingers to be blown off. Experience told John Henry how dangerous it could be to express one's allegiance in the War Between the States, so he lied and said a pistol exploded in his hand. The driver then wanted to know why he "traveled in this godforsaken country." John Henry did not answer.

"I take you to be a city feller." The driver indicated John Henry's derby. "Most likely a California one. I hear tell they rob stagecoaches left and right in California." John Henry smiled but gave no sign of agreement. "One particular fella named Black Bart is having a good time dispensing poems to his robbed stagecoach riders. Pinkerton detectives will get him, as they always get their man. Good thing that robber ain't in Texas, for those Texas Ranger boys will hang a man on the spot and then cut off his head to take back for the reward." John Henry did not respond to what he felt to be a mouthful of nightmarish words.

Coming around a horseshoe turn and climbing a particularly steep incline, the horses, snorting and sweating profusely, slowed to a crawl. Seeing his chance, John Henry placed the four-barrel derringer against the guard's head and spoke as calmly as he could: "I came here to rob this coach, not to kill a driver or guard." He pulled a single action hammer back, its metallic click a warning to the driver. "Be good enough to hand me your shotgun, dark man. Driver, hand me your holstered pistol."

"I'll be damned! Who would've thought a talkative fella like you would pull such low-down, dirty trickery?" the driver exclaimed.

"One weapon at a time. First hand me the shotgun, holding the barrel tips, and then hand me your pistol butt-first, driver." When they did so, John Henry ordered them to rest the horses. He holstered his derringer, checked the loads in the double-barreled shotgun, and pulled the hammers back loud enough so the driver and guard could not miss the sound of impending danger. "Toss that strongbox you are resting your foot on to the ground, and then the three of us will very slowly climb down without alarming the passengers. I mean no harm to you two gents or your passengers if you allow me to go about my business."

"Your business being to rob us?"

"I prefer to think of it as taking a loan from Wells Fargo. Now climb on down." When the two men reached the ground, John Henry, unable to handle two weapons at once, tucked the driver's Smith & Wesson .44-caliber pistol under his belt and then followed them to the ground. He leveled the big double-barreled Henry shotgun on the two men. "Tell your passengers there is nothing to worry about. You are just resting the horses, and they should use this opportunity to stretch their legs. Stand next to the stagecoach and stick your hands in your pockets."

Once the passengers—a bearded Mormon husband, his plainly-dressed wife, and a spruced-up cowboy using a crutch to walk—disembarked, John Henry searched the two male passengers for weapons. The cowboy turned over his jacket pistol, a small Dickerson 32-caliber single-shot that circulated among gun-toting men since the war. The Mormon man possessed no weapon, nor did his wife, violence being against their nature. The driver related that the middle-aged couple were on their way to Wyoming to teach the three Rs and proselytize the territory's young and old people, not sparing a soul.

The road ascended high enough for aspens and conifers to appear on the rocky terrain. John Henry instructed the three unarmed passengers to sit in the shade while he attended to business.

"Cut loose those two lead horses and saddle the bigger one. Leave the mouth bits in and the reins free," he ordered the two Wells Fargo employees. When they did as ordered, he demanded the freed horses be tethered to the stagecoach. He ensured the driver set on the stagecoach and then shot the lock off the strongbox with the driver's pistol. The horses stirred and neighed but held their ground. "Driver, carry that strongbox over into the shade where your passengers sit." He followed the driver and guard and made them place the strongbox before the female passenger.

"Mistress, be good enough to place the contents of that strongbox on the ground for all of us to see." She looked at him, nervously fingering her pulled-back hair. "I mean you and your husband no harm. I merely need your honest employment, and then we can both be on our way."

"How we going to make our way with only four hay burners that can hardly pull a dozing dog off the porch?" the driver complained, indicating the four horses hitched to the stagecoach. "Oxen is what is needed."

With hesitation, the woman, dressed in a coarsely woven black traveler's suit, removed three bags of what looked to be gold dust and a small stack of U.S. currency—payroll for Wells Fargo employees up the line, John Henry guessed. "Be good enough to count the money." She counted out $2250 in currency and $9 in coins and looked to him for more instruction. "Count out six hundred dollars in the smallest bills and hand them to me along with those loose silver coins. When Wells Fargo asks for an accounting, you will be able to say what money and gold dust I left. That way, I am not credited with more loan money than I took. No offense meant"—he nodded to the driver and shotgun man—"but we can't have any more money missing than what is." The stagecoach driver snorted, a hurt look appearing on his face.

John Henry dropped an unsigned IOU for six hundred dollars into the strongbox, promising to repay the borrowed amount at the first opportunity. "Driver, unhitch your team and let them meander up the road. They won't go far, but far enough to give me a head start." His attention fell on the injured cowboy, now dealing himself a hand of solitaire. "Cowboy, I reckon twenty-five dollars is a fair price for your saddle—more than fair for one as worn as it is." The cowboy, conditioned to circumstances beyond his control, took the money. "Driver and strongbox guard here is five dollars for the shotgun and another five dollars for your trouble."

"I'll be damned! Imagine paying us with money stolen from us. Who would've thought of it?"

"I'll leave your pistols up the road a mite."

Chapter 2

Mounted on the younger of the two stagecoach horses and leading the other, John Henry kept the animals to a trot moving up the mountain pass toward Wyoming. If he robbed a stagecoach in the Southland, near Los Angeles, he felt certain such a populated territory would immediately put a posse on his trail, pursuing him across a parched desert until caught. Traveling this far north gave him a good chance to lose any pursuit through mountain ranges on his way to New Mexico. Working for the rail line in Los Angeles taught him to estimate distances in the western territories. He guessed the distance to Wyoming territory to be less than a hundred miles across high rangeland where water from snowmelt still flowed, and grass still grew green. He could be in Wyoming within two days if he rode the two horses hard.

John Henry traveled the mountain summit road and, within the next five miles, spotted a Wells Fargo relay station. Keeping at a quarter mile's distance and careful not to be seen, he watched the station operator and his wife standing by a fresh team. A stable hand sat on the front porch, waiting, he guessed, for the overdue Salt Lake City stagecoach. The sun began to drop behind the western mountain ridge, telling him it was too late for someone to

21

ride west to check on the overdue stagecoach. They would ride out the next morning.

As night fell over the open rangeland, John Henry noted with relief that the sky appeared clear of clouds and the moon bright enough for him to read the terrain. He kept the horses at a full trot, alternating mounts every two hours. When the morning sun emerged on the eastern horizon, no movement appeared for as far as the eye could see. He continued to ride east until the sun began to set and then stopped to allow the horses to graze. After grabbing a few hours 'sleep, he rode through the remainder of the night until he entered what he thought to be Wyoming territory. He coaxed the horses onto a high plateau where he could view the landscape for miles. He saw smoke snaking into the northeast sky about two miles in the distance and headed in that direction until he determined the smoke came from the chimney of a crude one-room ranch house. When he came within about a quarter mile of the ranch house, he saw small corrals scattered about the barn that held frisky horses, and he knew he hit his mark. Experience told him more horse and cattle ranches than farms existed in Wyoming. The headstrong cowboys prided themselves in raising healthy beef and especially good horseflesh. Sheep ranches were thorns in cowboys' sides, hindering their prosperity; thus, the territory's sheep ranches faced a precarious existence.

John Henry removed the horses' reins and threw the saddle over his shoulder. He scattered the stagecoach horses, knowing they would graze for the rest of the day and then head west to the nearest barn. Saddle over his shoulder and shotgun in hand, he walked to the horse ranch, fully aware that he risked his life being on foot in a wild land. He gambled he could buy a good horse at the ranch. If not, he would have to take one by force.

As he approached the house, he saw a man his size, although looking as thin and hard as a fence post, breaking a wild mustang. John Henry looked on as the horse threw the cowboy in the dirt. The man picked himself up, cornered the snorting beast, and rode the animal until it exhausted itself. He then unsaddled the mustang and let the mare pace about the corral. The cowboy spotted him and grabbed his lever-action rifle. John Henry raised his shotgun overhead, signaling he meant no harm. The Wyoming rancher, who saw a traveler once or twice a year at most, continued to train his rifle on a stranger carrying a saddle over his shoulder and holding a shotgun above his head. He stayed overly suspicious.

"What do you mean coming up on me sneaky-like? I've got a good mind to shoot you where you stand."

Even though they were the same size and stature, all other resemblances between the men ended there. A scar ran diagonally across the cowboy's forehead where a horse probably kicked him in the head. When his one eye focused on John Henry, the other one meandered to the man's left. His tattered white shirt and patched overalls were ingrained with weeks of dust and dried bloodstains where he scraped his body when hitting the corral railings. He smelled like a wild critter and never experienced a haircut or shave in a year. A bath probably never entered the man's thoughts. A small pony could gallop between his legs, as bowed as they were.

"I mean no harm. I lost my mount a few miles back and need a replacement."

"What makes you think I got one to sell?" John Henry looked around the horse ranch, seeing a half dozen mustangs the cowboy broke and three unbroken; two brown and gray Appaloosas; a stunning brown, black, and white Choctaw; and two large chestnuts. Off in the distance, perhaps an eighth of a mile away, he saw a dozen or so horses grazing, their front legs hobbled.

"It looks like you have more than enough horseflesh about the place. I mean to pay a fair price for a good horse. I see you got a big mule shading itself by the barn. I am willing to pay a horseflesh price for that critter."

"You got money to back up your big talk?"

"You put down your rifle, and I will place my shotgun by my feet." John Henry took the chance the rough man would not shoot him and placed his shotgun in the dirt. After a moment's pause, the uncertain horse breaker leaned his rifle against the fence. John Henry removed a wad of currency from his jacket pocket and flashed four twenty-dollar bills. "I'll pay forty good American dollars for that big chestnut stomping the dirt in yonder corral."

"I won't sell her for less than three of those twenty-dollar notes you hold."

"I got four twenty-dollar bills that will be yours if you throw in that old mule that won't leave the shade unless a man pushes a Fourth of July firecracker up its rear end."

"Let me see that money." John Henry gave him the bills. "You sure this is good federal currency?"

"It is. To sweeten the deal, I am offering you one silver dollar for that motley, chewed-up, greasy piece of flannel you are wearing on your head."

The cowboy removed his grimy hat and admired it as if it were brand new from Sears, Roebuck. "What do you plan to do with that derby hat you're wearing? I'm partial to a dress-up hat. Throw that in, and I am inclined to sell you my prized horseflesh and favorite mule." John Henry nodded, thinking, *His favorite mule is his only mule.* "It's hard to keep my feet in the stirrups wearing these city shoes. I'll give you another silver dollar for those run-down, scuffed boots you wear."

The cowboy, who smelled like a vulture that stuck his head into a rotting carcass, crouched, his gnarled fingers caressing John Henry's polished shoes. "Throw in your store-bought city shoes, and we got a deal."

"These are genuine Montgomery Ward catalog high-top shoes, ordered less than a year ago."

"You don't say. I never wore city shoes." The cowboy stuffed the eighty-two dollars into a shirt pocket. "I'll grab the mule. You throw a rope on the chestnut."

The cowboy, now happy as a heifer in clover, invited John Henry inside to join him for a meal. He raised a few pigs behind the barn, and in the distance, a tiny herd of cattle grazed, guaranteeing meat on hand. After their meal, John Henry shared the remainder of his whiskey with the cowboy. He rode out that evening, but not before warning the lone rancher that someone would be showing up, asking him if he saw a stranger needing a horse. The ex-gunslinger advised the surly cowboy not to risk his life, misleading that someone who most likely would be a Pinkerton agent. On a fresh mount legally paid for, John Henry, after washing the cowboy's hat in a frothing stream, headed directly east for thirty miles to where he guessed the Green River and Rock Springs settlements to be. The gelded chestnut horse, a large thousand-pound Canadian bred for stamina, heavily muscled and standing fifteen hands at the withers, strode effortlessly over the open rangeland. He encouraged the gelding to gallop for a quarter mile to judge his speed. The big chestnut would not win any races unless they were greater than ten miles. The mule carrying his grip, rifle, and pistol brayed at the end of its rope but kept up.

*

The settlement of Green River appeared on a fertile rolling plain, its river flowing south. John Henry never rode this far south in the Wyoming Territory. He scouted farther north for General Connor's disastrous expedition into the Powder River country warring against the Sioux; and then for Colonel Carrington, an engineer who built three forts on the Bozeman Trail leading from the Oregon Trail to the gold diggings in Colorado, and later scouted for the army's supply trains during Red Cloud's War, set off by prospectors' incursion into Sioux sacred lands in search of gold.

The town of Green River, on the south side of the river, begun as a stagecoach station on the old Cherokee Trail, named after an unexplained Cherokee expedition from their southern homeland to the west coast. Later, the Union Pacific ran a rail line near the town. A new section of the town sprung up on the north side of the river, and that was where John Henry directed his horse. The Sweetwater County Courthouse, a mammoth two-story structure with Roman pillars fronting it, dominated the north side of the town; behind it, a massive weathered rock formation the locals called "Castle Rock" loomed over the courthouse. John

Henry noted the sheriff kept his jail in the courthouse, but jail business looked slow as the barred door hung ajar.

Only two streets, muddy from a recent downpour and intersecting each other, existed in Green River. On one end of the main street stood a weathered hotel, and on the other end, the train depot. John Henry avoided the half-dozen saloons in between. He looped the reins of his horse and mule to a hitching post in front of S. I. Field's general store. The store seemed too large for the town's size, but he was grateful for it. He saw the store, wood ceilinged with kerosene lamps hanging down, ran about thirty feet deep, with an eighteen-foot width. Everywhere John Henry looked, shelves held merchandise of one sort or another. The general store appeared well stocked with canned goods; bags of flour, beans, and coffee; and kegs of pigs' feet, pickles, and other preserved foods. Heavy coats and women's dresses hung on the wall. A moose head fixed to one wall of the room glared at him, and on the other side, an elk head stared back. There were showcases displaying tobacco and household utensils and even a showcase for men and women's boots. A quarter of the store space displayed coal miners' coveralls, hardhats, boots, lunch buckets, and gold prospecting gear nearby in a smaller area. The wood-plank floor creaked as he looked around the store that appeared better stocked than the ones he remembered in the village of Los Angeles.

He waited until two prospectors purchased their supplies for the trail and then beckoned the clerk, well-dressed in an eastern suit—maybe even S. I. Field himself—toward the side of the store that displayed guns. Whoever this S. I. Field was, John Henry noted he kept an ample supply of revolvers, rifles, and small firearms. The clerk first directed John Henry's attention toward an 1877 single-action .38-caliber Colt Lightning revolver and a Smith &Wesson .44-caliber, placing them on the counter. They were proven and dependable weapons, but John Henry knew what he wanted. He pointed to a newer 1878 model, a blue-steel Colt double-action .45 with a four-and-three-quarter-inch barrel. His damaged hand would not allow him to operate a single-action, which required him to thumb the hammer back. He held the pistol in his left hand, not wanting to draw attention to his three-fingered right hand. The weapon balanced effortlessly in his hand, half the weight of his old Navy Colt. He released the cylinder and spun it with a finger flick to assure himself that the pistol was unloaded. Closing the cylinder, he squeezed the trigger six times; the double action worked smoothly. As an old gun hand, John Henry should have felt elated holding such a precision weapon, but he knew the pistol was one more nail in the coffin he expected to fill.

S. I. Field wanted $110 for the revolver because it featured mother-of-pearl handgrips. John Henry paid the money after he requested the man exchange the grips for walnut ones, giving the weapon a plainer look. He wanted nothing flashy on his person. He took special care in choosing a leather cartridge belt and lefthanded holster and paid extra money for the best-tooled ones. The Colt .45 slid from the holster with ease. He next bought the latest Winchester rifle, a .44-caliber 1873 model that loaded from the side. Next, he insisted the clerk gather five boxes of cartridges for each weapon and 12-gauge shotgun shells, plus a cleaning and repair kit. An inch-wide leather shoulder strap became his last purchase.

He paid the bookmaker next door to stitch the holster to the right side of the gun belt, tilting it toward his left hand. He next rode across the Green River to a blacksmith in the old section of town, whom he paid to cut eight inches off the barrel of the shotgun he'd taken from the Wells Fargo guard and ordered the blacksmith fix two rings to it to hold the leather strap so he could sling the scattergun over his shoulder. He bought a meal next door to the train station and then headed east to Rock Springs, not wanting to linger in Green River, where he would be observed in such small surroundings.

*

Covering a distance he judged five miles or less, John Henry spotted Rock Springs scattered around the Union Pacific rail line. From his vantage point, it appeared a sizable town built on a rolling plain, at least six times larger than Green River. Unlike the smaller Green River, this town bustled with activity. Men loafed about under second-story porches and on wooden sidewalks outside saloons, hotels, and stores. Women, both painted and plain, carrying packages, moved from store to store. An army survey team, led by the explorer Jim Bridger, founded the town's after discovering a large coal bed nearby. This discovery motivated the railroad to direct a line through the valley, but not before the Holladay Overland stage line set up a stage stop near newly discovered water.

John Henry, shotgun slung over his shoulder, resembled a small-time rancher leading his mule to town for supplies. One side of the main street housed five saloons bunched together, from whence piano music blared over rowdy patrons' conversations. He thought a cold beer would be pleasurable but once again ignored the saloons and headed to a general store a distance away on the other side of the street. A balding, paunchy store owner met his entrance with a grin. John Henry bought sacks of flour, beans, coffee, and a slab of fatback. He picked out cooking utensils, flint, a box of matches, and two heavy blankets and paid the price with stolen money. On his way out, he noticed the confectionery counter, where the store sold a cold, sweet beverage mixed with carbonated water. He bought a glassful and told the clerk bring a bottle of whiskey from the shelf. He drank whiskey straight from the bottle and chased it with a mouthful of the sweet, carbonated beverage. Outside, as he loaded his supplies upon the mule, he heard gunfire coming from a low rise at a half mile's distance. The saloons emptied, and the male patrons and half the town rushed toward the disruption, some mounted, some running afoot. He asked the clerk, who, followed him outside, what caused the commotion.

"White miners fed up with come-late Chinamen stealing their wages and their livelihoods every which way a yellow man could think of. Boys went up there to take care of business, thinking to lay them Chinamen underground."

After finishing the western part of the transcontinental railroad, John Henry guessed the Chinese followed it east to find work, working for wages and under conditions the coal miners could not live with. He thought this conflict was none of his business; the ruckus outside of town was proving a distraction from his intent. He grabbed the clerk's forearm to get his attention. He gave the man a twenty-five-cent piece so he would be remembered. "Tell me, friend, how far is Julesberg?" John Henry would not travel there; he intended to create a diversion.

"Can't rightly say. It's a long ride east, though."

John Henry rode directly east on the trail paralleling the rail line for about twenty miles toward Julesberg until night fell, and then he cut back on his trail to sidetrack the Pinkerton agent he knew would be following him. He cut a wide swath around Rock Springs until he found the Green River again and followed it south into Colorado.

*

The part of the country he rode through existed as unexplored territory for John Henry. He rode over most of the Wyoming and Colorado Territories, scouting for the army in 1862 after he found himself deserted by Benevolence but never traveled this far south. After his release from the army, he remained in Kansas, waiting by the Wichita post office for back pay to arrive for the two years he spent as a prisoner. The Union Army pursued more important matters—mainly the rebel army's successes—and his back pay that never arrived, so he went to the nearest army post. The army first called Fort Hays, later Fort Fletcher to protect the Butterfield Overland stage line from Cheyenne and Arapaho attacks. The commander, unable to collect John Henry's back pay, offered him a job hauling hay and wood for the fort. The Dakota Sioux took to the warpath in Minnesota. After the army wiped them out, disgruntled Oglala Sioux farther west began slaughtering gold prospectors who invaded their territory in Wyoming. The army needed ex-soldiers like John Henry, who could handle a rifle and recruited him to scout Indian territory in Wyoming and Colorado under head scout Jim Bridger.

Bridger saw that the army issued him the latest Henry rifle, a high-powered repeating one, and the latest army pistol, a very heavy and powerful Colt .44-caliber. After arming him, Bridger cut him loose. He found the Oglala Sioux and their Cheyenne allies to be expert horsemen, deadly killers, brave and foolhardy beyond common sense. Alone on the plains facing such fearsome cavalrymen, he never thought he would leave Indian territory alive.

Two days into his journey south, John Henry found a sandbar covered with driftwood next to the river, with tree cover some thirty paces back. The trees obscured a box canyon that would dampen the sound of gunfire. There he set up camp. For the next forty-eight hours, he ate, slept, and defecated with the new Colt .45 pistol in hand. He cut a strip of leather from the rifle scabbard, made a thong, and wrapped it around his three-fingered hand and the pistol. The pistol must feel unobtrusive and a familiar part of his hand, so that when he held it his thought process would not be affected.

The weather favored him, and he built a crude man-sized figure out of driftwood in the canyon and draped a new white shirt he bought in Rock Springs over it. That very same day, he dismantled and assembled the pistol twenty times. There were forty-five parts he learned to recognize and name from a description sheet, some as tiny as a loading-gate spring or sear pin. The larger parts—the barrel, hammer, and trigger assemblies—he took apart until he could put them back together blindfolded. They became his chess pieces. Predominantly right-handed, he knew drawing the weapon left-handed would be awkward, but he planned to make the best of it. He next practiced drawing the weapon lefthanded from the holster on his right hip and tilted to his left, pulling the gun across his belt until it centered on his body. At such time he grasped the trigger with his right-hand index finger, wrapping the other two around the butt. His left hand cupped the pistol's butt, steadying his right hand's aim. He squared his body toward his target, legs bent at shoulder width. He did not fire one cartridge for three days, striving to establish a relaxed and smooth pistol-drawing motion. Once satisfied with his draw and aim, he fired at the shirt-covered effigy over the next four days.

His shooting, from twenty yards' distance, remained accurate, but over twenty yards, he could not always hit his target dead center. Using the new double-action revolver, he could fire two to three cartridges within a few seconds. He believed this rapid-fire that scattered an inch or two should bring down most men. The pistol's exceptional balance in his hands reduced the recoil to a slight kick.

At first, his shooting from a difficult left-handed draw only hit the shirt's edges. After twenty rounds fired, the lead slugs struck the middle, and finally, after using up four boxes of cartridges, he riddled the shirt's midriff to tatters. John Henry knew he would never be fast enough to beat those gun hands who perfected a fast draw. He practiced fluidity, a smooth motion that became instinctual, one that he did not have to think about. When circumstance dictated, he would simply react. From his adventurous days on the plains, he knew that in the split second before you squeezed the trigger, a gunman must surrender to instinct and fire within the blink of an eye at his opponent. Many men—braggarts, youngsters, and drunks, anxious to get off the first shot—would jerk the trigger, missing or, at best, wounding their man. Professional killers and seasoned lawmen would never be so foolish. The answer to killing a man was to remain calm, to practice and practice and practice until one achieved unruffled execution. He saved one box of the .45-caliber cartridges for the road.

John Henry did not need to fire the shotgun because it was an old companion. At the time of the Fort Hays City shootout, he carried a similar two-barreled shotgun slung over his shoulder along with two Navy Colt pistols because once fired, the pistols took too long to reload. The shotgun gave him two additional shots to knock a man down at close range. The newer, side-loading Winchester rifle he purchased in Green River functioned more smoothly and weighed less than the Henry repeating rifle he used on the plains. He fired off a box of .44-caliber cartridges to get the feel of the new lever-action Winchester. He would never be an expert with a rifle, his effective range being two hundred yards. The Winchester would be the choice weapon for him, because his

31

gunplay would be at close range. He intended the Winchester for hunting food and scaring off hostile Indians.

An old companion, he kept the Navy Colt—beautiful to the beholder, a long, sleek .36-caliber, seven-and-one-half-inch pistol, in his grip, cinched to the mule. Confident now in his gun skills, he rode to the place known as Grand Junction.

*

John Henry followed the Green River until he could no longer. He then rode south to where the Grand and Gunnison Rivers met. On the second day, rain began to fall, and then the wind kicked up. When he arrived at Grand Junction, slashing sleet met him. Except for deciduous growth along the two rivers, the valley showed few trees; the plain, not completely flat, sprawled to rolling foothills in all directions. John Henry spotted a large, wood-framed adobe structure, a barn, and a corral on a knoll one hundred yards from the confluence. The corralled horses were getting soaked. John Henry led his horse and mule to the side of the barn, out of the slashing sleet.

"Summerfield!" John Henry spun around, his hands on the shotgun. An exceptionally tall, lanky, and rawboned man watched him from inside the barn. "Whoa! Hold on, matey. It's me, Braddock—Bill Braddock, from our old days facing off against the northern heathens. Kind of edgy, aren't you?" Braddock observed, genuinely pleased to see an old acquaintance.

"I didn't recognize you without your hairy face and horsetail hair and critter smell," John Henry responded, relieved to see a friend rather than a foe. He remembered Braddock, now clean-shaven with a recent bowl haircut, as a hairy mountain man who hunted meat for the army when he scouted in Wyoming. Back then, the hunter shot only with a single-shot Henry rifle, a deadly long-distance shooter. They shared whiskey and traded stories around campfires, mostly his whiskey and Braddock's stories. He remembered how he enjoyed hearing the Englishman's tales. Braddock left England for good, but stories of the country's many battlefield victories accompanied him wherever he went. Instead of wearing greasy buckskins and a rank smell, the new Braddock wore clean clothing, a decent hat, and boots.

"Just being cautious. What are you doing down here in this godforsaken spot?"

"Came here with the army after savages massacred a religious nut named Meeker and a dozen other white nutcases crazy enough to attach themselves to him. The federal government appointed Meeker Indian Agent, and the dumb bastard tried to stuff his hard-ass religion down Ute's throats and turn savages into farmers, something as foreign to them as wild stallions hitched to a gentleman's coach. After a couple of years of Meeker ramrodding the savages and forcing them to praise the Lord, they did what they did best: They hacked Meeker and his party to pieces and burned their lodgings to the ground. Army wiped out most of the Ute and scattered survivors to the four winds. Their job done after a year's hard riding, the army rode back to northern quarters. If this storm hadn't kicked up, you could see what's left of the army's quarters in the distance. I tired of hunting game for the army and decided to settle down here, found myself an Indian woman and staked out fifty acres in all directions. My wife and I run a store for the few settlers along the rivers—prospectors, buffalo hunters, and the occasional traveler. I cannot say I care much for buffalo-skin hunters leaving good meat all over the prairie to spoil. The only thing the railroad did for the buffalo was to build tracks through the middle of their range. The buffalo don't gather in herds down here much, given they are reluctant to cross the tracks. I pick off an occasional stray, but I must travel north to get a good supply of buffalo meat. My place isn't much to see now, but someday when the railroad runs a line through here, my hard work will pay off. And then the squaw and I will travel throughout glorious England in style."

Braddock's three horses were neighing, trying to push the barn doors open. "Shelter your animals in the barn out of the weather. It looks like a sizable storm will hit. I put together a room in the barn to rent out to travelers. You can spend as much time there as you want. No charge. Get washed up. I'll put these nervous animals in the barn and then tell Missus Time of Flowing Water to get started on dinner." He chuckled, finding his wife's name humorous.

By the time John Henry washed the grime from his face and upper body, Time of Flowing Water spread fried pork chops, boiled potatoes, and carrots she earlier picked from her garden on the planked wood table. In his honor, she baked sweetened corn fritters. He thought Braddock's wife, decked out in a long-skirted white woman's dress, attractive for an Indian, taller than most plains dwellers. With coal-black hair and eyes and muscled like a she-wolf, she looked conditioned to the hard life of the plains. She featured the high cheekbones and copper-toned, broad face common to her race. The Ute woman sat opposite her husband at the table, never muttering so much as a peep, her eyes memorizing his every move. He did not know if she understood English, but she displayed a pleasant demeanor, not scowling at him like a predator as he remembered the women of the northern plains had.

After clearing the plates, Braddock set a jug of homemade whiskey and cups on the table. John Henry knew from experience he was about to praise England. Many men who lived through the Sioux wars came from notable backgrounds, and this ex-hunter was one of them. His father served as a ship's marine attached to the British warships that sailed up the Potomac in 1812 and joined the force sacking the nation's new capital. In the latter part of the eighteenth century, his grandfather served as a gunner on a British warship attached to Admiral Nelson's fleet that destroyed a Spanish armada at the seaport of Cadiz on Europe's western coast. Before that, his great-grandfather served to the English army that defeated the French in Canada in 1759 and sent them packing back to France. Braddock joined the navy when only fifteen. Finding ships too confining, he deserted a British frigate accompanying merchant ships supplying the rebel harbor at Charleston, subsequently fighting for the Northern Virginia Army. The Englishman anticipated the war's disastrous outcome for the South and once again deserted and made his way to the Great Plains. A crack shot with an English accent, not a southern one, he found it easy to find a job hunting game for the Union army in Wyoming. John Henry knew England would always be Braddock's revered home, but his fortune lay in North America.

The day's hard ride to Grand Junction and the flow of hard whiskey caused John Henry to doze on and off while listening to the English adventurer describe what he thought to be one of the greatest English military victories, which took place on the Saint Lawrence River over a hundred years ago. He listened as Braddock detailed how a bold gentleman general surreptitiously scaled the French embankment at Québec.

A born storyteller, Braddock lubricated his vocal cords by downing a cup of whiskey in one gulp. "Dispatched by General Jeffery Amherst, this gallant and very young brevet general and hero of Lewisburg sailed up the Saint Lawrence River with only nine thousand men on a few warships to attack the heavily fortified and manned French capital, Québec, in Canada. Wish I could've been there, matey. Six months later, short of provisions, Wolfe faced a freezing river that would isolate his forces' supply line. His staff of senior officers recommended sailing back to England before being trapped for months by a frozen Saint Lawrence River. Wolfe's boldness was English mettle standing proud: When all hope for conquest against French forces seemed lost, James Wolfe, so sick from a plaguing ailment he could barely stand, scaled the bluffs east of Québec, his army following, and with my great-grandfather marching close behind, caught the French by surprise, landing his forces on their unguarded flank. With a much smaller force positioned on the Plains of Abraham, General Wolfe decimated General Montcalm's larger army. He sent the French running, tails tucked between their legs. Wolfe paid with his life, but his devastating blow to French forces drove them from the New World."

Braddock spoke nonstop over cups of whiskey for two hours. His wife since retired earlier to the home's small loft. By the darkness descending outside, John Henry guessed the hour to be close to nine at night. He was about to head to the barn to sleep before the long ride to Las Vegas when his old acquaintance staggered him—but not before draining the whiskey jug.

"About two hours before you arrived, matey, a well-armed rider on a gray Appaloosa inquired if I saw a three-fingered man in the past week." John Henry figured a Pinkerton man hot on his trail rode past him while he camped in the obscure box canyon. "The only three-fingered man I know saw a portion of his hand blown off at Fort Hays City; if anyone ever did what you did in that shootout then I have yet to hear of him. I was hunting for Bear Coat Miles's troops chasing Sitting Bull's Sioux into Canada when word reached me of what you did those two days on the streets of Fort Hays City. You must have a few quarts of English blood flowing through your veins to kill seven men all by yourself."

"Damn, Braddock! How come you didn't mention that armed rider sooner?"

"I believe I wanted you to relax over a sumptuous meal and a good tale before you skedaddled like a stag with a bobcat tagging his scent."

John Henry pushed away from the table, taking his gun belt off the peg fixed to the wall. "We are friends, and that tells me you meant me no harm by delaying word of the man's whereabouts. In which direction did he ride off?"

"The man looked for a bed and a good meal, but he was a heavily armed, mean-looking bastard, and I wanted no part of him. I sent him three miles up the Grand River to an old skag's place. Told him he could get food and a bed there. The scraggly old woman is as daffy as a bat with rabies, and most men will give her a wide berth after five minutes' company, but she bakes a good rhubarb pie. This man who spooked you probably is fed up with her by now. Then again, he may stick around her place for the pie."

John Henry extended his left hand and received the ex-hunter's hand in turn. "Thank you for the meal and a good English story. Extend my goodbyes to Missus Time of Flowing Water." Braddock chuckled at the mention of his wife's colorful name.

*

John Henry rode into a fully-developed, hard-blowing snow storm. By the time he found the old woman's ranch upriver, wet snow covered his rain slicker, and he resembled a white apparition. From what he could see of the woman's house in the blinding snowstorm, it seemed well constructed, a two-room cabin probably built by a late husband. Kerosene lamps gave the interior a devilish glow. He stepped to the snow-caked window and through a clear patch of glass, saw a fire crackling in the fireplace, quite cozy on a stormy night. A large barn stood within one hundred paces of the house. John Henry figured the agent, wanting to rid himself of the woman, would sleep there with his horse. He turned his attention back to a sizable burly man seated near the fire, wearing a heavy sweater over his wool shirt. A small handgun, most likely a .38-caliber Smith & Wesson, hung from his shoulder holster. A Colt single-action .45 long-barrel hung on the man's right hip. He tucked a bowie knife into calf-high boots. The Pinkerton agent sat in profile to John Henry, and what he could see of him indicated his hair thinned to where he was almost bald. He displayed a substantial, dark handlebar mustache over thick lips and a heavy jaw. Sitting in a nearby rocking chair, the old woman showed a gaping mouth without teeth, more hag than a woman. The brazen red wig covering her bald head seemed a deranged companion to her pasty-white, wrinkled face. He noted she spoke nonstop while the Pinkerton man leisurely ate rhubarb pie and drank steaming coffee from a saucer. The man seemed relaxed and in no rush to resume his duty of hunting down a stagecoach robber.

The temperature hung around freezing, and the night wind knifed through him as he waited by the side of the house. After an uncomfortable hour in the storm, John Henry looked on as the agent slipped into a heavy outer coat and pulled his cream-colored, curved-brimmed hat down on his head. He placed a silver dollar on the table, which the old woman snatched. She followed him to the door, her toothless mouth moving nonstop, relating what John Henry suspected to be a stream of nonsense. The man hunter seemed unperturbed by her chatter as he bid her good night. Outside, the force of the snowstorm hit the agent full in the face, compelling him to hold onto his hat. Head down, he trudged through deep snow toward the barn.

John Henry removed the shotgun from under his slicker. He stepped away from the house, crept within fifteen feet of the man and yelled, "Pinkerton man!" Before the man could turn, John Henry fired a shotgun blast into his lower leg and sent a second blast into the other leg. The agent, crumbling into the snow, tried to draw his pistol, but blowing snow and the heavy coat covering the pistol slowed his action. John Henry rushed forward and slammed the stock of his shotgun into the man's forehead, stunning him; the wind captured his hat.

"Sorry I waylaid you, but crippling you is better than killing you. In a few months' time, you'll be limping good as new." Tossing the agent's pistols into a snow drift, he dragged the man out of the snow into the barn. Finding a kerosene lamp, he lit it and then inspected the agent's wounds. As many as three dozen pellets penetrated the man's heavily muscled legs from his torso down to his ankles. The main force of the scattergun's blasts hit flesh, creating a nasty fifty-cent-piece hole in each leg where blood streamed out. It appeared the pellets did not damaged the bones, but many of them embedded into both legs. Using the wounded man's bowie knife, John Henry cut one of the old woman's horse reins and made two tourniquets to slow the bleeding. Regaining his wits, the agent, pain twisting his face, glared at him. "I'll kill you for bushwhacking me, you son of a bitch."

"I reckon you might, but that day will be a few months off."

John Henry found a flask of whiskey in the Pinkerton agent's saddlebags. He forced the agent to drink, pouring the liquid down his throat to ease the pain. The gunslinger disinfected the pellet wounds with whiskey to slow infection. Neither he nor the man slept much that night as John Henry lay anxious for daylight and the man lay anguishing in pain. At dawn's first touch, John Henry saw the snowstorm abated after dropping a good foot of snow. The day would be frigid and gray, acceptable to the man on the road to a shootout. The Pinkerton agent being in no condition to sit a saddle, John Henry, after binding the man's wrists, threw him over his saddled Appaloosa like a bag of corn. The shotgun wounds in his legs were beginning to clog. With the agent's horse in tow, John Henry slowly picked his way through prairie snow to Braddock's place at the rivers' confluence.

He found Braddock feeding his horses in the barn. The mule he bought off the Wyoming cowboy whinnied at him while eating last summer's hay. He led his horse and the Appaloosa with the Pinkerton agent slung over the saddle into the barn's warmth. "I need a man and a wagon to deliver this Pinkerton agent to Mormon hands in Salt Lake City where he can be cared for. I'll pay thirty good American dollars for the service."

"That is a fair amount of money." The tall ex-hunter inspected the wounded Pinkerton agent, whose discomfort subdued his outrage. "What have you been up to, Summerfield?"

"I robbed a Wells Fargo stagecoach and that put this man on my smell. Saw no need to kill him—just to put him out of action for a few months." Braddock pushed his hat back on his head, seemingly amazed at what he saw and heard, and brushed his forehead with his jacket sleeve. "I'll be damned. Plan to rob more stages?"

"Don't reckon I'll have time for another. Can you find me a man to deliver him?"

"That won't be a problem, matey. For that amount of money, I'll deliver him myself."

Chapter 3

John Henry followed the Grand River southeast until it met a river flowing directly into a mountain range covering the northern part of the New Mexico Territory. He followed it until an Indian trail appeared, most likely Apache, and then picked his way through the mountains. The mountain range appeared green where streams flowed from low, rolling summits; otherwise, the land was dry, sandy, and rocky, with prickly bushes and scrub grass. For the last two hours, he noticed three male Apache following him on foot. They ran as fast as his horse and mule could trot. John Henry knew the Apache battled the U.S. Army since 1848 in Texas, New Mexico, and Arizona after the United States seized the territory from Mexico. Like the northern plains' warriors, the Apache produced exceptional, battle-hardened leaders— Mangas Coloradas, Cochise, Victorio, Geronimo, and Juh. Now only one Apache leader remained, supposedly hiding in Mexico. Except for the Chiricahua, the Apache, like the Sioux and Cheyenne on the northern plains, the army battered and starved tribes into submission by the army.

John Henry imagined the three young warriors strayed from a reservation. He knew from experience that any confrontation with Plains Indians, north or south, would end in the death of one party or the other. Apache would die to save face. There was no chance to ride away because the young warriors pursuing him would not give up the chase and lose face. He faced this situation before while scouting and thought it best to bribe his way out of conflict instead of shooting his way out. Bringing his large chestnut to a standstill, he dismounted and removed a sack of beans, a sack of flour, and his Winchester rifle from the mule. He held the sacks overhead and waved them with his left hand. He waved the rifle overhead with his right hand, signaling two options. The Apache, standing five hundred feet off, waved their hunting bows. From his distant view, they appeared a ragged bunch, wearing old shirts and loincloths over leggings. They wore no war paint or battle dress, just the customary rag headband, so he figured they hunted game before they came upon him. War paint or not, if they were Chiricahua, they were not restrained by a treaty, and he would be fair game for a day of torture and after that a welcomed death. He saw one Apache carrying a single-shot, Civil-War-vintage rifle—no match for his Winchester, but he did not want to challenge them in a battle. Even though the army relegated most Apache to reservations, he knew every one of them believed the land he traversed was theirs forever, and he was the intruder. He reminded himself that he was here to avenge Benevolence, not fight Indians. He saw the need to appease these three Apache, as he would be pursuing the murderers who abducted his daughter through their habitat.

He placed the two sacks of food on the ground and looked to the Apache for acceptance of his payment for passage through their land. They continued to wave their weapons, now in a threatening manner. He removed a small sack of coffee and a coffee pot and held them aloft, ensuring the metal pot gleamed in the sun. Coffee and a pot to brew it in being rare possessions for plains inhabitants, the three Apache lowered their weapons. This business concluded, John Henry mounted his horse and continued his pursuit.

*

Las Vegas, the town John Henry now looked upon, meant "the meadows" or "the fields" in Spanish. Enriched by the Gallinas River running through the town, the name seemed appropriate. The town still resembled a Spanish colonial one, displaying an old plaza with a flowing fountain and tall windmill. The steeples of an impressive Catholic church pierced the skyline. He saw a huge arch standing over one entrance to the plaza. The Atchison, Topeka and Santa Fe rail line ran near the far end of the plaza. Seeing no overhead wires, John Henry exhaled his relief that the telegraph did not reach Las Vegas. The town begun as a Spanish land grant, later captured by the American army during the Mexican-American War. It grew to its current size as a supply depot for the Santa Fe Trail running from Kansas to New Mexico. On the outskirts of town, he inquired at a freight business where the Claude Cardwell ranch once existed. The freight operator, curious about a heavily armed man asking about the ranch so long after outlaws destroyed it, nonetheless pointed to the location on a map tacked to his wall. He followed John Henry outside and watched him ride off in that direction.

About twenty miles southwest of Las Vegas along the Gallinas River, John Henry came across the burned-out remains of the ranch where his daughter and her half-sister's family lived and from whence the outlaws carried off the women. Only the outhouse survived. Gazing at the charred ruins, he saw the family built the house to be a respectable sizable. His daughter and Benevolence's second daughter carved out a good life, only to see it viciously taken from them. Likewise, the barn burnt to the ground, leaving only a charred shadow. The skeletons of milk cows could be seen broken and scattered among charred timbers. Smoker told him the smaller livestock, what the murderers did not taken, malicious men shot at it for target practice for. Wolves, coyotes, and other predators probably dragged off the carcasses. He saw that looters picked over everything that remained of the family's possessions; nothing that remained of their worldly goods—a broken washbasin, a burned hairbrush, a shattered picture frame, and a few other household items—were not worth having. Disgusted by the looting, he searched no farther. Under a large tub for bathing where he supposed the kitchen once stood, the grandmother's baked skeleton lay twisted by death's claws. Claude Cardwell's body, Benevolence's son-in-law, was nowhere to be seen. He assumed his ex-wife must have buried him before she traced his whereabouts in Los Angeles.

The Sioux and Cheyenne—as he imagined the Apache did—viciously slaughtered settlers and captured prisoners, inflicting the same horrors his daughter and Benevolence's family suffered. The Plain's savages could justify such atrocities; they were outraged over white people invading their lands. He could not fathom the motivation that drove white men to force an innocent husband into a shootout in which he knew he would die while his family looked on and then burn an old woman alive in her house. After destroying everything in sight, the marauders rode off with two grown women and two girls close to becoming women, so John Henry owned no doubt what the men intended to do with their victims.

A memory of the time in Kansas when a midwife handed him a small, red, and wrinkled baby, crept over him. That moment seemed to occur during someone else's life, as so much bloodshed and mayhem took place since the day he held the baby he later named after his mother, Jane. He deserted her before she could stand tall enough to be on a level with his knee. As he stood there among the charred remains, the stench of smoke soiling his nostrils, remorse long buried by the events of the past twenty years came to life and hit him with a vengeful hand.

He felt a rush of fury but subdued it; he needed a cool head to hunt down the killers. Anger would only get in his way. The guilt he felt over leaving Benevolence and his daughter on Kansas plains to fight a war gnawed at his psyche, but the uneasiness would give him the resolve to atone for it. He stood motionless for an indeterminate time, long enough for the sun to drop to the distant mountains before he pursued his purpose.

*

John Henry directed his big chestnut horse past the large arch leading into the Las Vegas plaza toward a livery stable on the outskirts of town. A fair-sized sign met him: NO PISTOLS ARE TO BE CARRIED WITHIN TOWN LIMITS. VIOLATORS WILL BE JAILED, JUDGED, AND FINED $25. He left his pistol, rifle, and shotgun with his stabled horse and mule, carrying only his hidden derringer. Las Vegas appeared to be a sizable town, somewhere around three thousand residents, he guessed. Most of the adobe dwellings were one story. The two-story courthouse and hotels stood prominently in his view, although dominated by a sizeable five-story hotel and high-rising church bell towers fronting the plaza. A line of saloons on a long, dusty street paralleling the plaza appeared. In the next street over, he took note of clapboard shanties and tents where he supposed the whores set up shop. Other dirt streets crossing one another hosted merchants, bootmakers, dressmakers, gunsmiths, wagon builders, blacksmiths, and various other commercial establishments. These shops applied too late to find space around the plaza where Las Vegas foot traffic tended to amass.

Confident word of the Salt Lake City stagecoach robbery failed to reach the town, John Henry made his way to the sheriff's office, a one-story mud-brick structure at the head of a street littered with saloons near the main entrance to the plaza situated behind the grandiose, high-rise Plaza Hotel. Wooden sidewalks paralleled both sides of the busy street where men milled about in front of saloons, smoking and talking. Several horses were tethered to hitching posts up and down the street. The street being a man's domain, not one woman could be seen. A towheaded, fuzzy-chinned deputy sat under a wooden sign with "Sheriff" carved in it in front of a window, watching the street's activity.

"Came to see the sheriff. Is he about?" John Henry sized up the deputy, a lean young man in the throes of an acne attack. He showed a recent haircut, and his shirt recently washed; the youngster appeared as freshly laundered as his clothing. The deputy cradled a shotgun and carried a single-action, long-barreled pistol on his hip. He looked too young to be a lawman.

"Sheriff is eating his lunch out in the back, but he doesn't like to be disturbed while relaxing. Best you come back in an hour or two."

"I don't have an hour or two to throw away. Be good enough tell me how to get out back."

"Suit yourself—don't say I didn't warn you. Sheriff can be mean at times, especially if he's riled. Go through the office, past the two holding cells, and out the back door."

John Henry saw a hungover prospector lamenting on a paper-thin bunk bed in one cell; the other cell stood empty. Once through the back door, John Henry eyed two young deputies pitching horseshoes in a neatly maintained and fenced-in backyard behind the five-story hotel. They must have used their lunch hours pitching horseshoes regularly because they both threw ringers.

Both deputies were immaculately-groomed and smartly dressed, and both wore pencil mustaches and slicked-down hair under straight-brimmed hats tilted back. They wore identical white shirts, black vests, and wool trousers; both displayed holstered pistols with ivory grips. The sheriff, a sturdy, compact, middleaged man weighing around two hundred pounds, leaned back on a hard-backed chair tilted against his office's adobe wall. His derby hat pushed back over thinning, white hair neatly parted down the middle. He chewed on a cigar under his large, snow-white handlebar mustache. He, like his deputies, appeared immaculately groomed. A white shirt buttoned to the neck covered his sturdy torso; he removed his suit jacket and draped it over the back of his chair. A gold watch chain draped across his vest, and a large Smith & Wesson single-action pistol hung from his shoulder holster. He seemed relaxed and accustomed to being the top dog.

"Sheriff." The cold-eyed lawman cast a scowl at the sound of his title, displaying an irritable disposition that signaled he could slap a man down for the slightest provocation.

The sheriff examined him as he would a man headed for the lockup. "What kind of business do you have that can't wait until after my lunch hour?"

"My name is John Henry Summerfield. My daughter was the one who was carried off by murdering marauders at the Cardwell place a few months back. I came to ask you what information you have on the men who burned the Cardwell ranch to the ground, murdered an old woman and a dutiful husband, and slaughtered everything in sight."

The sheriff took his time finishing a white-bread-and-sausage sandwich and sipping from a glass of beer, watching his deputies' horseshoes kick up dust. "Well, Summerfield, I see you're not wearing a pistol. That's a good start in Las Vegas. Troublemakers don't do well around here. I imagine you saw the big arch leading to the plaza. Once past there, you come upon a windmill; troublemakers swing from that windmill regularly. If I can't haul such troublemakers off to court to get them hung promptly and legally, vigilantes will save the town the expense of a trial. I'm told the windmill gallows is as famous as Roy Bean's courthouse."

"Sheriff, I didn't come here to cause trouble. I came here to find my daughter, her half-sister, and that woman's two young girls. I'm asking if you went after them, and if you did, why are they not swinging from that hanging windmill you warned me about?" Smoker earlier informed John Henry that the sheriff made little effort to pursue the killers.

"You have a smart mouth on you. John Henry Summerfield—why does your name crawl around in my memory? Have you been in trouble? Have you been imprisoned? Is there a wanted poster out on you? You strike me as a northern plains man. Is that so?"

"With all due respect, Sheriff, I'm not the bad man here. I'm here to find out who the bad men are. Did you pursue them or not?"

The compact man rose, brushed the bread crumbs from his vest, checked the time on his pocket watch, and put on his suit jacket. "Boys, time to go back to work. You can pick up your horseshoe game after duty hours." He turned to John Henry and replied, "We called for a posse to chase them, only a humdinger of a sandstorm hit the territory that very night the Cardwell ranch burned down and the murders took place. A storm wiped out all tracks, so I saw no reason to chase down folks I couldn't find, even if Apache blood surged in my veins. Whoever these killers are, they most likely headed south for Mexico or north into Oklahoma Territory. I have no jurisdiction in either place."

"Do you have names or a lead I can follow?"

"This territory abounds in badass men. Rustlers, robbers, claim jumpers, down-and-dirty back shooters. You name your poison, and it will be in Las Vegas. One particular badass exists by the name of Winston Williams who probably took part in it. We suspect he robbed a stagecoach over by Coyote Wash last year. He has been known to sell a Mexican women to the Apache. When he wants to cause mischief, he rounds up a few boys with no more morals than a pack of rabid rats. Rumer has it he and those boys recently sold white women to the Apache in trade for booty the Apache stole from white settlers. As long as Williams stays clear of San Miguel County, it ain't my business to go after him. With your crippled hand, you don't appear to be man enough to go up against that bunch."

"I'm man enough to use what skills I have left to find my daughter and her half-sister and those innocent young girls taken against their will. Man enough to die trying to put a bullet in each and every one of those killers, whoever they might be."

"Tough talk for a three-fingered man who I suspect does not know the territory. John Henry Summerfield—I can't place that name, but it will come to me. Don't cause me any trouble in this town, Summerfield."

His business with the sheriff finished, John Henry asked the deputy on the front porch where he might find a boardinghouse. The deputy, not more than twenty years old if he was that, gave him directions to the home of a widow and her new husband on the outskirts of town. John Henry thanked him and headed in that direction.

The deputy caught him up and volunteered, "My name is Tommy McGrath, and I possess a curious streak a mile wide. Someday it will probably get me into trouble, but I can't help myself. I eavesdropped on the conversation when you and sheriff jawed. I knew your daughter, Miss Jane Summerfield. I didn't connect you and her until you mentioned your name to the sheriff. When I was no more than a wet-nosed kid, she often substituted for my teacher, Mrs. Mayfield, when the old lady felt poorly. Miss Jane treated me kindly and helped me after school hours with my 3 Rs when I couldn't get the hang of them. My mom and I grew up poorly. Miss Jane always sent over a portion of her Sunday dinner. I owe her, and since she is gone, I suppose I owe you."

John Henry sized up the fair-haired youngster, who stood a few inches shorter than he. The boy possessed a trim physique and clean-cut features; he owned the look of a youth who would do no wrong but would be the first to respond to what he thought to be wrong. "If Winston Williams and his bunch are the ones that did poor Claude Cardwell and the old lady in and sold off innocent girls to heathens, then Damsel Dunbar would know if Williams and his gang were the women snatchers and what direction they headed because he is friendly with the Apache. Damsel mostly prospects in the mountains around here. He married an Apache woman, so he has Apache permission to search for gold under their noses."

"Know where I can find him?"

"He and his squaw put up a tent along Sandy Creek, where it flows from the Sangre de Cristo range. But you don't have to go

47

that far, as I saw him loading up his wagon at McDaniel's General Store on the other side of the plaza."

*

John Henry didn't need to look behind him; he could hear the sheriff's deputy's footsteps. Instead of intercepting the miner Damsel Dunbar buying supplies, he paid the widow for three nights' lodging at her boardinghouse. When the deputy left to report his movements to the sheriff, he followed Dunbar's wagon tracks from the meadows of Las Vegas into the foothills of the Sangre de Cristo range. The name of the mountains, a spur of the Rockies, meant "blood of Christ." The mountains did not look bloody, dry, and treeless to John Henry. Grass turning brown covered the ground as it rose gradually into the foothills. He followed Dunbar's wagon tracks until dark made it impossible to continue. Leaving his mule behind, along with his food supplies and blankets, he carried his Colt .45 pistol, repeating rifle, and a small jug of Braddock's homemade whiskey. He spent a chilly night huddled between rocks.

When morning came, he followed a creek farther up into the foothills until he spotted smoke coming from what he hoped to be Dunbar's mining camp. Summerfield eased his horse toward the smoke's origin where saw Dunbar pitched his tent between sizable boulders paralleling the creek. The miner's wagon sheltered the tent on the back side. His two hobbled mules grazed on a rocky hillside. A morning cooking fire blazed. John Henry walked the big chestnut toward a sluice, where Dunbar hunched, sloshing pebbles back and forth in a trough's flowing water. He spotted Dunbar's Apache woman a couple of hundred feet up the hillside, gathering firewood. A pistol belt hung from her waist, and an old Army Colt held sway in its holster. Holding both hands high above his head, he shouted, "Morning, friend!" The miner grabbed his rifle, which leaned against the trough, and trained it on John Henry.

"I don't want trouble, just a few minutes of conversation. As an indication of my good intent, I want to give you this jug of tasty homemade whiskey. With your permission, I will hand it over." Damsel Dunbar stood nonplussed as if he needed a few minutes to decipher the stranger's words. The miner, the same age as John Henry, stood as high and weighed as much. His features were not the rough ones John Henry associated with lone-wolf miners. The man's features were chiseled and better suited to a woman's parlor: blond hair, blue eyes, and a complexion naturally fair, though browned by the sun. He wore Apache clothing—a worn, flowery shirt and a loincloth over leggings and high boots—but still looked to be an odd mate for a dark Apache woman.

"You seek nothing else but conversation?" John Henry indicated that was all he wanted.

"Dismount and hand over what you have brought me."

John Henry dropped to the ground and tied his horse to a scrub tree.

"Pretty heavily armed for a man soliciting conversation, aren't you?"

"A bunch of low-living men grabbed my daughter, her half-sister, and two young girls at the Cardwell place. When I catch up with them, I will need all the firepower I have to lay my hands on the females."

"You don't mind if I strap on my pistol, just to be on the safe side?" Dunbar recognizing a gunslinger asked.

John Henry placed the jug of whiskey on the log bench before the breakfast fire, where coffee perked in a huge pot. "Tell your woman to stop pointing that cannon she holds on me." He waited while Dunbar spoke in Apache to his wife. She lowered the heavy pistol and joined her husband, carrying a full armload of dead branches.

"This is Onawa, my wife. Her name means 'wide awake.'" The copper-faced woman showed a small, squat body typical of her wild-living race under a long, flowing skirt and a man's shirt too large for her. She cut her black hair to shoulder length, exactly like her husband's. She dropped her load of firewood, sized up the visitor, smiled instead of shooting him, and then holstered her outdated pistol. Then she grabbed two water pails and walked to

49

the stream to gather water for the sluice. John Henry turned his attention back to Dunbar, who strapped his pistol to his left hip, indicating he was a left-handed shooter.

"A boy deputy sheriff in Las Vegas told me you have the Apache's ear and would know about the men who murdered Claude Cardwell and his mother and then traded two women and two girls to the Apache."

"I cannot say who did the dastardly deed at the Cardwell ranch, but I can say who traded two young girls to the Jicarilla Apache."

"Would his name be Winston Williams?"

"Can't rightly say it was Williams, but I know the names of two nasty brothers who ride with the Williams gang. I can say they were part of the party that traded the white girls to the Jicarilla. The Apache lost so many fighters battling the army their stringy bands needed young women for breeding. The traders were the Benson boys. Both bear a wild patch of red hair and freckles sprinkled across their faces—that's their calling card. Both carry hair-trigger pistols and mean tempers. There are a whole pack of Bensons holed up about fifty miles this side of the Mexican border, living like scrawny coyotes on desert land."

"Do you know exactly where they are living?"

"I suppose I can find out if you have a week or two to waste waiting. But you don't have to. The youngest Benson boy—younger brother of the redheaded women snatchers, who goes by the name of Benny—likes to rustle a few cattle and trade them off to Broad-Butt Betty, who stakes out a miserable patch of sagebrush and sand called Wild Wind Hole. He favors going there for a night of hell-raising and whoring. Miss Broad-Butt keeps a parcel of three shanties, one for whoring and two for gambling and drinking. Drifters and no-accounts are known to pitch tents on the outskirts. Unlike in Las Vegas, they can carry guns there. I went there once before I became a married man. It's a wild-ass place where a man can get shot for mumbling the wrong words—brawling, stealing, and backstabbing. There is one drinking well, but the water is so brackish you can't spit it out fast enough. I can't say I miss the place. When I bought supplies yesterday, a rancher complained to the store owner that someone rode off with five of his cattle. If five dollars somehow appeared in my pocket, I'd bet it that someone would be Benny Benson."

John Henry took a five-dollar silver piece from his pocket and extended it toward Dunbar. "Where is this place of ill repute?"

"Follow this creek out of the foothills to where it spreads to a sizable flow, and then turn your horse left. Go for about seven miles and you'll hear the commotion if you don't smell it first.

Chapter 4

John Henry rode the big chestnut up a dusty, rocky red-dirt trail to the three structures known as Broad-Butt Betty's, built up against a steep hillside covered in red rocks and scrub trees in the place known as Wild Wind Hole. The sun, hovering low in the late day, hit the structures, shooting long shadows across the ground. Two low-built, one-story saloons standing side-by-side looked to be about twenty feet wide by forty feet long; a two-story gave the saloons a grand appearance. Only solitary, heavy wooden doors broke the monotony of the front expanses. A genuine two-story, rose-colored structure with purple trim around the windows stood perpendicular to the saloons; the overripe-painted house must be the whorehouse, John Henry assumed.

As the mining prospector described, the newcomer noted that a half dozen tents of various sizes rose behind the saloons; a few men milled around their tents, dousing fires and washing up for a night's entertainment. Fifty yards from Broad Butt Betty's settlement, John Henry saw twenty or more horses kicking up dust inside a temporary rope-strung corral set up for visitors. A hard-looking, full-bearded man spitting tobacco juice into the dirt while sitting in a stiff-backed chair and cradling a shotgun stood watch over the horses. John Henry paid a one-dollar fee to corral his horse. He left his saddle, along with the rifle and the big chestnut, in the care of the guard and made his way toward the first saloon, name Gila Monster printed over the door. There a rambunctious rendition of "Camp town Races" greeted him. He hummed to the lyrics: *De Camp town racetrack's five miles long/Oh, de doo-da-day*. He stepped around two unkempt men, looking broke and hungover, who sat on a small landing and pushed open the saloon door. He expected to see a few men drinking at the bar. Instead, he saw at least thirty men—miners, ranch hands, roustabouts, and drifters—filling the long room's confines. Lively conversations, a buzz to his ear, stirred excitement in him, which he immediately subdued. Ten men lined up at the bar, heads bent over their drinks. The other patrons played cards, four or five to a table, or drank whiskey with prostitutes, and other drinkers sat alone listening to the music. To a man, they all wore hip pistols. There were at least ten women present, ranging from shapely to scrawny to porky, teenaged to middle-aged, wearing heavy rouge and mascara and dressed in very suggestive gowns that showed a lot of cleavage and leg. Some were past their prime, and some were entering their prime. They milled about the room, serving drinks and waiting to be propositioned. Cigar smoke hung heavy in the rafters.

Never comfortable with carousing in saloons, the man dispatched by a dying woman made his way to the bar and ordered a glass of beer. Behind the bartender, a loftily placed portrait of a naked woman reclining on a sofa under a thin sheet dominated the wall, her sumptuous breasts and exposed legs meant to arouse the viewer. Below the painting, John Henry observed his image in a prominent mirror advertising Santa Fe Red Cactus Beer. The words were written in an old-fashioned scroll around the mirror's edges. He studied his lean and somber reflection. Eyes hardened by a war-torn life stared back; the optimism that brought him to the plains of Kansas so long ago fled along with his youth. Wearing the Wyoming cowboy's beat-up hat and his worn, ten-year-old coat buttoned to conceal the Colt .45, he resembled just one more underpaid working stiff—thin and mean—so he felt he fit in with the crowd.

Seating himself at a table, he positioned his back against the wall. From there, he commanded a good view of the entrance, waiting for the red-haired Benson boy to appear. Presently two brawny, thuggish, and unkempt men caused a commotion as they entered carrying a huge older man, close to three hundred pounds, slumped in a chair. The beefy pair resembled each other enough to be brothers. Both were dirty and unkempt; homemade, clumsy tattoos covered their forearms and necks. Showing fleshy faces, wiry hair, and piggish noses under grimy prospector's hats, they moved and snorted as if boars sired them. An unsettled nature accompanying them spelled trouble. He heard one of the boar-like men say, "This here spot to your liking, Pa?" The fleshy man, an older and larger version of his offspring, obviously unable to use his withered legs, nodded his agreement, and the burly pair placed the old man at a table near John Henry.

The father, captive to his chair, appeared grossly fat and dirty. Tobacco stained his wild beard, and no brush touched his wiry hair for years. He wore a dirty derby, and his unbuttoned, stained shirt showed filthy underwear underneath. His suspenders connected to equally filthy trousers. John Henry thought the trio a curiosity but nothing more. He observed a prostitute joining the black piano player at the far end of the barroom and then singing the first stanza of "Jeanie with the Light Brown Hair." The romantic song signaled the prostitutes to approach unescorted men; their rehearsed movement provoked a smile to form on John Henry's lips. Thereafter, a prostitute wearing a skimpy red dress with a plunging neckline and a skirt barely dropping to her knees joined him. He agreed to her company, as it would make him appear just another customer settling in for a night's wickedness.

"I'm Marge," she whispered in a throaty voice. She sang to the music: I dream of Jeanie with the light brown hair/ Borne, like a vapor, on the summer air/ I see her tripping where the bright streams play/ Happy as the daisies that dance on her way. The prostitute's hand tapped out the melody on his inner thigh but failed to arouse him.

He guessed the brunette's age to be around twenty-five—she showed a puffy face—but her dark brown eyes reflected a much older existence. Shapely but soft around the middle, she displayed a warm smile and sweet voice that made her company agreeable. She appeared to have undergone a busy evening by the looks of her mussed, stringy hair, parted down the middle and pulled into a bun at her neck. She whispered in his ear, "I bet you carry a really big pistol. And I have just the holster for it." She massaged his groin. His eye on the Bensons, he pushed her hand away.

Despite the woman distracting him from his purpose, he enjoyed her company. He thought how nice it would be, to settle in for a night with this woman holding his hand, unruffled by his missing fingers, unfortunately, Benevolence forced him to swear revenge, and her words implied abstention for women.

"Why don't you and I go to Broad Butt Betty's house?" Marge placed his hand on her soft inner thigh. The heat from her groin and fleshy inner legs stirred his yearning for a woman. "All you have to do is pay me five dollars and Betty one dollar. Best deal you'll see tonight." He declined the offer and withdrew his three-fingered pistol hand from her soft, enticing thigh. But Marge did not give up so easily. "Because you look to be more man than anyone that will come along tonight, I'll reduce my price to two dollars and fifty cents." He again declined, and she feigned a pout. Not to be deterred, the woman calling herself Marge continued, "Maybe you're the shy type. Buy me a drink and we can get to know each other better." She owned a friendly way about her that attracted John Henry. Wanting to keep her at the table, he bought her a glass of watered-down whiskey served by another prostitute.

Marge swallowed her whiskey in one gulp, and John Henry signaled to the bartender to send over another. She nestled her head onto his shoulder and began to relate a tale of woe. "I came to this sad-ass territory from a farm in southeastern Ohio with my man, who said he would marry me. It wasn't hard for him to convince me to leave a life of toil that included milking cows, feeding chickens, hoeing weeds in fields that stretched to the horizon, cooking, canning, and cleaning until I fell asleep on my feet. Oh, I mustn't forget to say I shucked cornstalks until my fingers went raw. Paw worked me like a plow horse while my older and younger brothers barely did a lick of work." John Henry, believing Marge did not relate her past to every man or even if she did, gave her shoulders a supporting squeeze, remembering his time on the farm in Kansas. His touch encouraged the prostitute to continue her story. "The louse that brought me to Las Vegas ran off with a pack of miners to strike it rich, leaving me high and dry. What was a farm girl with no skills to do? I gained a nice hourglass body from working so damned hard on that miserable Ohio farm, so I got a job as a dancing girl in one of those Las Vegas saloons. But dancing was not what Salamander Sam, the owner, thought. In no time, I was dropping my drawers and spreading my legs for fifty cents a sticking. The rest of the three dollars went to Salamander Sam." The woman told a descriptive story that would arouse a lonely man, and no difference separated John Henry from any other lonely creature. "A reprobate wanted to tie me up and then strap welts on my behind with his belt so he could get a bigger boner. When he would not stop trying after I warned him a half dozen times, I stabbed him in the neck with the pointed end of my hair comb. He ran into the hallway, squirting blood all over both walls. The pervert made a huge mess that I cleaned up, and I didn't even get paid for it. It's a man's world in these hard-knock western towns, so the sheriff ran me out, and I ended up in this hellhole. I cannot go back to Ohio knowing I have laid on my back with half of the men in the western territories, and I cannot continue my life as it is."

John Henry heard her last words, but as she spoke them, a man he thought to be the redheaded Benny Benson entered and ambled to the bar, distracting him. The freckle-faced, red-haired boy looked to be in his early twenties and smartly dressed in black trousers and a matching vest over a white ruffle-breasted shirt. *A good-looking kid, but a sibling of the two snakes who probably stole my daughter,* John Henry mused, his hand massaging Marge's shoulder. The brother carried a single-action mother-of-pearl-handled revolver on his hip. He tipped his black hat back on his head, ordered a beer, and scanned the saloon for the most enticing whore.

John Henry signaled the bartender to send over another drink for Marge. He rose, intending to ask the red-haired youth if he went by Benny Benson. But before the searcher could confront the boy, the two beefy, swaggering brothers stepped into his path. He saw that malice in their hooded eyes possessed a hair trigger; they appeared to explode at the slightest provocation. The brothers charged him so fast that he fell back against the wall beside Marge. Both boar-like men pressed him so closely he smelled their distasteful breath.

"Our pa likes this whore that you have been spooning. Since you won't take her next door to where the beds be, we would like you to turn her over to our pa." Though the brothers resembled each other, with their broad, jowly faces, John Henry noted that the brother who made the demand lost his hair. He glanced at the instigator, the disabled, fat father, locked to his chair and then to the prostitute.

"I think I'll spend some more time with this gentleman," Marge replied, disgusted by the crippled old man. John Henry unbuttoned his suit jacket to reach his derringer that he felt undressed without.

"You Grayson boys, tell your pappy to find someone else. I am busy," Marge added.

"A woman is entitled to choose the man she wants to share company with. You two boys work it out with her. I've got some business at the bar." John Henry spoke, trying to separate himself from a dangerous situation.

Both of the Grayson men grabbed his arms. "Hold on, mister. You ain't going nowhere until we settle this matter. You got some explaining to do to our pa. You tell him why you locked up this whore, and she ain't no good to our pa this night."

John Henry stood four inches taller than the two brothers, so he could look past their bulk to see that the redheaded Benny selected a prostitute and moved to leave with her to go to the brothel's beds. He thought to pacify the filthy father and his sons to get at Benson before he finished his business. "You men got the best of me. I will speak to your pa if you take your hands off me."

"You apologize to him for your selfish behavior."

"I will do what is necessary for your pa to rein in you boys before someone gets hurt." An unpredictable shoot-out at close range with two ruffians in a saloon became the last thing John Henry wanted. He did not know what he would say to the old man slumped in his chair, but he needed to get some elbow room. He turned his attention to the chair-bound man, who eyed him like a crocodile. Resisting the urge to pull his derringer and make the two brothers back off, he went to the cripple to explain that he planned to leave the prostitute and everyone would be free to do what they thought best. A loud crack reverberated throughout his head, and then a staggering pain dropped him to his knees. He knew one of the brothers clubbed him, but the knowledge barely flickered in his consciousness. He pulled himself to his feet only to feel another thunderclap explode inside his head. John Henry's awareness went blank.

*

Someone shook John Henry's shoulder. He found his face pushed into moist dirt; his mouth and nostrils were full of foul-smelling mud. He saw a twinge of golden sunlight caressing the tops of three privies. The stench made a person retch. His head felt like it would split, throbbing so furiously he could not hold onto his senses. He spat out mud and wiped it from his teeth. His hands went to the back of his head, where he felt a mass of hair and blood caked over a sizable knot. His blood streamed into his hair and down his neck. The hands that shook his shoulder rolled him over. He looked up at Marge's dark, troubled eyes. She wiped the foul mud from his face with a handkerchief and then cleansed what she could from his nose and mouth. John Henry realizing someone mugged him, grabbed at the Colt pistol and then his breast pocket, where he secured the derringer. The someone stole both weapons and removed his wallet from his back pocket. He saw his hat tossing about in the dirt a few feet away.

"I am sorry to say, mister, the Graysons have rolled you and left you for dead. They performed this dastardly deed before. I suspected as much but couldn't warn you, because you would be gone the next day, and I would be facing the nasty bastards all alone."

"Help me sit up." Marge pulled him into a sitting position, and he noticed his boots were missing. "They made me watch while they pushed your face in the privy runoff until you stopped choking. When they thought you suffocated dead, they dragged me off with them."

"Where are the brothers?"

"Using your money. They put on a big party last night. One Grayson sleeps it off in the foyer of Broad-Butt Betty's establishment. The other brother is upstairs, still screwing one of the girls. I imagine both varmints are drunker than skunks by now. The old, fat monster kept me at his beck and call all night. He made me lick a limp prick that smelled like rotted fish and stuck his filthy fingers in me until I squealed in pain. When he finally fell asleep, I ran to you. Take this pistol and shoot the S-O-B in the head for me." The irate prostitute handed John Henry a short barrel revolver that appeared to be a .32-caliber. She helped him to his feet. "Come visit me when you get done punishing those three scoundrels. I will nurse and fornicate you back to good health and spirit."

The groggy man, his head aching fiercely, made his way to the roped-off corral. The corral rope and horses were gone, including his chestnut and Winchester rifle. Only wood stakes and the water trough remained. He plunged his head into the horses' water, trying to recapture as much of his thinking as possible.

The robbers took everything he accumulated after he robbed the Salt Lake City stagecoach, except the mule left behind in Las Vegas. He checked the loads in the single-action revolver and assured himself the pistol held five live rounds. Room dust covered the pistol, but Marge oiled the weapon. After checking the hammer action, he took the strip of rawhide wrapped around his wrist from the time he practiced shooting in Colorado and wrapped it around the .32-caliber revolver and his three-finger hand.

Subduing his anger, he entered the saloon where the robbers waylaid him, and found only one bartender and two solitary drinkers. Knowing he looked and smelled like crap, he inquired of the bartender where the corral attendant took residence. Taking in John Henry's dirty and disheveled appearance and the muddy hat he carried, the bartender sent him a condescending sneer, saying, "Buy a drink, or get your sorry ass out of here." John Henry glanced at the two drinkers at the far end of the bar; they traveled too far gone in their drinks to be interested in him. With his left hand, he grabbed the bartender's beard and pushed the bore of the prostitute's pistol into his cheek.

"He keeps a shanty and corral about half a mile off the trail that brought you here. You probably saw the horse tracks leading off the trail."

Barefooted and carrying the pistol, and in need of a good swallow of water, John Henry, holding his hat in the other hand because his head felt too sore to wear it, half-walked and half-ran to where the man who stole his horse and rifle kept a place. As much as he tried to keep an even temper, the previous night's waylaying left him furious. He spoke, "They should have killed me."

Two hours later, he spotted the one-room shanty with a small shelter for two horses attached to it. A small corral, perhaps thirty by thirty feet, held his saddle-less horse. He guessed the time to be about seven in the morning, as he could feel the sun's heat on his bare, aching head. Smoke from a stovepipe trailed up into the morning air. He smelled eggs frying and coffee brewing. The single window opening showed a piece of cheesecloth draped over it. He saw a man moving about, blurry behind the fabric, but could not tell if he carried a pistol.

Moving to the front door, he noted that rawhide strips held it in place. He guessed a wood slat secured the door from the inside. He placed his hat on the ground, and then, taking a chance the thief did not block the door with a plank, he kicked it. The thin interior slat splintered, and the door swung open, revealing the hard-looking corral attendant. The man froze in place, holding a coffee pot in one hand and a tin mug in the other. The eggs sizzled on a two-burner woodstove. The injured man fired a shot into the ceiling above the thief's head before he could lunge for his pistol on the table.

"Place the coffee pot and cup on the table." John Henry noticed his new Winchester rifle resting on two pegs fixed to the wall. With his free hand, he removed the rifle, slammed the wood stock into the man's jaw, and watched him stagger against the wall next to the stove. Placing the rifle next to the door, he grabbed the man's hair and rammed his face into the wall. Putting the pistol to the man's head, he ordered, "Place both your hands palms down on that red-hot stove."

"Are you crazy? I'm not going to do that!"

John Henry slid the pistol down to the small of the man's back. "The choice is yours: Cripple your hands for a few months, or never walk for the rest of your life. Hot metal over the fire or hot lead in your spine." It took a minute or two and a pistol slap across the back of his head to convince the horse thief to place his hands on the stove. John Henry could smell the flesh burning, and he heard skin sizzling. He made the man keep his hands there until he counted to ten. He then tossed the corral attendant's pistol and shotgun barrel into the stove's red-hot fire.

"Those pistol cartridges will explode," the injured man cried.

"Probably will. Consider yourself fortunate. Horse thieves being this far from the law get hung from the nearest tree." Satisfied the horse thief would be incapacitated for a couple of months, he saddled his big chestnut horse and rode back to Wild Wind Hole.

*

Nothing stirred, not man or beast, in the dusty, windblown, three-house collection of ill repute. He figured it to be about nine in the morning. Checking the two saloons, he now saw only two bartenders drinking coffee while waiting for the first flow of drinkers. Confident that no one would interrupt him, he went to the rear of Broad-Butt Betty's whorehouse and entered through the kitchen door. A fat Negro woman blocked his path.

"Too early for business, mister. Girls still sleeping off last night's ruckus." John Henry looked past the woman, whom he figured to be a housemaid and cook, and saw she prepared biscuits and coffee, frying three eggs for herself.

"Where are the Grayson boys and their pa?"

"What business is that of yours?" The heavy cook appeared disturbed by the interruption.

"They are every bit my business. Don't get yourself all in a rile; I mean you no discomfort." He placed a fifty-cent piece, taken from the disabled horse stealer, next to the place setting on the table. "You finish eating your breakfast, and by that time, I will finish my business here. Now tell me where the Graysons hole up."

The black woman studied the small pistol tied to his right hand and the Winchester rifle he carried in the left. "One is snoring in a chair in Miss Betty's greeting room. The father and his son carousel upstairs with the girls because they paid for a full night's business."

"Thank you. You be quiet now, and no one except those who deserve it will get hurt." He levered a cartridge into the Winchester, crept from the kitchen through what looked like a dining room, and then to the doorway. From there, he spotted the younger Grayson brother sprawled out in a chair, naked from the waist up. Dirty long underwear covered the lower part of his body. His meaty hand held an empty whiskey bottle; the other held John Henry's derringer. He saw his boots neatly placed near the chair.

Cradling the Winchester under his arm, he removed the derringer from the heavyset thug's hand and slid it into his coat pocket. He then took a pillow from a nearby sofa and pushed it against his pistol to soften the sound. He fired a round from the .32-caliber into Grayson's right foot. Although dulled by last night's debauchery, the man bolted upright, finding Marge's pistol pushed against his eye.

"Make so much as a murmur; you are a dead man. Where is my money and my Colt pistol?" The agonizing younger brother stared at the blood pouring from his shot foot. He cried out, "I ain't got your pistol. What's left of my. . ." John Henry slapped him

61

across the bridge of the nose, causing blood to squirt onto the man's filthy chest. He hit him a second time across the nose with the pistol iron and whispered, "I told you not to make a sound. Point to my money." By this time, the last blow subdued the brother. He pointed to his trousers, lying in a heap on the floor. John Henry removed what currency and coin he could find from the pockets, including a few filthy, wadded bills he guessed to be Grayson's. "How much of my money did you spend?" The man who waylaid him opened and closed his hand five times, indicating he spent around twenty-five dollars.

"You crawl out of that chair, get down on your hands and knees, and face me." John Henry sat in the chair, observing a very nervous man obeying his orders.

"Don't shoot me, I beg you." The menacing voice of yesterday degenerated into a whimper, and the eyes that reflected threat now feared threat.

"You are on a fast coach to hell, but I'm not today's driver. Very carefully put my boots on my feet, and then lead me to your lowlife brother and pa."

John Henry followed the Grayson brother as he limped a bloody path up the stairs to the second-floor hallway. The gunslinger took a minute to study the five closed doors. They stood peaceful, as if in repose after a night of debauchery. The brothel's morning requisitioned silence so thoroughly that a fly's landing against a window pane could be heard. "Your brother first. No tricks." The brother pointed to the door nearest the staircase. "Open it very slowly." John Henry nudged the hobbling man into the room. Following him, he saw the older and bald brother sound asleep with a naked, hard-looking woman, her face powdered white and lips painted crimson, sprawled across him. *Not exactly Romeo and Juliet*, he mused. Two empty whiskey bottles and dishes from a meal they ate during Grayson's nighttime orgy were strewn across the floor. Removing the older brother's pistol from its holster and pocketing the cartridges, he tossed it under the bed. He indicated for the younger brother to stand against the far wall within eyesight and then roused the prostitute awake. She gazed at him through blurry eyes. He touched a finger to his mouth, signaling silence, and then pointed to the wall where the Grayson brother stood. She, naked as a jaybird, did as instructed. He took the pitcher next to the nude prostitute's washbowl and tossed water on the sleeping man's face. When the brother stirred, he smacked him across the face with the pitcher, shattering it.

He suspected this brother clubbed him in the saloon. When the waylayer gained his senses, John Henry placed the .44 caliber rifle's muzzle on his forehead. "Grab that pillow behind your filthy head and put it over your right foot." The brother, dumbfounded by his situation, eventually did as instructed. "Where is my money and my Colt pistol?" Sensing his dire predicament, the older brother pointed to his pants slung over the chair and whispered in a voice far less aggressive than the one that confronted John Henry the night before: "Pa has your pistol."

John Henry placed the rifle's muzzle on the pillow over the man's right foot. "Sit up and wrap that pillow around the barrel of my rifle. No tricks, or I will blow off your wicky-wacky."

"What do you plan to do?" the brother asked in a shaky voice.

"Do it." By this time, the bald thug who waylaid him guessed John Henry's intention, he hesitantly placed the pillow where ordered. Assured the sound would be somewhat muffled, John Henry fired a round through the man's foot. The older Grayson yelped in pain. "You be the one who stomped my face into the piss-mud long enough to think me murdered?" The older brother dropped his head, whimpering.

"It doesn't matter which one of you belly-slithering snakes tried to do me in, you both will get the same comeuppance. Move to that wall beside your nasty little brother." He handed the prostitute's dress to her. "Get dressed, Miss, and sit on the bed until I finish my business." The older Grayson pitched his body off the bed and rolled next to his brother. He pulled on his brother's arm to right himself. The three men watched the frumpy woman put on her underwear and stockings and then her whore dress.

63

After the woman sat on the bed, John Henry, using the pillow to muffle sound, shot the older brother through his uninjured foot and watched him crumble into a bloody heap. He turned to the second brother who sobbed, his bravado broken. He shot his foot, splintering cartilage and bone. Both men gawked at their bleeding feet, too frightened to moan. "What room is your pa in?" The younger brother cried out, "Last room at the far end." John Henry retrieved what money they left unspent.

The prostitute, indifferent to violence, spoke. "This Grayson boy did not pay me for my services."

"How much does he owe?" John Henry patiently asked, assured the crippled father would not escape before he got to him.

"For an all-night romp, ten dollars for me and five dollars for the room." John Henry dug through Grayson's grubby wad of currency and handed her fifteen dollars.

A carpeted runner of Victorian design covered the length of the hallway, some thirty feet long. Behind the man seeking revenge, a full-length window and fresh-cut flowers on a stand lent a touch of class to Broad-Butt Betty's brothel. On the other end of the hallway, Summerfield saw the door to the room he suspected old-man Grayson occupied, where his Colt .45 waited for him. He imagined the old reprobate heard the commotion he'd created subduing his two sons.

Summerfield made his way to the closed door at the end of the hall. Even if he did not hear rifle fire, the disgusting parent would be armed. John Henry placed his ear against the door, hoping to hear some clue to the man's activity. Hearing only raspy breathing, he thought it foolhardy to rush in and confront the old cripple, perhaps kill him in a shootout. To date, he resisted killing anyone pursuing Benevolence's ultimatum—roughed them up some, but not instigated an offense that would motivate vigilantes to chase him down. He saw no reason to change his modus operandi.

He slowly opened a door on his left and gazed upon three very pretty young prostitutes under the bedcovers. They stared calf-eyed at him. Placing the barrel of the .32-caliber pistol to his lips to stop an unwanted scream, he whispered, "No reason to be alarmed, ladies, because I mean you no harm. I want to look out your window, and then I will be on my way." John Henry removed the sheet and blanket covering the three women, who wore only sheer night dresses. He determined they possessed no weapons.

He studied the outside of the house from a raised window catching the morning breeze. Much to his gratification, he saw that two sycamore trees grew to impressive sizes; Miss Betty obviously wanted shade for her working girls during daylight hours.

"Any of you ladies have a fondness for that old cripple, Grayson?" The three women looked like he asked them to eat a rat. Satisfied the prostitutes would not betray him, he slung the Winchester rifle over his left shoulder and climbed out onto a thick limb pushing against the house. Straddling the limb and scooting along it, as a child might do when caught up in horseplay, he changed limbs, bringing his person around the corner of the house to the window of the room Grayson occupied. Grayson raised the window six inches to gain the night air. The naked and sweaty old man lying athwart to the window sat upright in the bed, his back against the iron frame. Gun in hand, eyes fixed on the door, he resembled a bearded toad hoping to snag an insect. His filthy, meaty hand trained John Henry's Colt pistol on the door. John Henry's subduing of his sons did not alert him. His other hand held an empty whiskey bottle, into which he urinated.

John Henry raised the window as silently as he could and just as silently stepped into the room. Once he stood upright, he spoke to the unaware man. "You are a dead man if you so much as blink an eye. Your boys are temporarily incapacitated and won't be coming here to save your sorry ass. Finish your piss if you like, but first, very carefully, very slowly, toss my pistol to the foot of the bed." The pistol the old man held twitched toward his visitor. John Henry fired a bullet from the Winchester into the mattress next to the man's withered legs, and he tossed the pistol to the end of the bed. John Henry retrieved his pistol and belt, holding them under his left arm.

"I see my boys failed to send you to hell." The crippled man, not about to squirm, attempted to reason with his victim. "You got your pistol and belt. Now retrieve your money from my trouser pocket, and your business with me will be finished."

"Might be finished if you hadn't instructed your boys to cold-cock and smother me in piss mud."

"People don't take kindly to a man who murders a poor cripple like me."

"I have to agree with you on that. Then again, people don't take kindly to a nasty pervert, crippled or not, abusing prostitutes and robbing strangers."

"That pistol you hold belongs to the whore who took a liking to you?" The rough-talking father indicated Marge's pistol strapped to John Henry's three-fingered hand.

"Thank you for reminding me of Marge," John Henry replied icily. He undid the leather throng that secured Marge's pistol from his hand and buckled the Colt gun belt to his waist. He retrieved his money and what money the old man socked away in his trousers and then removed the old man's wide-very long leather belt.

"You intend to strap me for my naughty ways?" the old man asked, flashing his tobacco-stained teeth in an ornery grin.

"You're lucky I don't possess the strength to toss your flabby ass out the window." John Henry made a loop out of the belt and placed the noose-like loop around the degenerate's fleshy neck. He then put the belt's end over the top of the bed's iron frame and gave it a nasty jerk, causing his victim to gag violently. "I intend to warn you about inflicting your degenerate ways on Marge or any future whore you intend to terrorize." He pulled hard on the belt, whose leverage on the iron frame pulled the man's head above his massive body and held it until his corpulent face looked as if it would explode. Grayson's fleshy hands made nasty abrasions scratching at his neck's fleshy folds to ease his strangulation. "If I hear of you treating the whores any less respectful than a decent man would treat them, I will hang you slowly, lifting you off the ground until your eyes pop out and your tongue explodes, sending you on a path to death. When engaging whores, you pay the money and go about your business in a decent way. Is my meaning clear?" The old man could not breathe, let alone speak. He blinked his acquiescence.

Chapter 5

Whores filled the hallway as John Henry made his way to the kitchen. The black housekeeper's corpulent body bent over the sink, her hands washing breakfast dishes. John Henry grabbed a dishtowel and filled it with biscuits and a half dozen slices of ham to eat on the trail. He stuck an apple in his jacket pocket. The maid recovered from her shock at seeing an armed stranger in her kitchen and observed him without interfering. He tossed the prostitute's pistol on the breakfast table. "Please see that Marge gets her pistol."

He found his horse outside the brothel where he left it. Last night's carousers departed; hung-over celebrants slept it off in the tents or were long gone. He rode out on the same trail that led him to Broad-Butt Betty's whorehouse. Finding a hill covered in mesquite trees, he stopped there, intending to wait for the Benson boy to ride by. Before inflicting his brand of payback on the Graysons, he caught a glimpse of a red-haired man standing at the bar of the second saloon eating boiled eggs and drinking beer, his saddled horse tethered outside.

Later in the afternoon, the boy appeared, riding a gray range horse alongside a tall, skinny man in his twenties wearing a pencil-thin mustache, astride a black-and-brown gelding. The unknown man's hat bounced on his back, revealing slicked-down and carefully combed black hair that John Henry figured he took pride in. Both men, still dressed in their best outfits, rode with pistols and carried rifles attached to their saddles.

John Henry did not expect the Benson boy to ride with a companion. Rather than confront the two young men, he followed them, hoping they would lead him to the Benson ranch. On the way, he figured to formulate a plan that would incapacitate

Benson's companion without having to kill him. Having seen a lifetime of human carnage in the North versus South War and on the Great Plains, he possessed no inclination to kill incidental strangers.

Following the two men south, John Henry noticed the terrain changed from mountain streams flowing into grasslands to dry, dusty, and sandy rolling plains bleached brown by a relentless sun. Dry scrub brush that could tear flesh from a horse's flanks began to appear. Tumbleweeds rolled before the wind. Rocky wash beds and gullies cut out by rare downpours came into view. All around him, mountain ranges maintained an enduring distance, and those far horizons added to the feel of desolation in a windblown land that only lizards, snakes, and Apaches valued. It seemed to him the ubiquitous dry dirt and red rocks could grow nothing but harm.

The terrain occupied John Henry until he spotted the two men, three hundred yards ahead of him, spurring their horses into a gallop. The Benson boy employed himself as a cattle rustler, and ahead of him roamed a small herd of perhaps fifteen to twenty cattle. He watched as the men cut out four heifers and one small calf. They handled the cattle expertly, so he made them excowboys fed up with long hours and short pay.

That night he ate the last of Broad-Butt Betty's biscuits and ham while he watched the two cattle rustlers roast the small calf over a fire. The next morning came, and to his relief, John Henry saw the black-haired rustler herd two heifers east toward Texas, some leftover cooked beef wrapped in a slicker and cinched to the rear of his saddle. The redheaded Benson boy, carrying his share of the beef, continued south, pushing the remaining two heifers toward the family ranch. Damsel Dunbar informed John Henry that the Benson ranch occupied land fifty miles from the Mexican border. The ex-husband Benevolence dispatched to rescue her daughters estimated they were within twenty-five miles of that location. For as young as he appeared, the redheaded rustler showed outlaw savvy. John Henry surmised that the boy probably did not want the location of the family homestead, a sanctuary for three outlaw brothers known to an accidental viewer.

Around one in the morning, a bright waxing moon appeared, creating deep shadows. Within a half mile of the Benson boy's camp, John Henry secured his chestnut to a dwarfed tree and walked through shadows to the outlaw's sleeping place. He figured the Benson boy would be sleeping with a pistol in hand, a rustler's precaution. John Henry, concealed behind a clump of withered creosote bushes, waited for the first morning light. When the New Mexico sun settled on Benson, the cattle thief rose and walked a dozen yards along the gully until he found a spot to relieve himself. Pulling his trousers to his ankles, he squatted. The squat was the moment of vulnerability John Henry waited for. He crept behind a preoccupied Benson until he stood unnoticed at his side. He knocked the pistol out of the boy's hand with the rifle barrel. Trousers around his ankles, Benson could do little more than stumble upright, finding John Henry's rifle trained on his chest.

"Pull up your pants, cattle rustler. You and I are going to visit your home place."

"Who are you?"

"I'm a man who seeks recompense for injuries your brothers inflicted."

"What's that have to do with me?"

"You will learn in due time."

"Take my cattle and what cash I carry and leave me be."

"I can't do that. You can thank your two big brothers for your situation." John Henry did not give the boy a chance to ask why his brothers stood as the reason he waylaid him. After the Benson boy collected his gear, John Henry mounted Benson's horse and rode back to where he tethered his chestnut with the cattle and boy moving before him. The Benson boy, reluctant to guide him to his parents' ranch, nonetheless did so after John Henry threatened to turn him over to the nearest law official.

*

John Henry did not embrace violence, but having lived through three decades of it, he recognized its power. With his hands tied to his saddle horn, the redheaded Benson boy rode a few paces ahead, the cattle ambling before him. The boy led him to a rim overlooking a small box canyon, where a stream dropping off a mesa flowed near a sizable, crude, and roughly-built, timber-framed adobe ranch house. Store-bought windows decorated the front side. Nearby, a small corral and shed sat on parched ground. He saw two big wagon and two riding horses milling about the corral. Next to the barn, three pigs rooted in a pen, and two goats wandered about scavenging for food; a few sheep lay in the house's shade. Enough water flowed for a garden that provided corn, beans, and table vegetables. He took note that a hired hand split wood behind the ranch house.

Instead of riding into the canyon, the boy called Sidewinder Ravine, John Henry reconnoitered the mesa around the canyon. From his vantage point on the far side of the canyon, he spotted an old man, twenty years his senior, perched on a rock and holding a rifle, maintaining a watch over the canyon entrance. John Henry decided to ride into the box canyon and use guile to subdue the old man rather than shoot him. With the Benson boy, hands untied, leading his horse and the two cattle walking before him, John Henry walked beside his horse. As instructed, the Benson boy waved at his father and shouted, "Come on down, Dad, and inspect these fat cows I brought you."

The man, with blond and gray hair showing from under his hat, cradled his rifle as he descended from his perch halfway up the canyon wall. John Henry took in his appearance, perceiving a lean and weathered individual conditioned by a hard life.

"Who is this man, Benny, friend or foe?" Waving the rifle in a mock threat, the father flashed a crooked grin, indicating he joked. He then inspected the stolen cattle and cooked beef, smacking his lips in appreciation.

Walking toward the cattle, John Henry replied, "Foe, Mister Benson." Having previously lowered his rifle barrel to not alarm the elder Benson, he touched the back of the man's head with his pistol. "Empty your rifle and leave the lever open." Once the elder Benson did as instructed, John Henry ordered him to rope the two cows and lead them toward the barn. The hired hand— a squat, heavily built man exhibiting a large mustache and wearing a pistol belt, looked to be a Mexican national in his mid-thirties —walked to meet his boss and inspect the stolen cattle. When the hired hand came within ten paces, John Henry drew his pistol left-handed and then gripped it with his three-fingered hand, training it on the hired hand. The Mexican man's hand instinctively went to his pistol.

"Don't be a fool, Mexican. I have you dead to rights."

John Henry heard the older Benson shout, "Kill him, Manuel. Draw and kill him!" The man drew his pistol, but before he could level it, John Henry, standing less than ten paces distant, shot him in the stomach. He kicked the pistol from the Mexican's hand.

The shootout froze the elder Benson and his son long enough for John Henry to train his pistol on the pair. Angered that the elder Benson forced him to shoot the man, he slapped the father in the mouth with the pistol barrel. Until now, no one died by his hand, but chances stood the foolish hired hand would be the first. The gunfire brought an older woman and a middle-aged one carrying a little girl not more than two years old from the house; a young red-haired boy ran ahead to where the Mexican bled profusely.

"Everyone sit on the ground and put your hands atop your head." When they did as ordered, he tore open the hired hand's shirt and saw he shot the man in the left side of his belly. Turning the man on his side and seeing the .45caliber bullet passed through his body, felt relieved. "Missus Benson, tend to this man and see if you can stop the bleeding." The elder Benson woman, showing a mane of red hair streaked with gray, appeared hostile and unfrightened. She tore the hem of her petticoat, folded it, and pressed it on the wound to stop the bleeding.

"I'll need to pour whiskey on this bullet hole to sterilize it."

"Get the whiskey, but remember I train a pistol on your husband and son, these two children, and their mother. When you return, hold your hands high, carrying only a whiskey bottle." After the woman ran to the house, John Henry ordered the younger Benson boy to bind his father hand and foot. He allowed the younger woman—attractive at one time, now worn by frontier life—to hold her child while he tied her upper torso so it bound her against her prepubescent son's back. He then secured the young cattle rustler hand and foot.

While the older Benson woman tended the Mexican, he shot the Benson cattle, most of the ten chickens, and all the goats and sheep. Using lamp oil, he torched the barn and the low-built ranch house, leaving no structure standing, including the wash rack and smokehouse, and no livestock living except the four horses and stolen cattle. He tossed the old man's rifle and both handguns into the blaze. Lastly, he destroyed the garden. Ordering the older female Benson to saddle the range horses and hitch two more horses to the buckboard, he placed the wounded Mexican in the wagon bed. The man writhed in pain, his wound bleeding less than before. John Henry then ordered the woman to toss the carcasses of the three pigs and two goats down the well, fouling it. He made the Benson family observe their life's work burning to the ground.

Embers burning hot all around them, he herded the entire Benson family to a sizable oak tree by the road. The mother of the boy and small girl appeared to be in shock, fearing for her children's lives. Brunette and blue-eyed, the mother seemed a decent woman, but John Henry knew what must do. The elder Bensons' faces showed no fear, just fury over their situation. The younger Benson boy began to quiver as he guessed John Henry's intent.

"I destroyed your ranch because two of your boys rode with the gang of murderers that destroyed a ranch near Las Vegas, murdered an old granny, and kidnapped my daughter, her half-sister, and her half-sister's children. I mean to know who the kidnappers are and where they took the women and children."

"I don't give a rat's ass about what you mean to know," the gnarly Benson spat out between bleeding teeth and lips.

"I thought you might say that, you old lizard. Tell me where your sons rode off to, Missus Benson."

"You are a dead man when my two boys hear about what you did today. I'm not about to tell you where they are so you can waylay them like you did us."

"Sorry to hear you say that. Your son, bound hand and foot like an unruly calf, is a cattle rustler, and your husband a cattle rustler's accomplice. You'll notice I left the two stolen cattle alive as evidence of their crime. I am within my rights to hang them on the spot and save the sheriff the trouble. You, old man Benson, and you, young Benson, scoot up on the edge of that freight wagon and stand up." After some prodding them with the rifle, the two men stood on the wagon under the limb of the old oak tree. John Henry saved some livestock rope from the shed before he torched it. He made two loops and tossed them over the branch above the Bensons. He then tightened the loops around the men's necks, tying the ropes to the tree trunk, taunt enough to stretch the men's necks, forcing them to stand on their toes and gasp for air. "Your choice Missus Benson—tell me where your boys went, or I will lead this wagon out from under your husband and son." He then grabbed the forward reins of the two horses and moved to lead them away. The young boy looked on, fascinated; his mother, holding her infant child, appeared terrified. The horses began to paw the dirt, rocking the wagon on its wheels.

The woman's disposition, previously as hard as an iron oak tree, snapped after hearing John Henry's words. "Stop! I'll tell you what I know. Their names are Ben Apple, Wade Alsop, Charles Miller, Justo Trujillo, and my two sons, Bradford and Bryce."

"And the name of the man who leads this gang of cutthroats? Is it Winston Williams?"

"Could be Williams. Then again, it could be someone else. I heard tell some argued over who would lead those men." John Henry wrote the names on a small tablet he carried. "And where did these killers ride off to, taking the captured women and children?" The woman, uncertain of her boy's well-being if she complied, nevertheless spoke.

73

"I heard they sold the young girls to the Apache."

"Is that true?" He stirred the horses. The woman, her head drooping, nodded that it was. "And the two women, where did they take them?"

"Most likely, they used them to pleasure themselves before selling them off."

"Where would they sell them off?" John Henry demanded.

"There are outlaw canyons in the Oklahoma Territory, near where Texas and New Mexico meet. Most likely, they took them there to sell as whores."

"Be more specific."

"On the Black Mesa, near the Cimarron River."

John Henry untied the mother from her son and told her to mount one of the saddled horses and then handed her the small girl. He instructed the young cattle rustler mounted on a saddled horse to ride behind the small boy, mitigating his chances of escape. John Henry threatened the elder Benson's life if he did not deliver the wounded Mexican to the nearest doctor. The gunslinger waited until the surly man directed the wagon out of the box canyon and left the aging redheaded woman to fend for herself, knowing the Apache, like the Sioux and Cheyenne on the northern plains, would not take her; if he delivered the older woman to them, they would kill her, because she was past childbearing age and of no use to them.

Two days' ride from Sidewinder Ravine, he released the stolen cattle. Keeping the four Bensons riding ahead, he headed toward where he first saw the three Apache warriors and left a coffee pot, coffee, and sacks of grub on the ground to buy safe passage.

Chapter 6

John Henry herded the Bensons for three days to the greener plains north of Las Vegas, where he knew the Apache took refuge in the distant mountains. The woman and children stayed docile when they made camp at nightfall, but not so with the redheaded Benny Benson. John Henry hogtied him to whatever boulder, tree, or bush he could find. Having hastily left the destroyed Benson ranch in Sidewinder Ravine, the party carried no food and only water John Henry kept in his canteen. The children became cranky, complaining they were hungry. The mother begged him to find food. On the third day, Lady Luck smiled at the party. John Henry spotted three young bucks taking shade in a clump of bushes not more than one hundred yards distant. He quickly killed one deer with the Winchester rifle, scattering the others.

The venison satisfying their hunger, the Bensons became more complacent as they rode until John Henry halted their journey near where he previously saw the three Apache hunters. He ordered the mother and her son to gather all the brush and firewood they could find and stack it in a pile. He accompanied the Bensons as they gathered some sizable rocks to anchor a man's tether. After that, he tied the mother holding her two-year-old girl and hogtied the youngest Benson brother, wrists to ankles behind his back; he secured the boy separately. Having the woman and boy lie on their sides and Benny Benson a distance away, he lashed their ankles to heavy kindling and thereafter piled rocks on the sticks, prohibiting escape. When dusk settled on the plains, he torched the pile of brush and firewood, creating a large bonfire. He waited outside the fire's illumination until he heard horse hooves striking the ground. Satisfied he attracted some Apache on the lookout for prey, he rode off. He heard the young cattle rustler thrashing about, but he waited too long to escape.

*

John Henry felt he could not completely trust old man Benson to send word to his sons about the destruction of their home place; therefore, he would continue to provoke the outlaws. He became more unsure whether or not the mean-minded elder Benson would deliver the wounded Mexican to a doctor or dump him in the desert and ride back to his wife. In his mind, John Henry did the best he could for the Mexican because if the hired hand died, a killing would be attributed to him. Before he rode to Black Mesa in the Oklahoma Territory, he needed background on the five outlaws with whom the Benson brothers rode and who participated in kidnapping his daughter. He rode into the foothills northeast of Las Vegas to search for the Apache-protected Damsel Dunbar, who informed him of the redheaded Benson boy a few weeks back. After riding into Las Vegas, the general store owner informed John Henry that the prospector left his worked-out diggings, where John Henry first found him, to work the streams flowing out of the same Sangre de Cristo mountain range east of Santa Fe. Collecting his mule and camping gear from the stable, John Henry headed west toward the mountain range and into the heart of Apache territory. After two days' ride, he came upon the dryer side of the mountain range. The region, getting less rainfall than the western slopes, appeared arid. He assumed fewer streams flowed from the moderately high peaks, and that was advantageous, as he would only have to search a dozen streams, more or less.

The outlaws' hunter did not know the Apache trailed him on foot to the outskirts of Las Vegas after he left the Benson family staked out. In any civilization, savage or civilized, an unorthodox act such as giving four white people to enemies for unknown reasons created a high level of curiosity—enough curiosity to want answers—so the Apache, monitoring his movements, allowed John Henry temporary passage through their territory until they decided his fate. The safe passage could only come from those Apaches who benefited from his gifts; the other Apache bands remained unpredictable.

He knew about gold mining in the west since the gold discovery in Colorado set off the first Great Sioux War and brought about his years on the plains as an army scout. Initial gold discoveries were usually found in fast-flowing streams coming off mountain slopes, centuries of rapid water pushing large gold flakes and particles to lower levels—that is, if gold existed. Finding these streams in the Sangre de Cristos posed little difficulty for John

Henry, as clumps of aspen trees and other green foliage fed by water flow left a discernible swath of green trailing down mountainsides. A week out and crossing his fifth fast-flowing stream, he spotted early-morning camp smoke. Around noon, he picked up heavy wagon tracks switch-backing up the slope, following a fast-flowing stream.

When he came upon Damsel Dunbar and his Apache wife, Onawa, the unlikely pair stood knee-deep in the stream, panning gravel and rocks near the shoreline. As before, he held his shotgun over his head, shouting: "Afternoon, Dunbar, and a good afternoon to you, Missus Dunbar!" The Apache woman, conditioned to mistrust white men, cautiously drew her old Colt. Dunbar's hand touched his pistol. The prospector spoke in Apache to his wife. She lowered her weapon but did not holster it. Confident the woman would not shoot him, John Henry dismounted and tied his horse and mule to Dunbar's wagon wheel. The camp resembled the one John Henry previously visited: one tent pitched under a tree, a smoldering fire pit, a small pail for washing up, picks, shovels, and a sluice box scattered about. Dunbar hoisted the food stores in a tree to prevent bear thievery. He hobbled the two grazing mules a short distance upstream. Summerfield shouldered his shotgun and reluctantly turned his back on the woman while he pulled out a slab of fatback, a bag of coffee, and a tin of canned peaches.

"Like before, Dunbar, I've brought you some gifts to show I mean you no harm."

"And like before, Summerfield, I expect you'll be wanting information."

"I have the names of the men who kidnapped my daughter, her half-sister, and two little girls. I am told they hole up in some outlaw stronghold in the Oklahoma Territory. I would be obliged if you would give me what you know about the killers."

"I'm sure as hell know you know the backgrounds of the Bensons after leveling their ranch. The human gifts you staked out by a bonfire are on the minds of every Apache within two hundred miles of here. And what happened to the Benson ranch on that miserable patch of desert near the Mexican border put every rancher in the territory on edge."

"And why is that Dunbar, given the destruction of Claude Cardwell's ranch, dust barely stirred in Las Vegas?"

"Reason might be that one three-fingered man destroyed the Benson ranch, and it took seven of them to destroy the Cardwell place."

John Henry pulled the notebook from his coat pocket containing the names of the four other outlaws who rode with the Benson brothers and Winston Williams. "Sun is coming into its hottest time. Why don't we cook up some of that fatback you brought and find shade to look at the names on your piece of paper there?" Dunbar suggested.

While the Apache woman fried the fatback and made skillet-fried biscuits and coffee, John Henry unsaddled his big chestnut, relieved the mule of its load, and allowed them to graze on the grass near the stream. He and Dunbar, smoking a pipe, sat in the shade of a rocky ledge. Dunbar mulled over the names John Henry gave him.

"The two oldest Benson boys, as you know, are named Bradford and Bryce—Bryce, a bit of a dandy, being the older, but younger Brad by far is more ornery and deadly. Both of them, being carrot-topped, won't be hard for you to spot. They joined the rebel army at Vicksburg, then were captured by the bluecoats, and released after the war."

Dunbar put his finger on the name of Wade Alsop. "Another rebel and local boy turned bad. His family, low-living cattle thieves and claim jumpers, own a place a few miles outside El Pueblo. When it comes to outlawing, Alsop tried everything—horse stealing, cattle rustling, armed robbery. I don't think he's smart enough to rob a train or a bank, but that wouldn't stop him if he got the inclination. Ben Apple and Charles Miller are cousins, both sired by hardworking dirt farmers who tried their hand at ranching. Boys didn't take to work hard. One family lives outside of Los Alamos and the other outside of Mesa. Neither of these hamlets, not more than a wide spot in the road, ranch about thirty miles from Las Vegas. This Ben Apple is a tiny, fancy-dressing, and gun-toting crazy. Won't think twice about walking straight into gunfire because he believes he can't be killed. He talks to himself and likes to wear women's lavender water, so you can smell him before seeing him. Believe he became orphaned at a tender age when his pa got shot over a card game; after that, his mother went whoring in railroad camps, deserting the boy. Justo Trujillo is a half-breed from a Comanche mother and a Mexican father. He is deadly with a knife, with a gun, not so deadly. Probably because, when he grew up, those pisspoor Mexicans couldn't afford a pistol. The story has it that when his pistol went cold after missing his target numerous times, he threw his knife and hit his foe in the chest at a distance of fifteen paces. Except for Trujillo, most of these boys are ex-Confederates, disenfranchised after the war. They joined the Reb army so young that the only thing they ever learned to do was to raid, rape, and kill."

"This Winston Williams, what's his background?"

"He comes from a different cut of cloth. He rose through the ranks to be a Texas Confederate officer who accompanied John Baylor's successful Rebel mission to occupy Arizona. He later served under Sibley, who invaded New Mexico to cut off the Union supply line from California. The Texas Rangers hired him after the war to hunt down Comanche and Mexican cattle rustlers, plus every type of lowlife you can think of, but as it turned out, Williams preferred to work the shady side of the law. Saloon talk has it that bank, train, and stagecoach robberies were his preferred work. He's good at what he does, so good he hasn't been connected to a robbery yet. If still alive, his folks work a sizable ranch in the Yesalita Valley, east of El Paso."

Onawa brought the two men plates of sizzling fatback and fried biscuits cooked with enough sand and grit to wear down goats' teeth, but both men ate with relish, gulping down cups of hot coffee despite the warm day. A few hours of daylight remained for John Henry, so he saddled his horse and loaded the mule, thinking of riding north to the Black Mesa in Oklahoma territory. The prospector, believed to have immunity from the deadly

Apache because of his marriage to one of their women, caught John Henry by the arm before he mounted.

"I don't know if you know that the Jicarilla Apache gave you free rein to ride through their territory. But they despise the white man, and that free rein could change as quickly as spit dries in the dirt."

*

John Henry found the Black Mesa tucked away in the southwestern corner of the Oklahoma Territory; the mesa drew its name from its dark basalt spat out by an ancient volcano. He found the entrance to what he believed to be the outlaws' hideout after following horse tracks leading into a gulch that spread some ten feet across between two forty-foot-high mesas.

This pass, covered in sagebrush and small conifers, led to what John Henry believed to be a small meadow to graze livestock and protected by high bluffs where the outlaws could find sanctuary. He reconnoitered both sides of the mesas on foot, spotting two armed men guarding the entrance and two more down the passageway one hundred yards back. The entrance appeared impregnable, and the revenger possessed no idea how many outlaws were taking refuge there. He would not have determined that the hideout held the outlaws if he did not see old Benson, the man he spared, seated behind two horses pulling an empty wagon—the same wagon that hauled the wounded Mexican—out of the guarded hideout. Satisfied he found the right place and realized the old man informed his sons about the wrath perpetuated against their family, he waited for Bradford and Bryce Benson to ride out seeking revenge for their home place being destroyed. His promise to Benevolence to shoot down the seven men in the streets of Las Vegas loomed as unrealistic. Therefore, he thought to confront the two older Benson boys and shoot them once they exited the outlaw hideout.

Chapter 7

80

John Henry's mind traveled to his dying ex-wife and why she believed him capable of killing seven vicious murderers in a shootout. The army brass masked the shootout at Fort Hays City ten years ago to protect John Henry because of his continuous service to the Union during a precarious era in the nation. Even so, the retelling of the event over the past decade by town locals became exaggerated to the extent that it became local folklore, enough so to spur his ex-wife to track him to Los Angeles.

John Henry thought his scouting days for the army would be over when the United States government, suffering a soldier shortage on the plains because of the War Between the States, signed a peace treaty with Sioux chief Red Cloud, thus ending the first Sioux War. But the army requested him to scout for Colonel George Armstrong Custer's expedition into the Black Hills. Custer's subsequent announcement of gold deposits discovered there set off a mass migration of miners and speculators moving through the Sioux territory to the Black Hills, a sacred Sioux sanctuary.

Having become an expert on the Sioux due to constant encounters, John Henry knew the warrior-bred nation agitated by Sitting Bull and Crazy Horse, along with the Cheyenne, would begin attacking the whites moving through their territory, consequently triggering another plains war. In that war, he absorbed enough death and destruction to last a lifetime, so left the Dakota Territory for Fort Hays, Nebraska. At the fort, where he was known and respected as a Civil War veteran and where he first started as an army scout, he reapplied and hire for his old job driving freight wagons.

Fort Hays became one of the main supply depots for the army outposts spread across the Great Plains and a stopover for wagons traveling west toward the Smoky Hill Trail out of Cheyenne. The fort, occupied by two regiments quartered among a collection of barracks, kitchens, headquarters, and warehouses surrounding a parade ground and looked more like a settlement than a barricaded outpost. John Henry thought to settle down in

Fort Hays City and spend the remainder of his life working for the army, but events denied that thought's fulfillment.

In the process of returning from his home state—the newly established West Virginia, which separated from Old Dominion during the Civil War—where his mother, gravely ill from cancer, lay on her deathbed, he traveled in a Bloomfield stagecoach on the last leg of his journey to Fort Hays City. Accompanying him were a farming supply salesman, a major in the U.S. Army, and one very young and attractive woman, blond and petite. She introduced herself as Katie Craftsman from Cincinnati, Ohio, with a personality as sweet as store-bought candy and a tongue as lively as a kitten pawing a ball of string. The young woman said she traveled to Fort Hays City to marry her fiancé, who was mustering out of the army after two years of enlistment.

John Henry looked on as the young woman, holding a captive audience, questioned the army major about every aspect of army life on the frontier until she exhausted the man. An attorney's daughter and graduate of a women's finishing school in Cincinnati, she intended to be a writer who would chronicle frontier life. Next, she focused on John Henry, who was wearing a rough-woven suit jacket, denims, and scruffy boots; he removed his pistol belt and placed it near his feet. Ten years younger at that time, tanned and hewn by life on the plains, John Henry appeared as a striking individual who drew the young woman's attention.

One of her many questions most impressed John Henry: "Do you believe, Mr. Summerfield, that a woman can manage any task a man can do?" The question pressed John Henry back in his thinly padded seat. He heard of but never met a woman championing woman's rights. She probably supported suffrage, too. As pretty and as innocent as she appeared, dressed in a lowcut yellow dress revealing too much chest, she commanded a sharp wit and, to his way of thinking, an aggressive nature for a woman alone on the frontier. He answered, "It would depend upon the task, Miss Craftsman."

"I posed a simple question, stressing the word 'any.' Be good enough to tell me if you agree or not. And if not, what tasks are women not capable of?"

On the defensive, John Henry struggled for an accommodating answer. "The tasks a woman couldn't do would be physical, such as plowing behind a team of mules or building a sod house. Soldiering would be another task a woman would be incapable of doing."

"Mr. Summerfield, did it ever occur to you that the tasks you've declared women incapable of doing are out of reach not because of our inability to do them but because men deny us the opportunities?" The salesman laughed, ridiculing her question. The major seemed offended by it. John Henry could do little more than smile at the woman because he saw no safe reply to her query.

Katie Craftsman bubbled over with enthusiasm for the chance to begin frontier life in Kansas with her soon-to-be husband, Preston—whom, she explained, she waited for until he finished two years of soldiering; then, they would tie the knot; even though Preston's mother birth him in Louisville, Kentucky, across the Ohio River from Cincinnati, his family were Union loyalists.

She, bubbling with curiosity about life on the frontier, inquired about John Henry's part in it. He told her of his scouting days tracking Sioux and Cheyenne movements across the Great Plains, omitting the bloodshed and carnage inflicted by both the army and the savages. Dressed as she was in a very stylish, although provocative dress that revealed too much shoulder and too much ankle, she aroused John Henry; any robust man with eyes would be so aroused. Putting aside any sexual thought she provoked in him, he became entranced with the young woman as he would with his daughter had he been a father to her. He related the recent Sioux hostilities and advised Katie Craftsman to return to Ohio, where life was less dangerous. He saw that his advice would not persuade the young woman to give up her dream of building a frontier life with her future husband, especially since she would be settling down with an ex-soldier who knew how to use a firearm.

The stagecoach arrived in Fort Hays City as dusk fell over the town. A curious John Henry stood by while Katie's fiancé, dressed in an enlisted man's blue tunic and striped trousers, took her in his arms. John Henry noted the young man remained a private—the army dangling promotion as an incentive for reenlistment kept him at its lowest rank. He knew the young man, Preston Ambercet, a soldier earlier assigned to Fort Abraham Lincoln in the Dakota Territory. Red Cloud's Sioux would often raid the fort's livestock, and the dangerous task of tracking the raiders fell to John Henry. A squad of eight soldiers, including Preston Ambercet, accompanied him on one such occasion. The Sioux raiders, not more than five or six, ever anxious to score a coup, turned around and attacked the soldiers following them. The soldiers, excluding the sergeant, were raw recruits who turned their horses around in a desperate effort to escape the attack; the sergeant galloped after his panic-stricken soldiers. John Henry, giving chase, caught the reigns of one soldier's horse and turned the recruit to face the charging Sioux; The soldier happened to be Preston Ambercet. They took shelter behind a small rise on the open prairie with only dry grass to shelter them. The sergeant, meanwhile, managed to collect his squad and bring them to where John Henry and the recruit made their stand. Newly armed with Springfield breech-loading rifles firing eight to ten rounds per minute, the army detail held off the Sioux raiders, eventually scattering them. Subsequently, they recovered a dozen of the horses stolen from the fort. The commanding officer at Fort Abraham Lincoln believed John Henry's mission to be successful and congratulated each of the soldiers. After that, Private Ambercet felt indebted to the man who converted him from a scared boy into a respected soldier.

After embracing Katie Craftsman, Ambercet noticed his benefactor and led his fiancée to greet John Henry. The private explained the army would be discharging him this week, and within the same week, he and Katie planned to be married in the only church in town, a Methodist one still under construction. Thereafter, they would build a life together on the frontier. They invited him to attend the ceremony and the reception.

The town—made up of one long street with two shorter ones intersecting it and a couple of dozen crude cabins dotting the outskirts—appeared as another dusty and windblown plains habitat established by a railroad raging across the plains; the presence of nearby Fort Hays, offering protection against hostile savages, influenced the railroad route. The Union Pacific rail line ran parallel to the main street, just to the south of it. A depot and stockyards occupied the street's eastern end. The respectable Gibbs Hotel, a barbershop, and the Bloomfield General Store were close to the depot. The stagecoach station, corral, stables, and gun shop stood on the western end of the main street. That end of the street also housed the town Marshal's office, the jail, the tiny courthouse, and the *Sentinel*, the local newspaper.

A string of saloons congregated in the middle of the street; they were rowdy places with music pouring out their doors, serenading the town. The saloons serviced the fort's soldiers and the trail drivers delivering Texas cattle to the railroad and to the fort, a lethal concoction existed because both groups were hellraisers and enemies to each other.

The Kelly Saloon—a large, expensively decorated drinking, whoring, and gambling den—had become the most prominent of the two dozen saloons in Fort Hays City. Meat markets, saddle shops, and eating establishments interspersed across the street from the saloons; the brothels, of which there were at least a dozen, were scattered along perpendicular Fort and Commercial Streets. John Henry warned the young couple to be cautious on the lengthy walk to their hotel and to be on the lookout for troublemakers, advising the young woman to cover her bare shoulders. He then made his way to the stable.

John Henry collected the Mustang pony he captured on the plains and his saddle rifle and shotgun from the stable owner. The horse looked well-kept and fed, and all his possessions were intact. Half an hour passed since he said goodbye to the young couple, and he thought to check if they reached their hotel safely before he traveled to his room at a boardinghouse a quarter mile outside of town.

Darkness stood nearby as he slung his shotgun over his shoulder and, with his Navy Colt strapped to his hip, rode his horse at a walk down the middle of the street, casually peering into the windows of storefronts. Most of the saloons displayed only raw timber fronts and no windows. From experience, he knew that this close to autumn, most of the trail-driving Texas cowboys left Fort Hays City for home, but he saw maybe a dozen cowboy horses tethered to hitching posts lining the street. His stagecoach arrived on a Saturday, so he knew half of the soldiers stationed at the fort would be om a weekend pass. On the street, he mostly saw soldiers milling about, patronizing various shops; he knew they also filled the bars. He noted the usual enlisted man's horseplay and jostling in the street. He smiled, remembering his early soldiering days as he observed these horny kids longing for their hometown girlfriends, appearing more interested in finding female companionship than getting drunk. About two-thirds of the way to the hotel, he thought he heard faint sobbing—a woman's.

The gunslinger dismounted, tied off his horse, and crept into an alley between two saloons. What he saw did not shock him as much as it infuriated him.

While walking to the hotel, young Katie Craftsman's curiosity compelled her to open a saloon door against her partner's wishes. She stood fascinated, observing men drinking and gambling and prostitutes, dressed provocatively, sitting on men's laps. Standing transfixed in the doorway, she, young and shapely, caught the attention of three cowboys drinking at the bar near the door, all liquored up and wild with three months' pent-up energy. They misread her curiosity for promiscuity. The three men followed the young couple down the street and dragged them into the first alleyway they found. Thereafter, they pistol-whipped the resisting young soldier into submission.

John Henry saw that two young cowboys—all gussied up in new shirts, jeans, and chaps and wearing cattle-hide vests—fondled the breasts of Katie Craftsman. An older man, most likely an ex-Rebel soldier, still wearing his trail-driving clothing, held a pistol to the breast of a bloody and beaten Preston Ambercet. All three men were red-faced and sweating, indicating to John Henry they drank hard liquor for most of the day.

John Henry pulled back both hammers on his shotgun. The metallic clicks caught the attention of the trail herders. "You cowboys release these kids, and I'll let you go about your business. Otherwise, I'll use this scattergun on the three of you."

Fully confident that the odds of three against one were in his favor, the older cowboy growled confidently: "Looks like we have another Yankee poking his nose in business that doesn't concern him. The threat of a stupid jackass like you don't mean a tinker's damn to me. I'll shoot this fuzzy-faced bastard and then take you down before you can squeeze those shotgun triggers."

"Anything is possible if you're drunk enough to think it." John Henry turned half his attention to the younger cowboys, who continued to hold onto the young woman from Cincinnati. Terrified, she appeared roughed up. The cowboys tore the hemline holding her bodice, exposing her breasts.

"You boys deserve to spend some jail time for what you did to this woman, but that is much better than dying for being dumb drunks. Now you two cowboys release her, drop your pistols where you stand, and let me deal with your varmint sidekick." The two young men, not moving an inch, grinned menacingly. He turned his attention back to the older cowboy. "You did enough harm to this boy. Turn him over to me."

"You want this fuzzy-faced cur? Take him." Before John Henry could act, the drunken Confederate shot the boy in the heart, pushing him aside and aiming his pistol at John Henry. But it was a fool's play, for John Henry, standing less than ten feet away, fired his shotgun, hitting the cowboy directly in the chest. Instead of shoving Katie Craftsman aside to draw his pistol, the drunker of the two standing cowboys slit her throat with a knife. With no time to experience disbelief, John Henry fired the other shotgun load; the blast tore into the murderer's face, dropping him. He then hurled his shotgun at the other young cowboy, whose pistol stuck in his new holster, giving John Henry time to pull his sidearm and cock it. The young cowboy managed to get off one wild shot that nicked John Henry's shoulder. The man who tried so assiduously to avoid trouble, realizing it always found him, calmly squeezed the trigger of his pistol, hitting the young cowboy dead center in the chest. The shotgun blast and pistol fire immediately brought a crowd, which now surrounded John Henry and five dead people. Encircled by soldiers, prostitutes, merchants, and residents, John Henry knew it would not be long before the marshal arrived.

When the man—tall, lanky, and rough-mannered—did appear, John Henry pointed to the pistol-whipped baby-faced soldier, his blue tunic charred from powder burns around the bloody chest wound, and then to his molested bride-to-be lying dead nearby, blood seeping from her slit throat. Three Texas cowboys likewise lay dead: one with a hole in his chest; one with his face blown away, still clutching a bloody knife; and one with a bullet hole through his heart. Pushing back against the crowd pressing upon him, the shooter explained what happened to the marshal.

Amazed that one man could shoot three hardened trail hands at such close range without being mortally wounded, the marshal asked no questions. Marshal Matthew Pentz and John Henry were long-standing acquaintances who held mutual respect for each other; they thought of themselves as defenders of white women, children, and settlers in Kansas.

Marshal Pentz informed him that he would notify the cowboys camped outside of town that their cohorts were shot dead and ask them to collect the bodies; otherwise, they would be put underground at Boot Hill a mile out of town, a shameful place where dead-broke drunks and hell-raisers without friends or family were buried. Pentz related that less than a half dozen cowpunchers of the dead cowboys' trail bunch camped nearby. Having delivered the herd, the cowpunchers and the owner journeyed back to Texas. He advised John Henry to stay at the fort, where he could be protected until tempers cooled. After the mortician collected the bodies, John Henry rode toward Fort Hays.

*

But a half hour out of Fort Hays City, John Henry disconcerted that he did not accompanied the young betrothed couple to their hotel and thus prevent their deaths, dismounted and laid out his bedroll behind a clump of windblown brush. He checked his left shoulder and found the cowboy's bullet only grazed it. With water from his canteen, he washed out what looked to be a flesh wound and patched it with a torn shirtsleeve. He recalled that toward the end of the war, Rebel prisoners, many of them Texans, agreed to fight the Hunkpapa, Lakota, and other Sioux tribes warring on the plains in exchange for an early release from insufferable prisons. Having witnessed their camaraderie as a fighting unit, John Henry knew the Texan mentality enough to realize that everyone down to the last man would seek retaliation for a killing they perceived as wrongfully inflicted against one of their kind. Shooting three Texas cowboys certainly qualified John Henry for retaliation. He knew the cowboys' cohorts camped outside of Fort Hays City and, once notified of their brother Texans' deaths, would track him to the ends of the earth. He decided to track them first.

At the crack of dawn, with just enough light to put the Mustang to a trot, John Henry moved to where he thought the Texas trail drivers might camp. Within half an hour, he spotted their campfire smoke; dismounting, he led his horse in that direction. When he came within a couple of hundred paces of the campsite, he crawled on hands and knees through tall, dry grass until he could get a clear view of the cowboys. They finished their morning coffee and were now dousing the fire with the remainder of it. He watched as six men mounted range horses and galloped toward Fort Hays City. The six cowboys were heavily armed and outfitted in their rough trail clothes; one cowboy with long blond hair in his early twenties dressed much better than the rest, wearing a silver shirt, black trousers, hat, and fancy boots. He carried a mother-of-pearl-handled pistol coated in a silver metallic. Riding two hundred yards to their left, John Henry was tempted to pick off one or cowboys with his Winchester but concluded that he would scatter the rest. Even during the plains wars, when he tracked Sioux and Cheyenne bands, he never shot a savage from long range; to his way of thinking, that would be murder. As the band of cowboys neared town, a prairie wind kicked up, blowing dirt and brush horizontally, making it difficult for John Henry to see. When they reached the town, two cowboys rode to the stables, where they rented a wagon. The other four cowboys dismounted and entered the marshal's office; it became evident to John Henry that they were requesting a description of him and the direction he in which he fled. He stepped into a nearby eatery and sat near a window with a clear view of the marshal's office. Fifteen minutes later, the four men, looking disgruntled, exited the building; John Henry assumed the marshal, wanting to give him a good head start, gave the four men little information.

The four cowboys scattered to both sides of the street, questioning merchants and saloon patrons. At this early hour most saloon patrons were gone, and those who remained were either drunk or hungover. Nevertheless, he figured the cowboys gained a good description of him as he watched them collect in the middle of the street, appearing satisfied with their questioning. The men entered the Kelly Saloon, the only one with a large front window; from across the street, John Henry watched them throw down numerous shots of whiskey. Next, they made their way to a gun shop, where they purchased extra ammunition, and to a general store, where they bought provisions. They collected their horses and walked to the mortician's office on the corner of Main and Fort Streets, where a rented wagon was now hitched to a post. The wind kicked up to the point that debris blew horizontally through the streets, causing the mules hitched to the wagon to nervously paw the dirt and driving pedestrians to seek shelter.

The blowing dust and dirt minimized visibility; nevertheless, John Henry, standing across the street from the mortician's office, saw the six men load three crude wood coffins onto the wagon bed. Four cowboys, including the better-dressed one, stood by as the two others drove the wagon loaded with three hastily-built coffins out of town, heading south over the prairie toward Texas. The remaining four cowboys attempted to mount very agitated horses, tossing their heads about and trying to turn away from the blowing dirt. By now, the street appeared entirely deserted in both directions.

With the wind at his back, John Henry, shotgun in his left hand and pistol loose in his holster, walked across the street to confront the four men. He knew it was reckless to confront four seasoned cowboys alone, but he believed his years of trailing savages on the plains evened the odds. He often witnessed outnumbered Sioux and Cheyenne warriors turn on pursuers who outnumbered them, using an unexpected aggression to rout them. He counted on this same surprise to give him an edge. He knew he little choice existed but to end the matter here on this Fort Hays City street or else in some town and at some time when he didn't expect it, the cowboys would find him, and then the element of surprise would be on their side; the men, after questioning the street's occupants, obtained a good description of him.

When in town, John Henry always wore a suit jacket to conceal his derringer. He preferred to wear a plain white cotton shirt, buttoned at the neck, with a workmen's bandanna covering his throat. He pulled his denim trousers over boots that came up to his knees, appearing as another working stiff, and he always wore a worn, wide-brimmed hat to shield himself from the hot Kansas sun. These Texans were seasoned and un-intimidated men, soberer and therefore more brutal than the bunch he faced yesterday. All four wore heavy mustaches. Long ago, when sizing up those who appeared superior, John Henry learned to discard any disadvantage he felt so that the negative would not hinder him. He came within seven paces of the mounted cowboys, still trying to control their nervous horses. Their distraction encouraged him to cry out:

"You Texas boys looking to find the man who shot down your murdering cohorts? No need to look any farther—I am your man, John Henry Summerfield." All four men drew their pistols. It was the best move that John Henry could hope for. He would be defenseless if they charged him with their horses, but their wild ways and quick tempers favored him. Jittery horses made it difficult for them to get off clean shots; pistol shots hit the dirt around him. With the raging wind at his back, he fired a shotgun blast into the first cowboy, a tall and lanky range hand with a permanent sneer, before he could re-aim his pistol, knocking him from the saddle. The cowboy's foot caught in the stirrup of his saddle; spooked, the horse dragged him away. When the second cowboy's horse reared, John Henry stepped forward and fired a shotgun blast into his upper torso. The man, sleeves rolled up to reveal muscular forearms from a life of hard work, slumped in the saddle. The ex-army scout then dropped the shotgun and drew his pistol to shoot the remaining two mounted men, firing his Navy Colt while the third cowboy fired his pistol. John Henry's aim was truer, and the Colt's bullet struck the third cowboy, bald and mean-looking with his busted teeth and scarred lips flush in the forehead.

John Henry fired a split second ahead of the cowboy, unfortunately, not soon enough to divert the man's aim. The man's large-caliber bullet hit the grip of his pistol, destroying it and blowing off his ring and small fingers. The fourth cowboy—the well-dressed blond in a silver shirt, black hat, and fancy boots—had drawn and cocked his silver-plated pistol, but it jammed, the hammer frozen back. With his left hand John Henry pulled his derringer from his jacket pocket, but before he could get close enough to aim, the well-dressed cowboy spurred his horse into a gallop, disappearing down the first perpendicular street.

John Henry found his horse across the street and retrieved a second Navy Colt pistol from his saddlebag, a backup he always carried because once he fired five rounds from his Navy Colt, it was extremely laborious to reload. He cut a portion of the horse's rein and used the leather to strap the large pistol to his now three-fingered hand, which was bleeding profusely. Mounting his horse, he pursued the fleeing cowboy. Directing his horse onto the first perpendicular street, Fort Street, he found the cowboy, who, instead of escaping, reloaded his pistol to face John Henry. The cowboy fired a round into the dirt to check the pistol's function. He then spotted John Henry, now facing him forty yards away.

The wind kicked up, blowing papers, porch furniture from second stories, and any item not secured along the street, tossing the cowboy's fancy black hat from his head. John Henry got a good glimpse of the well-dressed cowboy's face, a well-formed, good-looking one, handsome enough to be on stage. Viciously spurring his horse in the flanks, the cowboy excited his mount into a full gallop, firing wildly at John Henry. Having faced such charges from plains warriors, John Henry thought it best to charge the man charging him. When he came within twenty yards, he maneuvered his horse to the right side of the cowboy's. Using a tactic he witnessed expert Sioux horse riders employ, he leaned to the left of his horse, his upper body behind the animal's sizable neck, firing his pistol as his foe, charging within five feet on Army veteran's right,. He missed the cowboy but slew his horse with two bullets to the head; reining his mount to a skidding stop, he saw a stunned cowboy sprawled in the dirt, his pistol some ten feet away. Shot in the neck, his horse staggered and collapsed.

Dismounting, he placed a foot on the man's pistol. Prior to the previous day, the ex-Union Army veteran and plains scout never intentionally killed a man outside the line of duty. He would break that precedent again by forcing this man into a pistol fight—and to do that, he knew that the man must face him so he could avoid a murder charge.

The dust-covered cowboy pulled himself onto his hands and knees to regain self-control. John Henry kicked the silver pistol forward until it rested within a foot of the cowboy. "Pick up your pistol and face me." He looked down at his hand, blood streaming from where a bullet blew off his two fingers. The grip of his pistol felt wet and sticky, slimy with blood, but securely fixed to his hand. The oscillating wind blowing in from both sides of the short perpendicular street caused debris and trash to blow to and fro between them, the windstorm favoring neither foe. He held his pistol so that the muzzle pointed to the ground and waited until the cowboy followed suit. He did not wait for the cowboy to move first; swiftly elevating his handgun, he took sure aim and fired. The expert shooter shot the well-dressed cowboy squarely in the chest and watched him pitch facedown into the dirt, never getting a chance to level his pistol.

John Henry, a nondescript freight driver, shot four men in addition to the three men he shot yesterday over an incident he could walk away. Some of the whores who formed a circle around him and the dead girl and her fiancé yesterday now braved the wind and looked on from second-floor balconies. He noted that his wounded horse looked set to drop to the ground at any minute; he removed his saddle, his saddle bags, rifle, and the reins and bit from the horse's mouth. No choice existed but to shoot the animal in the head. Then he moved out of the wind to where one of the whores could hear him; she recognized him from his frequent whorehouse visits when he was free from delivering freight for the army. He tossed her a silver dollar. "This is for the liveryman to haul away these dead horses."

He made his way to the marshal's office, noting that only a few people lined the streets because of the early hour. Grateful for the lack of attention, he saw the marshal holding a rifle as he exited his small office at the head of the street. Carrying a saddle and an attached rifle over his left shoulder, saddlebags over the other, John Henry noted the marshal studying the pistol dripping blood strapped to his bleeding hand and the three cowboys sprawled out dead on the dusty street in front of the mortician's establishment. He trained his rifle on John Henry, who slowed his approach, uncertain of the lawman's intentions.

"There is one more dead cowboy on Fort Street under the whores' balconies."

"Summerfield, I respect you as a past protector of white people on the plains, but seven dead bodies in two days, not counting those poor youngsters, sure does test that respect to its limit." He lowered his rifle and held it in the crook of his right arm. "If I hold you for the judge, I reckon you will hang, that is, if the Texans don't lynch you before that time. James Knox Ulsterman's only son was one of the cowboys I talked to yesterday. If you shot him, God help you. Is he killed?

"If blond hair fell to his shoulders and he dressed in a silver shirt, black hat, and fancy boots, I shot him through the heart."

The marshal grimaced, untied the leather strip securing the bloody Navy Colt pistol, and placed the weapon in John Henry's holster. He then wrapped the mangled hand in a bandanna taken from John Henry's neck. "I see you are on foot." "My horse lies dead next to Ulsterman's son."

"Best you start walking to Fort Hays. Soon as I clean up your mess, I'll catch up and deliver you to the fort."

*

Once the marshal delivered him to the fort, John Henry's boss—Major Brandenberger, in charge of supplying the army's frontier forts spread across Minnesota, Colorado, Wyoming, and Montana—ordered him taken to the army surgeon, who cauterized and bandaged his wound. His escort then took him to Brigadier General Wills, an advocate of protecting Union war veterans, who ordered him placed on the first supply wagon heading north into the Montana Territory. The general advised John Henry to begin a new life in Canada because his career working for the army was finished. For the next five years, John Henry did just that, as a tracker of renegade savages and outlaws for the Royal Canadian Mounted Police in Saskatchewan and later guarding stagecoaches traveling between Regina and Saskatoon.

On one such stagecoach journey, a hunter from Texas spotted his three-fingered hand. John Henry heard a two-thousand-dollar reward for information regarding his whereabouts, James Ulsterman posted from Kansas south throughout Texas. He decided to get as far away from the volatile plains as possible and headed for Los Angeles, where he thought to live a normal life in a civilized town. It would be a life without a wife because he could not jeopardize a woman by asking her to live with a man on the run. He knew that somehow and in some way, he would run into James Knox Ulsterman if the man did not find him first.

*

Rehashing the shootout in Fort Hays City that changed his life, John Henry waited another day for the Bensons to ride out and would wait for days if he did not spot vultures circling a half-mile behind him. In all probability, the scavengers found a dead animal, but given the vicious attack on the Cardwell ranch, John Henry felt he could not leave any stone unturned. With his mule in tow, he rode to where the vultures circled over a small, dry gulch that at one time of the year captured enough rainfall to keep a few mesquite trees alive.

As he neared, he saw a naked body dangling from the limb of a gnarled tree, dead from thirst but too far away to determine the sex. A pack of eight or nine coyotes jumped about the body and tore off strips of flesh from the lower legs. Closing the distance, John Henry saw the hanging body was a female. When he rode within fifty yards of the tree, he shot the largest coyote through the head with his rifle; he shot two more predators before the pack scattered. The body hung for days, exposed to the sun and wind, and badly decomposed. The woman's back faced him, intensifying his anxiety. He cut the rope that bound her hands to the tree limb and caught the body in his arms. What he saw horrified him: the kidnappers slit her abdomen from vagina to breastbone after slicing her flesh about the arms and legs.

He guessed the woman suffered this torture for refusing to show the kidnappers a good time. He thought he witnessed almost every kind of heinous acts a man could handle, but this was the most sickening. Dismounting as gently as he could, careful not to drop the corpse, he placed the dead woman in the shade of a clump of mesquite trees. After that, he retrieved his small tent from the mule and laid the woman on it. Forcing himself to gaze upon the dead body, the woman's remains appeared tall with hair that resembled his own before it began gray. His stomach turned when he saw the woman wore no wedding ring—there was a good possibility she was his unmarried daughter—though a second thought reminded him the kidnappers stripped her of all valuables, including a wedding band.

He very carefully wrapped the corpse in the canvas tent. Unsure whether or not the dead, mutilated woman was his daughter, John Henry felt more guilt than revenge well up in his hardened psyche. He knew he wronged Benevolence when he deserted her and a two-year-old child with only a hired hand to help them on the harsh Kansas plains. The memory of the time he hired on as an army scout when he saw his daughter exiting from the church with her new family compounded his guilt. He could gain permission from his commanding officer to leave the formation and visit with his daughter, but he chose not to. No matter how hard he searched his memory, he could find no justification to relieve the grinding guilt abandoning his daughter brought on. Guilt would be a chain that bound him to his vendetta sworn on behalf of Benevolence. But he saw now that avenging Benevolence by waylaying anyone who rode out of the canyon must wait for another time. First, he would ride to Las Vegas and bury this woman, most likely his daughter, in a proper manner.

*

He waited the remainder of the day and the first few hours of the next morning, with the dead woman still wrapped in his canvas tent, for any sign of outlaws who might be alerted by his rifle fire and might pick up his trail. No curiosity seekers appeared. For whatever reason, the Benson boys chose not to follow their pa to retaliate for the destruction of their home place.

A few days later, in the late afternoon, John Henry spotted Las Vegas' large arch overshadowing the plaza and the plaza's windmill, infamous as a hanging spot for bad men. As he rode by the sign forbidding pistols in the town, he recalled his encounter with the hard-nosed sheriff and, wanting to avoid another such encounter, rode directly to a funeral parlor on the town's main street. He reverently removed the woman's body slung over the mule and carried it inside. The mortician, a tall and very thin balding man owning a hooked nose and sunken cheeks, took the body from John Henry and moved it into a back room. He paid the mortician twenty dollars to make the woman as presentable as

97

possible and another twenty dollars to purchase a respectable lot in the cemetery on the outskirts of town.

He next rode to the stables, leaving his horse, mule, pistol, shotgun, and rifle, keeping only his derringer. His family raised he as a Presbyterian; Benevolence raised a Catholic—a blending of venerable opposites. He possessed no idea what faith the dead woman observed. He found a Catholic church dominating the plaza and arranged for a priest to say proper words over the woman. He next walked past several two-story adobe dwellings surrounding the plaza, hosting a variety of merchants from wagon builders to bootmakers. As usual, men milled about in front of saloons on the main street leading into the plaza, smoking pipes and cigars if they could afford them and jawing. Numerous horses tethered to hitching posts along the street indicated that Las Vegas was enjoying a busy day. John Henry purchased a fashionable Eastern dress in a dressmaker's shop; taking the dress to the mortician, he waited until the crane-like man properly made up the dead woman. He paid thirty dollars for a cherry wood coffin, even though the amount considerably reduced his cash reserve. Satisfied that everything was in order, he sought the towheaded, fuzzy-faced sheriff's deputy, Tommy McGrath, to tell him if this woman was his daughter or half-sister.

He found the young deputy sitting on a bench outside the sheriff's office; being the office attendant seemed to be his assignment while the sheriff went about his business. The youngster remembered him and flashed a welcoming smile, which faltered when John Henry informed the deputy about the woman he found in the Oklahoma badlands and asked him to identify the corpse. When they arrived, the mortician performed a decent makeup job on the dead woman's decomposing face. He washed and dried her hair and arranged it so it hugged her forehead and cradled her chin. Heavy pancake makeup covered her decomposed face, although her well-proportioned features remained evident. Laid out as she was in a fancy pale blue dress, she looked like a woman who led a respectable life. The deputy stood there staring at the corpse, his eyes locked on the reddish-brown hair and the woman's long fingers intertwined across her chest.

"That woman is Miss Jane, who helped me with my three Rs. I am sorry for this town's loss, especially yours, Mr. Summerfield." The deputy choked on his last few words.

John Henry sank into a hardback chair near the coffin, his fear realized. "Thank you, Deputy."

"My mom and me will be at the funeral if there is to be one." John Henry indicated there would be. "Is there anyone else I should ask to be there?"

"Loner" would be the proper description for John Henry. Therefore, he was heartened that his daughter partook of Las Vegas society, acting as a substitute teacher and probably very active in church affairs. "I would be obliged if you would inform those who knew my daughter Jane that the funeral will be tomorrow at noon. Do you know which church she attended?"

"Catholic one on the plaza's far end, same as me." John Henry made the right choice, although this fact did little to cheer him. "Best you get moving about informing Jane's friends, Deputy."

"You can count on me. I'll be off duty at five." John Henry sat stiffly on the wooden chair in the parlor until well after six o'clock, when the mortician closed shop for the day.

Standing in the street outside the mortician's office, the sheriff and his two brawny deputies faced him as he exited. The deputies looked to be seasoned lawmen, their eyes flat like those of predators on the prowl. As before, the compact sheriff appeared perfectly groomed, and his white mustache waxed to perfection. "I heard you were back in town. A lot of very interesting but troubling incidents occurred since you showed your face here last time. Some three-fingered stranger rode into Broad-Butt Betty's place of ill repute and blew apart four feet belonging to two hoodlums. Bad blood ran through those Grayson boys, and I suppose they deserved that. Good thing for that person that Broad Butt's den of iniquity is just across the county line from my territory and out of my jurisdiction, or I would be obliged to question the shooter. I also heard tell of a man who rode south in New Mexico territory, close to the border, and burned the Benson place to the ground, shot the livestock, and left family members staked out for the Apache to find. Again, that is out of my jurisdiction, although the Otero Sheriff would like to question the villain. Trading with hostile Apache is a hanging offense to towns around here, white women trading being the worst such crime." John Henry's eyes traveled from the gold watch chain draped across the lawman's vest to the large Smith & Wesson pistol the man carried in a shoulder holster that bulged under his expensive suit jacket. "Man involved in those happenings liked to carry a shotgun. The stable owner told me you own a shotgun. It seems to me, Summerfield, that trouble follows you wherever you go, and to my way of thinking, that makes you a troublemaker. As I warned you before, I don't tolerate troublemakers in my territory, and especially in this town."

"As I told you before, Sheriff, I obey the law when I can. Once I deal with the men who murdered my daughter and kidnapped her half-sister and those two little girls, I will be out of your jurisdiction forever."

"Some time back, some Texas boys collecting short pay and a bunk at a ranch outside of Waco dropped off some reward posters and asked after the whereabouts of a man who shot seven of their cohorts in Kansas. Are you from Kansas, Summerfield?"

"I am."

"I don't rightly see how a three-fingered man could kill seven hardened Texas cowboys face-to-face in two days." He turned and indicated to his deputies that his business with John Henry concluded. And then, on second thought, he turned back to John Henry. "I just remembered those Grayson thugs took a derringer off the man they nearly beat to death. You carry a derringer, Summerfield? You been warned no weapons are allowed in this town." He gestured to his two oversized deputies to grab John Henry by his arms; the sheriff frisked the restrained man, reaching inside his coat and removing the derringer. Fingering the four-barreled Sharps pistol, he smiled menacingly. "I really dislike lawbreakers—my job is to teach them a lesson." He slapped John Henry across the cheekbone with the small pistol, causing blood to stream from an inch-long gash in his cheek, and then pounded his fist into John Henry's belly. When the taller man failed to collapse, he dropped the derringer's four cartridges into his hand to give it more heft and then used all his compact weight to drive his fist two more times into the restrained man's lower belly. John Henry sunk to his knees.

"You can pick up your toy after you pay a twenty-fivedollar fine. If I'm not around, you can pay my young deputy, the one that's taken a shine to you."

When the lawmen left, John Henry rose and walked to a stonecutter's shop, thinking too much existed on his plate to deal with the hard-nosed sheriff. He purchased a tombstone and ordered it inscribed:

Jane Rose Summerfield
Beloved daughter of John and Benevolence
1859–1885

Tommy McGrath, the sheriff's deputy, accomplished what he told John Henry he would; John Henry counted thirty-one residents from in and around Las Vegas paying their respects at his daughter's burial the next day. They were the hardworking people who rarely spoke unless spoken to, people who avoided the iniquity found in saloons and whorehouses. He imagined they only drank liquor at Saturday night socials and then went to church on Sunday mornings, resting on the Sabbath as their God commanded. He spent ten years avoiding attention; now, after the priest said his holy words, John Henry gained the attention of the entire gathering as they queued to offer their condolences to him. John Henry considered his person to be well known in Las Vegas. After the crowd dispersed, he stood by while the gravediggers filled the hole where his daughter lay. Alone with thoughts of payback, he walked a mile to the stable and collected his horse and mule. He still needed to smoke out the seven murderers of his daughter

Chapter 8

Once a man steps over civilization's line into anarchy, there is no stepping back, and this holds true for John Henry. With his mule in tow, he rode south toward Clines Corners, a crossroads leading to Santa Fe or Las Vegas from southern New Mexico Territory. Once there, he rode east across a desolate stretch of parched land to where he believed the Alsop spread to be; the ex-Rebel Wade Alsop would be his next target. Less than a decade ago, Apache raiders overran the area he rode through, but now it was rare to see a raider. The prospector's information described Alsop as coming from a family of low-living cattle thieves and claim jumpers. He told John Henry the father, going by the name of Ben, could shoot down a man at two hundred paces with a rifle. Given that knowledge, he carefully circled the Alsop spread, which consisted of two hovels on a miserable patch of rocky, alkaline land, not a ranch that offered a decent living.

The wretched spread showed evidence of years of neglect. The corral appeared in desperate need of repair; the barn door hung off its hinges, and the livestock looked miserable and underfed. He spotted six family members lounging in the shade and drinking what looked like hard cider. The father, a droopyeyed, slovenly dressed man, stood about five feet eight inches, his sandy brown hair falling over his forehead. His wife, thin as a rail, was a sharp-faced woman who wore a bonnet and a threadbare dress that hadn't been washed in years, as filthy and unkempt as her husband and children. John Henry counted four younger females—a dirty, pregnant woman in her middle twenties and a girl just a few years past puberty, along with what he guessed to be eight- and ten-year-old dirty-faced girls. Barefooted, the offspring learned their hygiene from their parents. The Alsop offspring looked to come from different sires, as their hair coloring ranged from black to brown to sandy blond.

While waiting for nightfall to surprise the Alsops, John Henry spotted two cowboys riding range horses in the distance, traveling toward Las Vegas. They stopped before a pole with a crude sign tacked to it. On his way to the Alsop place, John Henry read the sign: SHORTCUT TO LAS VEGAS, SAVE MANY MILES. The shortcut, if indeed it existed, ran right past the Alsop hovels. The youngest of the scrawny girl perched herself on a rocky rise, reconnoitering the landscape with a small telescope. Once the cowboys directed their horses down the shortcut path, she threw a stone with uncanny accuracy and hit a washtub, alerting her family. The chaps-wearing cowboys, little more than teenagers and as carefree as wildcat cubs, carried pistols and saddle rifles. Two cowboys plus the Alsop family being a total he could not handle, John Henry thought no choice existed but to wait until the cowboys rode past the Alsops, but to his surprise he now saw the family tacking two signs to the front of their shanty. One handmade sign read WHISKEY 10 CENTS, the other, WOMEN $2.

The cowboys, dusty and hot from the trail, dismounted before the Alsop hovel. After half an hour, John Henry led his horse and mule into the shade of some juniper trees stunted by the alkaline soil and prepared for a long wait. He chewed upon a strip of hardtack as night fell. Lanterns lit the main hovel. Thereafter, accordion music could be heard; the cowboys, accompanied by female giggling, shouted more than sang some made-up lyrics to the music. John Henry listened to the raucous parents and children clapping their hands and stomping their feet. John Henry figured after the two travelers drank their fill of whiskey, one or both of the older sisters would service them, so he reluctantly waited for the morning, when he hoped the cowboys would be on their way.

When the next morning's sunlight shone over the New Mexico Territory for an hour, he looked on as the parents carried one unconscious cowboy, bound hand and foot. The two older girls carried the other victim, equally tied up and indisposed, to a rickety wagon and placed them in the bed. He thought the family using low-down trickery slipped the unsuspecting travelers a Mickey Finn—chloral hydrate—not an uncommon act on the frontier. The oldest girl hitched two mules to the wagon, and all six Alsops climbed aboard the wagon and rode off into the parched prairie. John Henry followed them. About five miles out, the family rode onto a rocky mesa with numerous washed-out ravines cutting through it. They directed the wagon up a ravine that snaked about and stopped after three hundred paces.

Following at a distance, it took him about ten minutes to come upon the wicked family. When he did, the two oldest girls were scratching out shallow graves; the parents, becoming satiated buzzards, stripped the cowboys bare-butt naked and now eyed the grave digging, smoking pipes, and sipping rotgut from jars. A harmonica and a worn deck of cards sat atop two piles of the cowboys' clothes. The senior Alsop's rifle leaned against the wagon behind him. The two youngest girls, looking as wild as wolf cubs, sat on the wagon's tailgate, playfully swinging their feet and humming, "*Jeanie with the Light Brown Hair*." Whether the family intended to bury the two cowboys alive or dead remained unclear to John Henry. He waited until the two older girls stood knee-deep in the holes they carved out and then dismounted. There were six Alsops, so he strapped his Colt pistol to his right hand and carried the sawed-off two-barreled shotgun in the other.

The children's off-key humming and the older girls' digging in the dirt created enough noise to enable John Henry to creep up behind the parents as they supervised the grave digging. Within three feet of Ben Alsop, John Henry fired his pistol into the air, hoping to take the family by surprise. "Everyone stay put!" The senior Alsop lunged for his rifle where it leaned against the wagon; John Henry smacked him in the back of the head with the barrel of his Colt, causing the man to stagger. He hadn't noticed before, but Alsop's wife carried a small pistol in the pocket of her dress. She pulled the weapon out, but before she could aim, John Henry slammed his pistol barrel on her wrist, dislodging the pistol. He trained his shotgun on the two females standing knee-deep in the makeshift graves to keep them in place. The two younger girls darted up the washout, disappearing around the first bend.

John Henry ordered the two remaining daughters to remove the ropes binding the unconscious cowboys and then hogtie their parents, one with a sizable knot on his head and the other with a sore arm, so that their wrists and ankles were secured behind their backs, rendering them immobile. He then rolled the squealing parents facedown into the shallow graves. He ordered the two grown girls to carry the unconscious cowboys into the shade, place them upright, and leave the cowboys' clothing next to them. Feeling secure, he unstrapped the Colt pistol from his hand. He mounted his horse and ordered the two older females to board the wagon. Subsequently, he ordered them to follow their sisters up the washed-out ravine. Farther up the ravine, John Henry noticed at least a dozen oblong places where the family disturbed the ground; the Alsops were an accomplished family of way-layers and murderers, he concluded.

The two girls, wearing ragged dresses over coveralls, ran into a dead end about half a mile up the gully. John Henry ordered them to climb into the wagon, but they were defiant, throwing rocks at him. Anticipating their resistance, he sent their older sister, carrying the cowboys' harmonica and playing cards ,to bring them back. The three sisters sat in the dead end for an hour playing poker and taking turns blowing into the harmonica, but the younger girls refused to return to the wagon. Within the next two hours, the hot New Mexico sun accomplished what the bribes could not; the younger sisters, overheated and thirsty, followed their older sister back to the wagon. With the four sisters riding ahead of him in the wagon pulled by slow-walking mules, John Henry directed them back to where their parents were bound and the still unconscious cowboys positioned under a tree. Scratching out a note, he informed the cowboys of the Alsops' murderous intent and the probability of numerous graves farther up the ravine. Whether or not the cowboys disposed of the senior Alsops or turned them over to law enforcement made little difference to John Henry. Hanged would be their fate.

Just as he did at the Benson ranch, John Henry torched the Alsops' two hovels. He shot the smaller livestock, destroyed a

105

neglected garden, and then hitched three horses on a rope line to the wagon. Learning from experience, he secured enough flour, beans, and fatback to feed the four females on the journey north to the Jicarilla refuge.

*

The party traveled at night on a slow ride to the mountains north of Las Vegas. The Alsop girls remained troublesome: The younger girls spat at him every time he rode near the wagon; the older girls kept taunting him by pulling up their dresses and exposing their vaginas, telling him the many clever ways in which they could please him. Finally, he bound and gagged all four females and drove the wagon, his animals secured behind. Once John Henry reached the spot where he staked out the Bensons, he ordered the four females to collect firewood, and then as before, he staked them, bound them hand and foot to the ground, and left them for the Apache. He left the wagon and the Alsop mules and horses as an extra bargaining chip. When night fell, he lit the collected wood, waited until it blazed into a bonfire, then rode off a short distance, out of sight, and waited for the Apache to collect the females.

Most of what John Henry knew about the Apache he read in the Los Angeles newspapers. As fighters, they were every bit as formidable as, if not more so, than the Sioux he tracked on the northern plains. And unlike the Sioux, who heavily depended upon the buffalo for food, clothing, and shelter, the Apache were not dependent on one source. For centuries they lived off the harsh southwest land, eating snakes and insects, mescal cactus pulp, and anything that crawled or sprouted, making it difficult for the army to separate them from their source of food as they did with the Sioux. With the Apache, the army faced a new type of enemy who could cover thirty miles in one day on foot over harsh desert terrain, going without water and running after the army's dehydrated and exhausted horses collapsed. Raised to be raiders and killers from the time they were old enough to walk, the Apache were ferocious predators, attacking American settlers and miners who moved onto their land. They perfected what they did best:

Murder in the most atrocious ways, burning habitats, and stealing livestock.

Yet John Henry knew that by 1885 the Apache, like the Sioux, had been all but decimated by the U.S. Army. Now only small bands held out. For centuries Apache tribes raided Mexican villages and battled Mexican armies; subsequently, they battled the U.S. Army when the Americans took over Mexico's northern territory in 1848. Five distinct bands—the Tonto, Jicarilla, Mescalero, Chiricahua, and Mimbreño- comprised the bulk of the Apache nations, occupying lands in Mexico and the Arizona and New Mexico Territories. Because of the lack of abundant food in their harsh homelands, the Apache roamed in small bands, with sometimes as few as twenty-five men protecting fifty or more women and children. As the Sioux bred great war chiefs in Red Cloud, Crazy Horse, and Sitting Bull, so did the Apache in Mangas Coloradas, Cochise, and Geronimo. Yet, all except the latter the government betrayed and subsequently killed. Most of the other Apache in 1885 the army hunted down, killed, subdued on reservations, or sent to faraway prisons.

The U.S. Army in the southwest, led by General George Crook, conquered all the bands except for a handful of Chiricahua who occupied the mountains of Mexico and were led by their war chief, Geronimo. John Henry didn't know that General Crook was a masterful Indian fighter who long since realized his army could not keep pace with the Apache on their harsh terrain. Therefore he recruited enemies of each tribe, Apache, who could track those warriors Crook called renegades. Seeing their own people stalking and then ambushing them demoralized the renegade Apache and caused them to surrender—that is, all except Geronimo's Chiricahua. Damsel Dunbar informed John Henry that the Jicarilla, long since tamed, still occupied portions of the Sangre de Cristo Mountains, but only in small bands. Although historical enemies of the Chiricahua, they now sheltered the tribe's escapees from reservations, mostly the San Carlos and White Mountain, warriors anxious to join Geronimo in Mexico. In order to strengthen Geronimo's band, these Chiricahuas needed horses and weapons before they made the long trek to Mexico.

John Henry hobbled his horse and mule, allowing them to graze in a small canyon, before hiding all his weapons except the derringer to avoid losing them to a band of desperate Apache. Carrying a bag of coffee and a pouch of tobacco he'd collected at the Alsop ranch, he went on foot to where he saw the Apache leading the girls and livestock into the mountains. They saw no use for the wagon and would send the women down later to tear it up for firewood or wickiup material. Feeling secure in their remote territory, the Apache made little attempt to cover their trail, so John Henry found no difficulty following them to their camp. In all that he did, he kept in mind his dual purpose: Disturb the Williams gang enough for them to come after him by destroying their families, homes, and livelihoods; and gain the release of Benevolence's granddaughters. To accomplish the latter, he must determine if he could trade with the unpredictable Apache for the girls and, if so, how much it would take to secure their release.

*

He reached the Apache camp unhindered in the dead of night; like the northern plains tribes, this band of Apache posted no sentries. It looked as if the band roasted and ate one of the mules, because only the skull and bones remained, stacked neatly next to a smoldering fire for making a broth the next day. He guessed they also drunk a good deal of fermented mescal to celebrate their good fortune, finding four females and a soon-to-be-born infant to breed or trade. In the tinge of morning light, John Henry counted at least twenty wickiups, crude domelike structures framed by tree branches and covered by brush, inhabited by families. He estimated the camp held about forty men and sixty women and children.

Having left the Jicarilla gifts of Anglo humans, he counted on being recognized as the donor; even so, he knew he gambled with his life because, from what he read, the Apache were as explosive as unsettled nitro. He went unnoticed by the few Apache who rose with the dawn, relieved themselves in the wooded

108

terrain, and returned to their wickiups. When the sun's rays hit the wickiups in full, the women, dressed in long, multicolored skirts and long-sleeved shirts belted at the waist, and their children, dressed as little warriors without weapons, exited their shelters; the older children searched about for firewood, while the younger ones clung to their mothers. Within minutes, a woman noticed John Henry leaning against a rocky ledge and screamed an alarm. He raised his hands above his head, one hand holding a sack of coffee, the other a pouch of tobacco.

He spoke no Apache but guessed that because of the demands of Apache reservation life, someone would speak enough English to communicate. The warriors, still groggy from the effects of drinking mescal, surrounded him. Before long, they began to taunt John Henry, seizing the coffee and tobacco and then striking him with their fists. They stripped him of his hat and jacket. Knives flashed before his face. Other blades pricked his skin, enough to stain his shirt with blood. One warrior held John Henry's derringer over his head, provoking a chorus of laughter from the others; they saw the small weapon as a child's toy. Eventually, a headman pushed his way through the commotion surrounding John Henry. He noted the gift of coffee and tobacco. Believing he recognized John Henry, he ordered the four Alsop females brought forth. When they appeared, the headman inquired: "He the one?" The younger Alsop girls spat at John Henry, but the older girls, noticeably subdued by the situation, indicated John Henry was indeed the man who brought them to the Apache.

The headman, showing a mane of gray hair on an angular head and taller than the rest, returned John Henry's hat and coat. He examined the derringer and then fired a round into the sky. The demonstration provoked laughter. He fired the weapon thrice; then, deciding the derringer was useless, he returned it to John Henry. He then spoke to the crowd surrounding the unexpected visitor. John Henry did not understand a word of what the headman spoke, but his words calmed the mob surrounding him, and they fell back, the women preparing morning cookfires, the men dividing up the coffee and tobacco. Two warriors carrying rifles

109

guarded John Henry where he stood. When their morning meal was ready, the Apache men, some armed, and the women, carrying knives, sat in small circles eating a corn mush of some sort and leftovers from the roasted mule. A woman gave John Henry a bowl containing a boiled strip of mule flesh floating in a broth.

After everyone ate, the Apache formed a large circle before their wickiups. The sun bronzed their faces, and the wind weathered their skin to leather. The men, long dark hair falling to their shoulders and held back by strips of cloth tied around their foreheads, appeared lean and muscled, more than capable of conquering their environment. Mostly, they all wore long-sleeved cotton shirts cinched at the waist with cartridge or pistol belts and loincloths draped over bare legs. Moccasins tied below the knees covered their feet. Some of the warriors held a rifle; those that went without carried bows and arrows. Half the men stood apart, indicating to John Henry they might be from a different band. The women dressed distinctively in multicolored and patterned skirts, homemade or stolen. When everyone assembled, including the children, a few warriors herded John Henry into the circle's center.

The headman spoke. "I am called Nantan Lupan. Why you leave white people?"

"Other white men, bad men, traded two small females to you a few moons back. The little females are part of my wife's family. I want them back."

Silence fell over the headman and those who understood English. John Henry waited for what seemed an eternity for the headman to reply. Finally, he spoke. "The little women are with the Navajo people."

John Henry tried to absorb this considerable setback: the Apache traded Benevolence's grandchildren to a Navajo band who probably resided far north of these Apache. "How much to bring the two little women back?"

Again, silence prevailed. Finally, the headman replied, "Many more white people."

"I can bring more, but we must agree upon how many." The headman upped the price. "No number important. Need horses. Need many rifles."

"Many horses I will bring. Many rifles I cannot." Giving rifles to the Apache would be a hanging offense, and John Henry held no desire to take that risk. But the more significant consideration was that these unpredictable Chiricahua, the Jicarilla sheltered, could kill Americans on their way to Mexico. Suddenly the Apache men began talking among themselves in the Athabaskan language. And then shouts sounded in English of "Kill him!" and "Give him to me!"

The tall headman stood up and signaled for silence. "No rifles, no little women."

John Henry departed from civilized conduct into lawbreaking when he robbed the stagecoach and later shot the Pinkerton agent in the legs. Now no end to savagery seemed in sight. "I know the Chiricahua need rifles to join Geronimo in Mexico. I must know they will not kill Americans on their journey to Mexico. I will need the word of the Chiricahua that they will kill no Americans." The headman's insistence on rifles in exchange for the children gave him no choice but to push the possibility of hanging out of his head.

The headman spoke at length in Athabaskan to the Chiricahua surrounding him. Seventeen of the men stirred—only a few held rifles, which were Civil War vintage. One by one, they repeated the headman's words, "They agree. They say, no kill *Americanos*, kill *Mexicanos* below the unseen line dividing the lands."

*

John Henry figured fortune smiled on him when he left the Apache stronghold alive. Now the terms were clear: the Apache needed horses and rifles. The horses would be problematic but obtainable; the rifles loomed like a problem much harder to solve. He found his big chestnut and mule where he hobbled them, noting the Apache did not follow him. He rode to the outskirts of Las Vegas, near where he buried his daughter, and set up camp, intending to wait a week to see if the Winston Williams gang would show their faces in town now that he'd destroyed the Alsop ranch. He camped out of sight in a clump of bushes growing along a dry stream, well aware that having destroyed two ranches and delivered white children to the Apache would prompt law enforcement to look for him, especially the Las Vegas sheriff who bullied him. But he knew that seven hard-natured and well-armed men riding into Las Vegas at any hour of the day would create a stir, enough to gain the town's attention, and word would filter to him.

While he waited, John Henry avoided the sheriff's office near the plaza, checking daily with the general store owner for any news of the Williams gang. He realized that he reached middle age, and gunslinging, sacrificing white captives to the Apache, and putting his life on the line held little appeal for, especially when he knew a Pinkerton agent trailed him and sooner or later would trace him to via the Las Vegas sheriff. He wanted to quit the unsavory business of burning ranches to revenge Benevolence's family. But after a visit to Jane's grave, the image of her tortured naked body hanging from a dead mesquite tree, her flesh being ripped off by wild animals, haunted him. This image of her strung up by ruthless killers and left to die miserably resurrected a burning need for revenge. Before he left to join the Union army in the nation's capital, he recalled carrying the little bundled Jane, a week or two over one year of age and screaming piteously in pain from infected ears to the doctor in Lawrence. How frightened and helpless Jane appeared, bonding him to her like no one before. These images of the daughter he deserted on the Kansas plains cemented his need to complete the dirty business that lay before him.

The Williams gang never appeared. He figured they were up to no good somewhere, probably pursuing some criminal business raiding ranches, or else they would seek him out to avenge the destruction of their families. Desiring to inflict more transgression to bring the cutthroat gang to him, John Henry rode east again, picking up the Pecos River that ran from the Sangre de Cristo Mountains for a sizable distance through New Mexico

Territory's parched land where a few ranches existed and then flowed into Texas; there the river eventually joined the Rio Grande. Most years, after a short rainy season, the Pecos dried up fto a mere trickle, if that much. But it was enough for a few poor ranches to exist. John Henry reconnoitered two ranches on the way to the Miller place and saw the inhabitants dug wells to water their livestock and nourish gardens near where the river's water trickled over rock formations embedded in the sand. He followed the thin, flowing river until he came upon the Miller ranch, a windblown strip of sand and sagebrush running along the western bank of the Pecos River. He understood why Charles Miller joined the outlaws: Insufficient substance existed here to sustain another adult on the harsh and unforgiving land.

John Henry knew little about Charles Miller other than he participated in the raid on Benevolence's family. As he spied on the man's home place, he observed a middle-aged man attempting to break a wild Mustang in a corral. Five unbroken horses milled about in a second corral, and off in the distance, another half dozen broken horses grazed, their forelegs hobbled. He knew the elder Miller broke and sold horses for living. A woman—Miller's wife, John Henry assumed—hoed a small vegetable garden near a one-room adobe bungalow. He ascertained from his vantage point across the river that the Miller maintained spread and the Millers appeared to be hardworking settlers.

At this time of year, the Pecos River was a mere six-inch-deep trickle, barely enough to give a thirsty horse a wet nose. John Henry rode across the shallow water, hands out at his sides, plainly signaling that he was a passerby who meant no harm. The woman discontinued her garden work and approached him, curious but friendly.

"What brings you about these parts, stranger?"

"I am looking for the Miller family, who I hope will tell me where their son Charles currently spends his time."

"You got business with him?" She gave him a dubious look, noting the weapons he carried.

"My business is with him and those men he rides with."

"Can't rightly say I know where my boy is, given that he has taken up with a wild bunch. Let me fetch my husband, Carl, though I suspect he knows little more than I do. Why don't you dismount and treat yourself to a dipper of water while I bring him to you?" She gave him a welcoming smile, unusual for a woman living such a harsh life. She stood about five feet, four inches tall, and was well put together, a good-looking brunette despite the hard life she chose for herself. John Henry helped himself to a dipper of water from a water barrel in the shade of the low-built adobe ranch house and then used his hat to dip out a portion of the water for his horse and mule. Thereafter, he hitched them to the corral's crude railings.

Carl Miller met him with a handshake that John Henry took in his left hand, seeing no need to advertise his handicap. The man appeared tall and lean, displaying the same build as John Henry. He seemed embarrassed that his son took up with such bad men, stating he did not know Charles's whereabouts except that he liked to frequent the Mexican villages south of El Paso. The Millers invited John Henry to stay for supper in about two hours. The couple reminded the stranger of his parents: his mom, a farm girl with little education and little wherewithal to better her station in life, and his hardworking dad a carpenter turned laborer, strong as a plow horse and stubborn as a mule, more handyman than a builder, a laborer who could not keep food on the table and a roof over his and his wife's heads. Under the Millers' hospitality, he felt his determination to accomplish his mission softening, so he acted quickly, leveling a shotgun on the unarmed couple. The double-barreled shotgun leveled at their midriffs stunned the pair into silence.

"Sorry to do this to you, Mr. and Mrs. Miller, but I'm out to take revenge for the terrible deed your son Charles inflicted on my daughter, my ex-wife's second daughter by another man, her husband and her mother-in-law, and two grandbabies at a place known as the Cardwell ranch, north of Las Vegas. Mr. Miller, you round up your horses and corral them." He found an old single-shot, heavy-barreled Henry rifle by the door and fixed it to his

114

mule's pack. "Mrs. Miller, you put together some food and water, for we face a long journey ahead of us." John Henry forced himself to torch the ranch house and barn and trample Mrs. Miller's garden. Gnashing his teeth in self-disgust, he fouled what he thought to be a good couple's well, knowing he crippled all hope they held for the future.

The Millers were expert horsemen, riding effortlessly and driving ten horses before them. John Henry rode a few paces behind them, following the Pecos River south toward where he believed the Apple ranch to be. Even though John Henry indicated he meant Charles Miller harm, his mother sensed that he intended to kill her son. She nudged her horse next to his. "My husband and me tried to give Charles a good upbringing and to raise him to be a God-fearing boy, but he was soft-headed, easily swayed by other boys. That's why he took up with that no-good Ben Apple, crazier than a bug on a red-hot skillet. Whatever my son has done, it was not of his making. I ask you to be mindful of that when you find him."

After riding a twenty-mile stretch, they came upon the Apple property. John Henry spotted a four-year-old towheaded boy playing with a miniature wooden horse in the shade of a scrawny tree. The boy appeared small for his age, prompting John Henry to recall Damsel Dunbar's description of Ben Apple, a tiny, gun-toting madman who thought he couldn't be killed. The blond, blue-eyed, fair-skinned boy carried a squint and a lopsided halfsneer, half-grin: Ben Apple's miniature, he guessed.

The aroma of fresh-baked bread emanated from the small ranch house; the Apples were eating their supper. The property, a well-maintained barn with sturdy corrals, showed the same dutiful maintenance as the Miller ranch. Upon hearing a small herd of horses approaching, the curious Apples emerged from the house and appeared pleased to see the Millers pass by. Ben Apple's dad stood a brawny five feet two inches tall, carrying a huge belly that tugged at his shirt buttons. Rolled-up shirtsleeves revealed heavy arms; he wore wide suspenders to keep his patched and worn trousers in place. John Henry saw that smiling did not come easily

115

to him, but he gave it his best attempt upon seeing the Millers. His wife, skinny and plain as a fence post, towered over her husband. She looked to be a taciturn woman who did not attempt to smile, but this soberness came from her personality, not her intent.

John Henry saw that the Apples were poorer than the Millers: he counted just five horses in the corral. The barn door was open, and only one milk cow tethered inside. A few chickens pecked at the dry dirt. Without asking the Apples' permission, he ordered the Millers to herd their horses into the corral alongside the Apples' horses; he saw no need to waste time on introductions. Once again, adding waylaying to his list of misdeeds, he trained his shotgun on Mr. and Mrs. Apple. "Let us go inside and collect what food you prepared because the five of us and your little one, who I take to be your son's boy, will need it on our travels." After ordering the woman to collect the toddler, he escorted the men and women into the sizable one-room dwelling, where he spotted a shotgun resting on pegs pounded into the wall. Breaking it apart, he checked it for loads, then handed the empty gun to Mrs. Apple. "Turn over what other weapons you have." The big-bellied rancher removed a worn single-action .38caliber pistol stuck into an equally worn holster from a chest at the foot of his bed. John Henry removed the cartridges from the pistol, slinging the holster and weapon over his shoulder.

"What's this all about, stranger? You sneaking onto our place with our neighbors and robbing us?" the male Apple demanded.

"You will find out in due time. Now, you and Mrs. Apple grab what you need for traveling. I'm sorry to say that I must burn down your holdings."

Feeling trepidation as he did when burning the Miller place, he destroyed the dwellings, crops, and domestic animals that made up the Apples' simple home place as the disheveled families looked on. He lifted the boy to eye level. The fearless kid, pulling on his nose, gave him a screwy look. After hoisting the four-year-old boy onto a horse in front of his grandmother, he ordered the two families to direct the horses north to the Apache territory in the Sangre de Cristo Mountains.

*

Gazing upon the mountain foothills that shielded the Apache, John Henry circled the horses, some still not broken, until they milled about in one spot. He ordered the Miller and Apple families to dismount and unsaddle their horses. He reached the same spot where he left the Alsop and Benson family members and ordered the man to loop a rope around the horses' necks to keep them under control. He then placed the out-of-date weapons he confiscated from the two families on a saddle blanket. Except for the little boy, the families looked unsettled, reacting to the wild location. He took the tiny toddler from Mrs.
Apple, ordered the adults to take what food and water they needed, and pointed in the direction of Las Vegas, ordering them to walk there. They all protested, especially Mrs. Apple, planting their feet and refusing to move.

"The Jicarilla and Chiricahua Apache will appear as soon as I start a signal fire. They will accept the boy, but they do not need you four adults, as you are too old to be of any practical use to them. What use they will find for you will be to skin you alive, stake you out under the sun, and enjoy hearing you beg for death. But that death won't come until wild predators find you."

His words convinced the four adults to depart and carry what succor they could. He watched them walk, heads bowed and shoulders slumped, across the wild plains, feeling disgusted with his person—the Millers resembled his parents, and the Apples those of earlier pioneers settling on Kansas's untamed prairies. John Henry once again waited for the Apache to show, this time not hiding himself or his animals. In an hour, perhaps two, after he ignited the bonfire, three Apache riders and seven warriors on foot appeared, led by their headman Nantan Lupan, a name that meant gray wolf John Henry discovered. The mounted trio dropped to their feet, pleased with the horses but disappointed in the few outdated weapons spread on the ground. After leaving his shotgun slung over his saddle, John Henry escorted Ben Apple's tiny son

117

to Nantan Lupan. The pugnacious tot, barefooted and shirtless in tattered coveralls, shook off John Henry's grip and stomped forward to meet his fate. The warriors around Nantan Lupan laughed at his bravado, but their solemn-faced leader appeared dubious at the gift, noting the boy's tiny size.

"He will grow to a fine warrior in your wickiup. Look into his eyes and you will see Apache bravery." John Henry did not exaggerate—fear found no place in the boy.

Nantan Lupan lifted the boy to eye level and studied his defiant glare and the screwy twist of the mouth; the squirming boy pulled on his head scarf. Still unsatisfied, he carried the boy to where some weathered red rocks crumbled and urinated on the debris. He then wiped the red mud over the boy's face and upper body. He wrapped his head scarf around the boy's blond hair. After a minute, Lupan grunted his approval and carried the boy back to his followers. They seemed pleased at the boy's transformation.

"I will wait here until you return the little women to me," John Henry volunteered.

Nantan Lupan mounted his horse, placing the boy behind him. "We welcome your gifts, bad-hand man. The tiny warrior pleases me. Need more rifles before little women return to you." With those words, he turned his horse and galloped toward the mountains. His ten warriors followed, racing their new mustangs at full gallop.

*

John Henry rode into Santa Fe at the beginning of December; the hot weather simmered to the high eighties. He could see the town remained faithful to its distasteful setting, a hot, dry settlement of some twenty-five-thousand residents, with streets so narrow a wagon wheel's hubs brushed the building fronts. The town, at the end of a railroad spur and supplier to distant mines, symbolized disappointment—so much expectation but so little return. He thought *quite a contrast to Las Vegas* as he searched out Smoker's hog business, his horse and mule kicking dust into the curious town dwellers' faces. He saw no "pistols forbidden" signs riding down the main street. He knew Santa Fe once reigned as the regional capital for the Spanish conquistadors north of Mexico, and Mexicans predominantly occupied the town, although the white race controlled political power. He traced the appealing aroma of smoked hog to Smoker's Hog Slaughterhouse and Smokehouse Emporium on a backstreet off the main thoroughfare. John Henry counted three well-constructed, whitewashed buildings, one a slaughterhouse, one a smokehouse, and the third a retail store. He counted thirty employees before entering the smokehouse, impressed by Smoker's accomplishment. He found Smoker, dressed in a suit and vest and wearing a small-brimmed Eastern hat, supervising four meat cutters. John Henry spoke affectionately, "Hello, Smoker." Benevolence's Los Angeles escort's small, wiry frame, bent even farther by maturing arthritis, spun on his heel, a crooked smile lighting up his face. He embraced John Henry, arms around his waist and head buried in his former employer's chest, as he stood no higher than the man's chin. "I miss Benevolence," he prattled. "She treated me good." He then pulled back, anger clouding his face. "I would stay with her permanently if not for her damn third husband, who turned me out because my fits bothered his evening porch drinking. If only she didn't smoke those damn black cigars. Smoking tobacco is what did her in, John. She died like a hellcat, clawing at the air."

John Henry unpeeled Smoker's arms from around his waist and waited until Benevolence's lifelong companion wiped his tears on his shirtsleeve. "Let's talk outside, Smoker. I need to collect an old debt owed me."

The successful businessman beckoned to an employee to take over. "Need my help? Glad to be of service."

"Might be more service than you expect." Outside, under the intense morning sun, Benevolence's first husband spoke. "I need for you to buy twenty of the latest Winchester rifles and hide them until I can collect them. You will buy them separately in Santa Fe and probably travel to Tombstone and Tucson to buy the remainder unnoticed."

"What do you need twenty rifles for?" Smoker's already weak legs turned rubbery.

"I need them, and that should be enough reason for a friend to help a friend."

"Jesus! Law authorities will think I'm buying them for the Apache and hang me on the spot."

"Not if you go about it one rifle at a time."

"Can't do that, John."

"Remember that time in Lawrence when Benevolence, you, and I were young, that one particular day when we drove into town for our monthly supply run and an evening of beer drinking and a burlesque show? Later that day, you woke up in the doctor's office, confused, your face and body battered and bruised. We told you you'd experienced a fit and collapsed flat on your face."

"I recall you and Benevolence told me a well-meaning fib. I found out later from Henderson, the old gossiping stable hand, that the town rowdies found me fitting on the ground and hung me upside down by the ankles from the barn's hayloft lift to watch me shimmy and shake like they would a mad hog. Those varmints poked me with sticks and kicked me so I would spin and writhe on the rope to get a laugh. Things got out of hand, John. They stripped me down to my birthday suit. Henderson told me they were boiling tar and plucking a chicken to tar and feather me, hang me on display for the town to ridicule. He told me, you went looking for me and saw what the bullies did and how you rifle-whipped two men and drove off the others. You saved me from a life of shame in Kansas. I ain't ever said thank you, because I thought you and Benevolence wanted it left unsaid. I'm thanking you now, John, but I ain't buying your rifles. You could try to convince me six days to a Sunday, and I still would not be foolish enough to buy you twenty rifles."

John Henry led Smoker through town until he came upon a very narrow dead-end street blocked off by adobe bricks cemented to a height of six feet. "I don't got 'six days to a Sunday' to collect on that thank-you, Smoker." He positioned his old friend against the brick wall. "I got no choice but to ask you to give me an ass-to-brick-wall commitment."

"What in the world would that be?"

"Try taking a step backward. Now try stepping to your right and then to your left. Not anywhere to go but forward, is there, Smoker?"

Chapter 9

John Henry rode out of Santa Fe unnoticed, heading south toward the border town of El Paso and then into Mexico to find the family of Justo Trujillo, the half-breed who rode with Winston Williams. Damsel Dunbar related to John Henry how expertly Trujillo handled a knife; he wondered if Trujillo's knife mutilated his daughter. The possibility of Trujillo's involvement in Jane's death was enough to heat his fervor to accomplish what he proposed to do: Destroy the sixth murderer's family and home place. He crossed the Rio Grande River at El Paso, the town known as "El Norte" or "the Pass," where the river cut a swath through the ancient mountains the Spanish called la Sierra de los Mansos, and headed east to a tiny village named Zaragoza, where he learned Trujillo's Comanche mother and Mexican father eked out a living raising goats south of the border.

*

The rancher whose son John Henry gunned down in Fort Hays City, one James Knox Ulsterman, sprang from proud ancestry. Ulsterman's great-great-grandfather accompanied Daniel Boone of English blood, who scouted for General Edward Braddock on his disastrous attack on Fort Duquesne in 1755. A few years later, Ulsterman's Scot-Irish ancestors migrated out of Virginia to Kentucky. Born in Boonesborough around 1776 during a Shawnee attack on the settlement, Ulsterman's great-grandfather came into being amid savagery. A generation later, his grandfather, once reaching his teenage years in Kentucky, enlisted with John William's Volunteers to fight Creek and Seminole renegades, later joining Andrew Jackson's army during the 1812 war. After the war

121

with Britain ended, he sought unoccupied land in Tennessee on territory near Nashville in 1815. His son Henry, born in 1800, fathered two sons, one of whom was James Knox Ulsterman, born in 1820. A user of enslaved people, James Knox Ulsterman joined the Rebel cause against the Union. He fought in the raging campaign at Nashville led by Rebel general John Bell Hood, a commander known for attacking whatever force stood before him. Mortar fire severely wounded Ulsterman as he led a charge up Montgomery Hill. After Ulsterman was sent to a hospital behind Rebel lines, General Hood promoted him to brevet lieutenant colonel. Ulsterman, his face badly burned by the explosion at Montgomery Hill, kept the title but after being released from the hospital and never returned to a war doomed to be a Confederacy loss. The Confederate president, Jefferson Davis, and his cabinet already escaped south from the rebel capital of Richmond to Georgia. The Union president, Abraham Lincoln, waited on the outskirts for the rebel capital to fall.

After the Confederacy surrendered at Appomattox, James Ulsterman collected his slaves, livestock, furniture, and family and migrated west to Texas, settling near Abilene. Ulsterman carried grief with him—Yankees killed his oldest son at Wheelers Station in a foolhardy attack against heavily fortified Union trenches.

He viciously fought the Comanche on the open prairie, driving them farther west and subsequently taking over their territory as he spread his land claims farther and farther across open Texas rangeland. As a middle-aged man wielding 220 pounds of hardened muscle and carrying the title colonel, he appeared insurmountable to the enemy. His bigger-than-life image struck fear into his enemies once they took in the red scar covering the left side of his face, accompanied by his long, blond, flowing hair and wild beard. Ulsterman was hell on horseback, riding and firing from the saddle as well as any expert Comanche horseman. Having perfected the leadership skills in the Rebel army, he became a born leader even of the most brutal, undisciplined men. He paid his riders well, training them to be butchers fiercer than their enemies.

Ulsterman, leading a hundred Comanche haters, caught Dog Lope's unaware Comanche camping along the Clear Fork Brazos, killing seventy-eight warriors and fifty women and children during the attack and subsequently torturing another twenty-five captives before hanging those who did not perish. Echoing what he observed of Comanche torture at numerous burned-out ranches spread along the Texas plains, he would, alongside his men, skin savages alive; others he buried shoulder-deep in anthills, a procedure he'd seen the Apache perfect, who learned it from the Mexicans. Ulsterman favored roasting Comanche upside down until their brains cooked, leaving them to languish slowly, simmering over coals buried an inch beneath the sand.

The Comanche learned to avoid his cattle herds, occasionally stealing a cow here and there. As much a thinking man as a killing one, Colonel Ulsterman, after years of confrontation, finally favored giving the Comanche a few hundred heads of cattle each year rather than continually fighting them. Ulsterman became one of the first cattle drivers to push cattle north out of Texas toward an ever-expanding railroad line running across Kansas, Nebraska, and Colorado.

Known as a brutal but fair man, Ulsterman dispensed a frontier justice that usually meant hanging cattle rustlers on the spot and destroying sheepherders, whom he thought to be a plaque inflicted on good rangeland. His men were devoted to him, viewing the Confederate war hero as a demanding but generous employer. Texans admired him, and politicians sought his money. Surrounded by his ever-expanding array of bunkhouses, corrals, and barns, he shunned comfort, living in the original four-room ranch house he and his wife built 20 years ago. Ulsterman's wife died giving birth to his youngest son, the one John Henry shot down. James Knox Ulsterman relived his son's death every night, having his foreman depict in detail the shootout at Fort Hays City, down to John Henry's fingers blown off. Now aged into his middle sixties, he still sat strong in the saddle.

It was on a saddle cinched to a large gray horse that Ulsterman rode west toward El Paso, leading ten pistol-savvy cowboys. He heard about a three-fingered man appearing in the New Mexico Territory. His cowboys poked around the destroyed ranches belonging to Benson, Alsop, Miller, and Apple families in New Mexico. Given what he found out about the Cardwell ranch and subsequently burned properties along the Pecos River, he believed the latter were the victims of this same three-fingered man, and he surmised that the parents of Winston Williams would be the next targets. He sent his cowboys to distribute reward posters for information leading to a three-fingered man, extending his search from West Texas and around Las Vegas and Santa Fe to smaller towns into the Arizona Territory. An informant—Benson's hired Mexican, whom John Henry wounded and placed on a buckboard, the wounded bounty hunter Bill Braddock transported to a doctor. The man survived his gunshot wound and collected a five-hundred-dollar reward after spotting John Henry crossing the border into Juárez.

*

John Henry decided to cross into Mexico as soon as possible at El Paso, confident men would trail him after he destroyed the skimpy ranches along the Pecos River. And the ominous possibility existed that the wounded Pinkerton agent he left in Colorado recovered and would be on his trail by now. In Mexico, his pursuers would not enjoy law enforcement's cooperation. Approaching the border town, he rode through vast fields of hay, alfalfa, and wheat spreading from the Rio Grande to the mountains. Although a breeze blew over the fields, the temperature soared above one hundred degrees, forcing John Henry to frequently water his horse and mule as he crossed the numerous irrigation ditches the Spanish dug a century ago. He rode past a sombrous string of mud huts with straw roofs and into a border town strung out along the river, passing among the expanding town's two-story commercial structures. Nearing the border, he took San Antonio Street, avoiding the sheriff's office at its head, where the notorious Dallas Stoudenmire, an aggressive, gunslinging law enforcer, presided. Like the main streets in most Texas towns, saloons, hotels, and brothels—to John Henry's way of thinking, the places where danger always lurked—overloaded San Antonio Street. He kept riding and took a one-lane bridge crossing the Rio Grande River. Federal guards on both sides of the border paid little attention to him; commerce flowed freely between the larger Ciudad Juárez and El Paso. He followed a trail east along the Rio Grande River to where he believed the Trujillo goat ranch to be.

He figured he rode about fifteen miles before he came upon an old man, arthritis bending his upper back so severely that it forced his head downward. The man tended a herd of goats about a quarter-mile from his hovel. John Henry saw his hands were bloody to the elbows and guessed he recently slaughtered a goat and sold it to one of the fly-infested butcher shops beside the river. He took the man, who he assumed was Justo's father, by surprise. Without removing his shotgun from his shoulder, he spoke calmly, in unaccustomed Spanish. *"¿Es usted el papá de Justo Trujillo?"* The uneasy man, unable to raise his head, indicated he was. *"Vamanos a su casa."* Without removing his shotgun from his shoulder, he gestured for the deformed man to herd his goats back to his dwelling. There he spotted a young woman he figured was Justo's wife. A hacking cough attacked her as she carried a crippled daughter to a blanket laid out in the shade where the girl could catch a breeze and find relief from the insufferable heat. The little girl appeared to be about seven years old, with a deformed hip and a crooked left leg. Dressed only in a ragged slip revealing thin, bony shoulders, the small girl weighed no more than fifty pounds' she fingered her long, dark hair braided into one large ponytail. Her eyes shone like lively coals—the child appeared a defective little beauty to John Henry's way of thinking. The mother, thin as a rail, placed an old deck of playing cards on the blanket for the girl to play solitaire.

Keeping the old man and his goats in front of him, John Henry studied the mud-brick hovel unfit for human occupation: a tattered blanket covered the doorway; large black flies buzzed back and forth through an open window. Chickens scratched in the dust surrounding the mud brick dwelling. John Henry directed the old man to release the goats to where a smaller herd of tame goats milled about in the back. He could smell the makings of tequila simmering in a homemade still beyond the goats; he figured the old man sold the concoction to locals to make a few more pesos to supplement his meager livelihood. Behind the crude home, John Henry came upon Trujillo's Comanche mother. Toothless and wrinkled, she tended a chicken sizzling on a brazier just outside the open rear entrance.

Speaking Spanish never became a study for John Henry picked up only a few words of the language from the population along the railroad line in Colorado. He summoned the adults to assemble in front of the mud hut through gestures and rough Spanish, leaving the crippled girl comfortable on her blanket. He spoke, "Move to the front of your house." The wife of Justo translated his words into Spanish: *"se trasladó a la parte delantera de su casa."* He then motioned the adults to enter the one-room dwelling. The home displayed a dirt floor; Justo piled hay-stuffed burlap sacks for sleeping into two corners. A worn sofa pushed against one wall and an eating table with a missing leg, supported by a packing crate, occupied the room. To John Henry's right, a blanket on a cord separated the sleeping quarters of the senior Trujillos from the rest of the room.

He addressed the three adults before him: *"¿Tienen ustedes rifles o pistolas en la casa?"*

"No, señor," the old man replied.

The idea of following his practice of vengeance—destroying the meager mud hut, chicken coop, and scrawny animals outside—gave John Henry a knot in his stomach. Annihilating a family already beyond destitution was not in his makeup. Scanning the room, he discovered a photograph of a young man dressed in a vaquero outfit touched up in color, wearing a full handlebar mustache under a short-brimmed sombrero. He believed the picture to be that of Justo. The vaquero wore a tight-fitting short-waisted brown jacket with green contrasting cuffs and lapels over a white, frilly shirt; silver studs covered the jacket's shoulders. He wore cattle-herding leather chaps unbuttoned at the knees to reveal fancy boots with silver spurs. Brown and green, skin-tight silver-studded trousers completed Trujillo's flashy outfit. He tucked a large knife under a fancy red and green sash wrapped around his waist.

"Your son rides with the bad men who killed my daughter and her half-sister and sold the sister's children to the Apache. He is lost to you; I will shoot him down when I find him. This will be your punishment for giving birth to such a bad person. You, wife of Justo—find another man." Justo's wife gasped, then repeated his words in Spanish to her in-laws. John Henry, unsure if any of them grasped the full meaning of what he said, repeated his epitaph to her: "Find another man." He did not destroy one brick or one animal belonging to the meager goat farm.

Leaving the family, he mounted his horse to ride back toward El Paso, scattering goats in his path. The bent old man ran after him, firing an ancient pistol until he emptied it, missing John Henry but hitting the mule in the rear haunch. John Henry, annoyed, dismounted and disarmed the old man, who was thoroughly shaken by his failed attempt to intervene on his son's behalf. Under normal circumstances, John Henry would punish the old man, but he decided to try a different approach: He pushed the man back into the hovel and beckoned to Justo's terrified wife to translate. He demanded of the old man, "Tell me something about your son, so I don't have to pistol-whip you." The bent man remained silent, his head bent even farther toward the ground. "If I beat you, you will be unable to provide for your family, and they will go hungry. Tell me something about your son."

The father spoke to his daughter-in-law, who translated for John Henry: "My son rode through here with six men and a captured woman, heading south toward the Cantina of the Happy Winds. I am told they sold the woman to the owner of the cantina, who makes money off of *putas* who sell their bodies to those who can pay."

When he left the goat farm for the second time, John Henry tossed the poorly maintained pistol, a Civil War ball-and-powder Smith & Wesson, onto a distant sand dune. The wounded mule would hold up for a day or two before gangrene set in on the rear haunch; he hoped he could find a Mexican animal doctor before then. Changing his plans, he rode south toward the cantina, where he believed Clara—Benevolence's second daughter, a woman he never met—was being misused.

*

A few miles south of the Trujillo goat ranch, he came upon a horse breeder whom he paid to remove the slug from the mule's haunch. Satisfied the mule would hold up under its load, he eased his way farther south to the Cantina of the Happy Winds, which sported a green- and red-painted, low-built mud-brick exterior. A straw roof topped the structure, and a solitary, lit kerosene lamp swung in the wind next to a red door. A few saddled horses and work mules stood tethered to a hitching post on the side of the building. John Henry tied his horse and mule to a mesquite tree a short distance from the hitching post. Carrying a shotgun, he entered a smoke-filled, lantern-lit room. The proprietor painted the rough-plastered room red, which, time faded to a patchy rose. John Henry went to a long bar that occupied one side of the rectangular room. Farmers displaying rough hands and hovering over glasses of beer and tequila occupied a dozen scattered and scarred wooden tables. Three vaqueros standing at the bar carried pistols; the laborers carried machetes. Two Mexican prostitutes drank with the vaqueros or bandits—John Henry could not determine what persuasion they followed. An older, frumpy female ballad singer strumming a Mexican guitar and voicing gut-wrenching sounds of the proletariat drenched the room in melancholy. John Henry ordered a beer in English to determine if the bartenders spoke the language. The pocked-scarred-faced man behind the bar, whom John Henry took to be the proprietor, replied, "*Una cerveza, señor. Muchas gracias,*" but then spoke in understandable English: "We have many women for your pleasure, señor."

"When I find the right woman, I intend to pleasure myself."
John Henry turned his back to the bartender and fixed his eyes
upon a flaxen-blond woman with icy blue eyes, now clouded by
drink, sitting at a corner table waiting to be propositioned. Even
though she wore a saloon girl's scanty red outfit that barely
contained her full bosom and ripe hips, her somber face and
unapproachable demeanor discouraged solicitation. John Henry,
taking his beer with him, approached her. Standing over her, he
saw deep bags under her eyes and fresh bruises on her left cheek,
as well as a black eye left over from a past encounter. She was
drunk, but not enough to calm the twitching hands she clasped
around her drink.

"May I join you?"

She glanced at him, seemingly indifferent to the fact that
he was American. "It'll cost you two tequilas." She quaffed what
was left in her glass. John Henry motioned to the pock-faced
owner to bring two more tequilas. After a prostitute delivered the
drinks, he sat opposite the woman he believed to be Clara, cradling
his shotgun in his lap. If the weapon or his nationality made anyone
uncomfortable in the dimly lit room the south of the border, its
occupants gave no indication. Until this moment, John Henry did
not noticed the bouncer—a young, well-built Mexican teenager
sitting in the corner, away from the bar. He wore two pistols and
cradled a rifle. The bartender also wore a pistol, and the Anglo felt
certain a shotgun rested behind the bar.

"I believe you to be Clara Cardwell. My name is John
Henry Summerfield. I am the first husband of Benevolence, your
mother and the grandmother of your two missing daughters." The
woman emptied one glass of tequila. "I'm sorry to say, I believe
your mother passed away since I last saw her a month or two
back." The woman looked upon him with interest for the first time,
draining the second glass of tequila. "Your half-sister, Jane, is also
dead. The monsters who kidnapped you saw that she died
horribly." This time, the thoroughly sodden woman gasped and bit
the knuckles of her hand. "That murdering gang sold your two girls
to the Apache." Tears streamed down the debased woman's face.

"I mean to get them back for you. But first, I came to take you away from this den of iniquity and send you to Santa Fe, where you can reclaim your life."

"Look at me—I am a grieving widow who has fallen into the depths of depravity, a wife and mother turned into a ten-peso whore. I don't deserve to reclaim my past life."

"What has been done to you can't be undone. You can stay here and drink yourself senseless, and within a year, you'll be so sodden that the owner will sell you off, most likely to the Mescalero Apache. No slave drinks tequila in Apache wickiups—you will find unstopping work and constantly birthing Apache babies. I intend to return your young girls to you, and then they will be yours to raise—that is if you find the courage to pull yourself from this life of debauchery. "

"How can you possibly get me out of this damned imprisonment?" She indicated with her eyes the armed bouncer and equally armed men standing at the bar.

"I'm going to try. Will you go along with what I plan to do? If not for yourself, do it for your daughters." She nodded tentatively, very uncertain that anyone could free her from forced prostitution.

A worker dressed in homespun white cotton garments approached the table, his sombrero in his hand. He spoke in broken English: "Pardon, señor. I paid for this woman's time."

John Henry, determined to avoid confrontation before he was ready to act, replied, "I will wait my turn." Clara accompanied the laborer through the back door to where the cantina's fornicating rooms were located. He nursed his beer and tequila for the next half hour, undergoing the scrutiny of the teenage guard. The young gunman posed little threat to John Henry, given the ex–army scout's gun fighting experience. Nevertheless, he kept his attention away from the boy and on the drinks before him.

*

Clara returned to the barroom, following the contented Mexican laborer, and took a seat opposite John Henry at the table. Benevolence's second daughter seemed unfazed by giving her

130

body to a man for a few pesos. John Henry went to the burly, pock-faced bartender and paid ten dollars in silver coins to purchase Clara's entire night. The bartender greeted the offer with a succulent smile—he never received a price that high for such an uncooperative whore. "Take the larger tent, señor." He gave a broad smile to the man he thought to be a big spender. "Nothing but the best accommodations for you on your night of pleasure." John Henry ordered a bottle of tequila and a full pot of hot coffee. He escorted the drunken woman through the rear door to an assembly of small tents for night-long copulation. He noticed a six-foot-high rickety wooden fence built around the tents to keep out interlopers. Pulling the flap back on the larger tent, he saw it housed a full-sized bed, table, and chairs for eating.

His first task would be to pour coffee into Clara until she became sober enough to ride his mule. He collected an old shirt and a second pair of denims in the saddlebags strapped to the mule and ordered Clara to dress in them; since he paid a handsome sum for Clara, neither the bartender nor the guard gave his movements a second thought. To disguise her, he put his short-brimmed hat on her head after she fixed her hair into a bun. Then the pair waited until about four o'clock in the morning, at which point they moved to slip outside unnoticed and make their way to John Henry's mule and horse. All Cantina of the Happy Winds' customers exited through the bar, as the back of the property had been fenced off. But John Henry saw he could escape through the kitchen if he could get by the armed cook, though the man appeared more formidable than the average cook, perhaps a Mexican outlaw going straight. Acting decisively, John Henry trained his Colt on the cook's head before he could take his hands from the flank steak he was cutting for the next day's burritos. Forcing the cook outside, he wrapped a rope around his neck and bound his wrists before him. Off to the side of the cantina, he placed an unsettled Clara on the mule and gave her the more deadly shotgun for protection. The mule's wound seemed to be healing enough to carry her, but to be safe, he removed sacks of flour, dried beans, and cornmeal from the animal to lighten its load. "Ride directly west, following the river trail, until you reach Ciudad Juárez. From there, cross the Rio Grande bridge and take the first stagecoach out of El Paso for Santa Fe. Once there, your adopted uncle, Smoker, won't be hard to find— follow the smell of cooked pig." He sent her ahead, telling her to urge the mule along as fast as possible. Satisfied Clara was safely off, he rode the chestnut while pulling the cook alongside him at a brisk walk.

With the cook's rope in one hand and the reins of the chestnut in the other, John Henry began the sixteen-mile ride to Juárez, confident the owner of the Cantina of the Happy Winds and his bodyguard would be trailing him. He was not disappointed: within ten minutes, he heard the galloping of two horses some three hundred yards behind him. He tied his horse to a clump of bushes and hogtied the cook next to the trail. He stood in the middle of the road, sure the two Mexicans did not possess the expertise to shoot him while moving at full gallop; if they planned a shootout, the odds favored him. The young Mexican bodyguard was first to rein in his horse, five feet from where John Henry stood. He held his pistol in his right hand, having ridden so fast and furiously that his pistol hand shook.

"Best to holster your pistol until your hand steadies." Aware of his unsteady hand and John Henry's left hand on his pistol butt, the youth followed his advice.

The burly, pock-faced proprietor galloped in a moment later. "Where is my blond-haired prostitute?"

"She is out of your reach. And you will must go through me to pursue her." The bartender appeared uncertain about what to do next, but the young Mexican did not lack courage and, acting as if he knew how to use his pistols, grabbed for his holstered right one. Using his practiced left-handed cross draw, John Henry got off a shot before the boy leveled his weapon; wounded, the overanxious gunmen dropped his pistol. The veteran gun hand's bullet hit the boy in his right shoulder. His off-target aim did not please John Henry, but on second thought, he reflected that it pleased him to know he did not fatally shoot the youngster. Both Mexicans were awed by the speed with which John Henry fired his

Colt and promptly ceased their aggression. "How much did you pay Winston Williams for the woman?"

"I paid a man two hundred pesos, and they drank another hundred pesos in liquor, señor."

"It seems you likely made more than that much in trade, but I will pay you the equivalent of fifty pesos in American, which should amount to ten dollars. Do we have a deal? I will pay now if you return to your cantina now and forget the woman and I exist." He picked up the wounded Mexican's pistol and confiscated his second weapon. The young gunman, traumatized by his wound, offered no resistance. John Henry then relieved the proprietor of his shotgun and pistol; the older Mexican, desiring to escape an unpredictable situation, was likewise compliant. "You'll find your weapons three miles up the trail but not before tomorrow morning. Now you two hombres take your cook and return to your cantina and consider yourselves lucky you are not dead." He tossed ten dollars in coin at the scar-faced proprietor's feet.

John Henry instructed Clara to leave his mule at the stable next to the stagecoach station in El Paso; he intended to reclaim the animal there. He thought to gain Ciudad Juárez before the first touch of light, eat some food, travel to El Paso, and pick up his mule and shotgun. From there, he would head out to destroy the ranch of Winston Williams's parents, the last on his payback list. Thereafter, he believed Williams and the six murderers could no longer ignore his destructive ways and would hunt him down in Las Vegas, where he planned to wait.

*

On the trail a half mile east of Ciudad Juárez, John Henry came upon a Mexican *el camino vente*, the path sale in English, a small mud-brick roadhouse with a kitchen serving breakfast. He failed to eat during the last three days, so he ordered eggs, ham, a stack of tortillas, and a pot of coffee. He soaked his first tortilla in an egg yolk when a large old man with long, gray hair and a full beard took the chair opposite him. One side of the man's face displayed a bad scar. He carried two pistols, the left one turned toward his right hand. A look of toughness emanated from the man—John Henry guessed him to be a hard-nosed cattle rancher. Soon after he sat opposite John Henry, ten more cowboys sat at tables on the dirt patio. "I take you to be the three-fingered John Henry Summerfield, the killer of seven men at Fort Hays City ten years ago. In that time, not a single day passed when you were not in my thoughts." John Henry's worst fear, one he ran from for ten years, suddenly came to life. "And now you are in my grasp. I am James Knox Ulsterman, the father of the twenty-five-year-old boy you shot down in cold blood on a side street called Fort. My boy's name was James McCoy Ulsterman—McCoy being his mother's maiden name. May they both rest in peace."

"Your boy could've ridden off, but he chose to make a stand. He held a gun in his hand when I shot him."

"My boy took no part in the affair with that poor woman and her undeserving husband-to-be the day you shot three of my men. I grant you the low-living cowboys who did the murderous deed deserved to die for what they did that day. And you saw that justice was served. Why didn't you let matters rest there? On the next day, after the marshal informed him of the death of his men, my boy came to Fort Hays City to collect the bodies. When you attacked his men outside the mortician's office, he felt obliged to protect the three men you shot down."

"All three cowboys held pistols in their hands."

"And you shot all three while they controlled spooked horses, and then you chased my boy onto a side street to murder him. Being my son, he was not about to turn tail and run away. The whores told me how you used a Sioux maneuver to de-horse him. He was just twenty-five years old—sprawled on a dusty street, dizzy from the fall, and not a match for a seasoned plainsman like you. You could've spared his life, but you kicked his pistol to him. Being my son, he saw no choice but to face you in a shootout." John Henry saw how the old man treasured his son's decision to fight rather than run. "There are ten pistols trained on you now, so I suggest you place your pistol, your rifle, and that little Derringer you prefer to carry on the table. You and I must conduct business, which is best conducted on the plains where the

Comanche once rode."

*

John Henry soon found himself running behind Ulsterman's trotting horse, his big chestnut keeping pace beside him, to a deserted stretch of the desert a few miles south of the Mexican roadhouse and some seven miles from the border. Ulsterman's ten hardened cowboys rode at a slow pace around him. The Texan rancher found a small clump of oak trees illuminated by the moon and reined in his horse; the cowboys followed suit, stopping in a cloud of dust. John Henry fell to his knees, exhausted, dust filling his parched mouth. Two cowboys immediately yanked him to his feet, and two more ripped his clothing and boots from his body until he stood naked. Two ropes were looped around his wrists and then wrapped around the saddle horns of two horses. The horses were led away from each other, stretching the captive to a breaking point. Then the vengeful father stepped forth and slammed his fist into the side of John Henry's head. He delivered a vicious blow for a man in his sixties, stunning the captive.

"That's the first blow you will receive as recompense for my son's death." Immediately after that, with John Henry stretched like a human clothesline, the ten cowboys took turns beating him from his neck to his ankles until every part of his body was beaten to the extent the captive wished he could die. Then Ulsterman stepped forward and, using his whip's handle, beat John Henry's face to a bloody pulp.

"I am tempted to use the horses pull your arms out, but I devised something special for you." Ulsterman then ordered his men to bind John Henry's arms to his side and hang him upside down by the ankles from an oak tree branch. He then took his knife and slowly and methodically removed the skin from the captive's back, enjoying John Henry's wincing under the pain. "This will make an appropriate flower basket for my son's tombstone so that each day when I place a flower into your skin hanging off the tombstone, he will get some gratification knowing retribution has

135

been exacted for his murder. Now let me give you a special treat." Ulsterman poured water from his canteen on his captive's bloody face to revive him. "Since you prefer Plains Indian maneuvers, here is one of their favorites. My boys are preparing a slow-burning fire just for you." John Henry felt himself being hoisted higher, still upside down, so his head was about eighteen inches off the ground. A cowboy quickly scooped out a hole underneath his head and placed glowing embers there. "I'm sure a seasoned plainsman like yourself will recognize my favorite means of putting a man out of his misery—only this brain baking is meant to prolong your misery, to slowly dismantle your body functions until your brain turns to gravy and your eyes melt in their sockets." Ulsterman seated himself on a nearby rock, prepared to watch John Henry slowly expire.

A shrill sound streaked across the prairie, reverberating off of canyon walls. The Texans knew the sound well—*El Degüello*. It sent cold chills down their spines, for less than fifty years before, *El Degüello* sounded death for the defenders of the Alamo, where not one man escaped. *El Degüello* declared the Mexican army's announcement that no quarter would be given to those they planned to attack. The sound paralyzed Ulsterman's men, who knew they would soon be caught deep in Mexican territory by a cavalry patrol of at least platoon strength. Mexican patrols were made up of brutal troops who felt no remorse when chopping off gringo heads.

Realizing they were no match for the Mexican army, the cowboys quickly mounted their horses. Not given to such panic, Ulsterman tried to calm his men long enough to throw the tortured captive over his saddle, wanting to take him along and continue the slow death. But the cowboys rode off to a distance and waited for their boss to join them. The Civil War veteran and Comanche Indian fighter next pulled his pistol to shoot the man who shot his son, but the trumpet call sounded a second time, ominously close—too close to risk the sound of a pistol shot. Finding no other choice, Ulsterman mounted his horse and rode off with his men, stealing John Henry's horse.

*

Pain dulling his senses, a semi-conscious John Henry felt himself lowered to the ground. A big, clean-cut, clean-shaven, well-dressed man wearing a Texas Ranger's badge stood over him. "You are in sorry shape, partner. But I am here to help you. My name is Winston Williams; I am the man you believed murdered and sold off your wife's family. I came to tell you it was not me who did the hideous act—for that reason, I've been following your movements around El Paso so that I might explain that very truth before you burned down my family's ranch." Williams dressed the injured man, who winced in pain at the slightest movement of his limbs, in extra clothing he retrieved from his saddlebags, reversing the shirt to leave his back bare. He then cut off two branches from the oak tree, limbs strong enough to make a Plains Indian transport that early French explorers called a travois and weaved smaller branches onto it for support. Because of John Henry's skinned back, Williams positioned him face down on the travois.

Williams knelt beside the suffering man so that his face could be seen. "As I said, I am the man whose family ranch you intended to burn to the ground, and I've been following you for the last day to explain that I was not connected with the burning massacre at the Cardwell ranch up north in New Mexico Territory. The man you want is called Bolingbrook. He is a butcher, a veteran scout of the northern plains, just like you. Talk has it he hails from Kansas. I left the gang after Bolingbrook persuaded my followers that burning ranches and raping women would be more rewarding and less dangerous than robbing public transport. My specialty feature me robbing stagecoaches, stealing range cattle, and robbing a bank where a man could get out of town without getting shot. The Texas governor pardoned me if I would rejoin the Texas Rangers. I am now a proud officer of those Texas Rangers."

John Henry's mouth was so swollen the words stumbled from his lips. "How did you find me?"

"I trailed you from that Mexican *camino vente* after the Texas cattle baron, Ulsterman, and his men rode off with you. After seeing what those cruel men intended to do to you, I rode back to

137

the roadhouse and paid a Mexican trumpeter to sound *El Degüello* to scare those men back to Abilene. A shrill Mexican trumpet's blasting sure did the job. Now let me get you to a doctor in the United States."

"No doctor."

"Are you a wanted man?"

"I am a man some men would be interested in catching. Take me to El Paso, where I can collect my mule."

"Where do you intend to go?"

"A place northeast of Las Vegas, New Mexico, called Wild Wind Hole, where Broad-Butt Betty's brothel offers gambling and whoring. There is a prostitute there named Marge who said she would fornicate me back to health. I'm hoping she'll change her intent to nursing me instead."

"I'll see to it that you get there."

"Why would you want to do that?"

"I view us as comrades in a mess that neither of us wanted to be involved in."

"Why help me?"

"You and I are white men drawn by the need to see a wrong made right."

Chapter 10

The severely injured John Henry Summerfield could only imagine, but never really know, the slaughter that occurred that dreadful day at the Cardwell ranch. The man who ousted Winston Williams, Francis Bolingbrook, along with his gang of six—the redheaded brothers Bradford and Bryce Benson, the half-crazy Ben Apple, the outlaw cousins Wade Alsop and Charles Miller, and the deadly Justo Trujillo—sat mounted on the rise overlooking the Cardwell ranch at the breakfast hour. Bolingbrook wanted to gun down Williams, but the man's proficiency with a pistol and his ex-gang's loyalty to their former leader convinced him to let the man ride out of their outlaw lair. He convinced Williams' followers that raiding prosperous ranches would be more entertaining and safer

138

than robbing stagecoaches, trains, and banks because they were less likely to get Pinkerton agents and possies on their trail.

Possessed of a butcher's reputation, Bolingbrook wore his hair long to where it rested midway down his back. Two braided pigtails fell from his sideburns under a black, wide- and flat-brimmed hat. He possessed a big man's six-foot-three frame and weighed nearly 220 pounds. A childhood bout with smallpox left his face pockmarked around a bulbous nose and dimpled, square chin; his ice-cold blue eyes gave him a fearsome bearing. He preferred to wear a black shirt under a red vest, with buckskin trousers tucked into knee-high leather boots. Bolingbrook carried two pistols, the left one reversed so that he could draw it with his right hand if he emptied his main pistol.

Francis Bolingbrook experienced his first killing as a teenager when he followed in the path of his older brother, who accompanied John Brown during the slaughter of Southern sympathizers in bloody Kansas. An anti-slavery fanatic, he rode with the Kansas Red Legs, decimating Southern sympathizers in Missouri. If Bloody Bill Anderson, the Southern guerrilla who excelled in senseless slaughter, knew a counterpart on the Union side, it would be Francis Bolingbrook. After the Civil War, Bolingbrook hired on as a scout for the army, especially adept at discovering Sioux and Cheyenne villages, where inhabitants, women and children included, were shot and chopped down. He rode with John Chivington, who ignored a recently signed peace treaty, during a deliberate massacre of Black Kettle's peaceful Cheyenne at Sand Creek in the Colorado territory and later on Nelson Miles's mission to eradicate Crazy Horse's following. Massacring and killing any Plains Indian that walked became a way of life for Bolingbrook, to the extent that he could not stop.

At the conclusion of the Sioux wars, Bolingbrook took to robbing stagecoaches and frontier trains, leaving a bloody trail across Arkansas, Nebraska, and Oklahoma. Federal marshals eventually captured him in a Fort Smith, Arkansas brothel; the court sentenced him to ten years in the U.S. Disciplinary Barracks at Leavenworth. A favorite of Civil War veterans because of his strong Union loyalty, the guards allowed Bolingbrook to escape while on a wood-gathering detail outside the prison walls. He returned to robbing stagecoaches and small banks, rarely leaving any survivors.

The gang of seven looked down from their vantage point on a large and well-maintained, freshly whitewashed, timbered five-room ranch house fronted by a large porch with a rocker and chairs. A short distance away was a small bunkhouse—occupied by John Henry's daughter, Jane. A newly rebuilt barn housing six milk cows and a bull stood a short distance from the ranch house. Two corrals held at least twenty horses, some yet to be broken; a pigpen with two families of swine bumped up against the barn. A large vegetable garden growing beans, carrots, and corn the women maintained spread out behind the ranch house. Nearby, a well with a windmill could be seen.

The murder-minded gang of seven was spurred to action by the smell of fried ham, eggs, and fresh bread. Bolingbrook's gang dismounted and led their horses to the ranch house; splitting up, the gang entered the house through the front and back doors, confronting the Cardwell family at their breakfast table. Renegades Bradford and Bryce Benson promptly grabbed the two young girls and hogtied them while Wade Alsop beat Claude Cardwell to the floor with his rifle butt. Bolingbrook, training his pistol on the three women still seated at the breakfast table, ordered the ex-Confederate Ben Apple and his cousin Charles Miller to loot the five-room ranch house of any cash and valuables, including heirlooms, jewelry, and pocket watches. During the looting, the two men found two rifles, a shotgun, and a recently oiled .38-caliber pistol. Outraged at the robbery of her house, the grandmother attacked Bolingbrook with a broom. Amused, he knocked her unconscious with the butt of his pistol, leaving her to lie motionless on the kitchen floor.

The vaquero-outfitted Justo Trujillo and the younger, more sinister Benson brother, Bryce, grabbed the two adult females and dragged them to the bedroom. When the women resisted, they slapped their faces raw and punched their bellies until they were rendered compliant. Except for Francis Bolingbrook, the entire gang took turns sexually assaulting Jane and Clara; Bolingbrook, his promise to his gang fulfilled, was content to feast on the unfinished breakfast. After the looting and raping, Bolingbrook ordered everyone outside, leaving the unconscious grandmother on the kitchen floor. The raiders then torched the ranch house, cremating the grandmother. Thereafter, they set fire to the bunkhouse, barn, and windmill, shooting cows and pigs that would only slow them down if stolen. As the structures blazed, the gang herded the raped women, the hogtied children, and the beaten Claude Cardwell near to the burning corrals. Not finished with the murderous morning, Bolingbrook strapped Cardwell's holster to his waist.

"If you own a drop of manhood in you, you will defend your family." He handed Cardwell his pistol and five cartridges, ordering him to load the firearm. He then backed up fifteen paces and ordered Cardwell to draw the pistol, telling him that if he refused, his wife and sister-in-law would be gutted before his eyes. Cardwell—a rancher, not a gun hand—reached for his .38-caliber pistol but was no match for Bolingbrook's fast draw. Two shots—one to the forehead, the other to the heart—dropped him dead. Whereas John Henry Summerfield killed only when forced to kill, the maniacal Bolingbrook killed to feed his bloodlust. Thereafter, the gang of seven, the Cardwell Ranch blazing at their backs, rode off with their captives and stolen horses, headed for the Apache camp in the Sangre de Cristo mountain range.

*

Winston Williams, mounted on a weary horse at the crack of dawn, dragged the travois bearing a severely injured John Henry to an El Paso livery stable. He collected John Henry's mule and shotgun, rented a buckboard to transport the injured man to Wild Wind Hole. Williams served as an Confederate captain with an inherent sense of right and wrong regarding killing. He earned a distinguished record in the Texas Confederate Army, taking part in the successful Rebel mission out of Texas to occupy the Arizona Territory during the war. Later, Williams accompanied General

Sibley's invasion of New Mexico Territory to cut off Union supply trails to California. After the war, the Texas Rangers eagerly recruited him to hunt down Comanche and Mexican cattle ranchers. Underpaid and overworked as a Ranger, he took to working the shady side of the law, robbing stagecoaches and small-town banks.

"Damn, I've seen it all now. I can see why people call this patch of sagebrush and sand Wild Wind Hole." Williams brought the buckboard to a halt before the encampment's fancier saloon. He jumped to the ground and examined the two saloons and the rose-colored two-story structure where Broad-Butt Betty's prostitutes conducted their business. "I can see why this place has a reputation for being lawless, remote as it is." He unpinned his Texas Ranger badge and pocketed it. He next checked his single-action Colt for loads. "You stay put while I hunt down your prostitute using the name of Marge." He went to the two-story house of prostitution, only to be directed to the tents in the rear of the saloons.

For the badly beaten John Henry, it became a torturous and painful ride bouncing along the rough dead-end road that led to the remote Wild Wind Hole. He rolled off his side so that he lay upright, his weight resting on his elbows. He noted the bearded horse thief, the man whose hands he burned, setting up his rope-strung corral for the evening's business, wondering if the corral tender would seek revenge. Lying in the buckboard, hatless and shoeless, he felt battered and bruised; his back stung like the pangs of hell, and his hair scorched off the top of his head; blisters formed there. Circumstances spared him broken bones. He retained his mule and shotgun, though he lost his Colt .45 pistol, his derringer, and his money, along with the big chestnut horse and saddle. Injured, he felt near to the end of his life, vulnerable to any trigger-happy drunk—or worse yet, the revenge-seeking Grayson brothers he crippled and their nasty pa, whom he threatened to hang. He was relieved when Williams appeared with Marge at his side. She wore a flimsy robe that highlighted her hourglass figure. Her dark brown eyes lost their ennui and brightened when she saw John

142

Henry. Without her heavy makeup, Marge was handsome, presenting a smooth forehead, high cheekbones, and full lips.

"I knew if I played my cards right, my lanky revengeseeker would return to me." Her warm smile and sweet voice gave John Henry hope. With those words, Marge cupped the injured man's swollen face in her hands, her eyes full of tears, indicating that she harbored genuine affection for the man reclined in the buckboard. "Don't you fret none, mister, this runaway farm girl will nurse you back to health just as soon as you tell me your name."

"John Henry Summerfield." A swollen mouth made him slur his name.

"My name is Marge Hillbrandt." She kissed John Henry's forehead. "Help me carry him to my tent, Mister Williams." Williams and the prostitute assisted the banged-up man to her tent behind the saloons. The tent appeared more extensive than the other, temporary ones—Marge traded her body to a gambler for the tent; he in turn, won the tent from two prospectors in a card game. Williams and Marge positioned John Henry on a full-sized, iron-framed bed so that he lay on his side facing them. "You and I will be very cozy in bed, Mister John Henry Summerfield. Now I will undress you and heal your battered body."

"Well, Summerfield, it looks like you are in good hands. I'll be returning this buckboard and heading back to Texas, where there is plenty of outlaw business to be terminated. You and I forged bond in blood that I won't forget. By the way, here is your old Navy Colt." He revealed the charred but still functional pistol wrapped in a rag. "It got burned a mite in the fire Ulsterman prepared to get the hot coals to bake your brains, but it shouldn't be a problem for a three-fingered gunfighter like yourself to handle." John Henry thought the old pistol forever lost. He held it like a prized possession.

*

True to her word, Marge nursed John Henry during the daylight hours, applying a cool, moist poultice with an unknown liniment to his skinned back to prevent hard scabbing. She gave him laudanum for his pain and fed him soup through his swollen mouth. By day, she became a nurse to heal the man who enamored her and returned to prostitution at night, servicing customers to procure money for John Henry. The injured man never asked her for money, but she knew, he being robbed, needed clothing, a horse, and a saddle. Ever since her Ohio lover deserted her in Las Vegas, Marge hungered for intimacy and set her sights on John Henry, even as drably dressed and low-key as he presented himself. No rhyme or reason existed for the attraction. There were better-looking and wealthier men, flashier and more exciting, but John Henry possessed the chemistry that stirred affection in her. Enhancing the appeal was his ultimatum to old man Grayson, which kept the reprobate from abusing her, and his wounding of the Benson brothers, which moved them to give her a wide berth during their bouts of saloon drinking.

John Henry fought loneliness since 1861, at age twenty-one, when he deserted Benevolence on their Kansas farm and joined the Union Army. He used Sioux women who traded their bodies for food during his long enlistment as a plains scout for the army, and during his low-profile years in Los Angeles, he treated himself to a whore once a month in a house of prostitution on Temple Street. In 1885, twenty-four years without intimacy weighed heavily on the forty-five-year-old man. Having Marge sleep with him for a few hours each night and constantly nurse and entertain him during the day created a desire for her within him, despite her life of prostitution. She massaged his muscle-stiffened body and rubbed ointment on his singed head and back, which grew scar tissue before healing. Each night after working in Broad-Butt Betty's rose and purple-trimmed house of ill repute, she would snuggle up to John Henry, nestling her head to his and holding his hand. After four weeks of healing, when the muscle bruising and stiffening in his body subsided and new skin, although scarred, grew on his back, John Henry made love to Marge with a passion that he only remembered experiencing with his young wife, Benevolence. For her part, Marge felt the same passion she dreamed of as a young girl on an Ohio farm and never found in her carnal customers.

For the next two weeks, like young lovers, they became enamored with each other, kissing during the day and making love every night. John Henry reconciled himself to sharing Marge with other men, dwelling on her pleasant demeanor and giving nature. But as John Henry came close to a full recovery, his promise to Benevolence to avenge her for the dastardly deed at the Cardwell Ranch occupied his thoughts. He realized he needed more firepower than his shotgun and Marge's underpowered .32-caliber pistol, and more mobility than the mule. He also realized he must leave the woman he fell in love with, and no certainty existed that he would return to her.

*

The woman John Henry loved appeared at his side, buoyant in the morning hours. He sat up in a wooden rocker, sipping coffee. To his surprise, Marge presented him with used boots and a western hat. She bought the items from the barkeep at the Gila Monster Saloon; the saloon made side money collecting and selling clothing, boots, and pistols lost in poker games or seized after a cowboy found himself shot dead in a pistol fight. Grateful to wear boots allowing him to move about outside the tent, he pulled them on and stood. "A good fit, Marge."

"Here's another surprise for you." Beaming a contented smile, she held out a small box tied with a red ribbon. "This I saved up to give to you." After handing him the gift, she gave him a big hug. John Henry undid the ribbon; a neat roll of currency inside the box met his inspection. "There's enough cash there to buy you a horse and saddle. The corral tender has collected two or three saddle horses from liquored-up men shot dead."

John Henry remained speechless—the notion of accepting money from a woman was a new concept for him. His first instinct compelled him to return the money, but he knew he desperately needed money to pursue the revenge he'd promised Benevolence, and robbing another stagecoach was out of the question. Seeing the conflict etched across his face, Marge rushed to him and peppered him with kisses. "I know you intend to hunt down those men who inflicted a savage beating on you. I don't intend to whore the rest of my life, so I am praying you will return to me after you finish your business, and we can settle down somewhere peaceful. I don't mean you must marry me, me being a whore and all. But we could live together and spend the rest of our days making love. Can you see yourself doing that, John Henry?"

Marge's words emotionally stirred John Henry even though he owned no thought of hunting James Knox Ulsterman; after he finished the business with the Bolingbrook murderers, he felt ready to settle down. He also felt regardless of Marge being a prostitute, he would not find a more giving, devoted, and passionate woman anywhere. He put the money in his trouser pocket, thinking that he would repay the gift in countless ways once they were together.

"There is land to be bought in California, south of Los Angeles. A man and a woman can buy cheap acres there and grow oranges for sale. You can work as much or as little as pleases you. Would that suit you, Marge?"

She swooned in his arms. "Oh, yes, it would, my darling! It most certainly would."

*

John Henry never left the tent since he arrived in Wild Wind Hole six weeks ago. With Marge accompanying him, he walked to test his healing body and regain stamina. Mindful that he inhabited a lawless patch of sand and sagebrush, he strapped Marge's .32-caliber pistol to his injured hand and tucked it under the secondhand suit jacket Marge bought for him. Marge linked her arm with John Henry's as the couple made their way to the temporary corral that filled up with patrons' horses by this time of day. John Henry approached the corral tender and spoke: "I will pay you hard cash for a good horse and saddle."

The man John Henry forced to burn his hands on a hot stove recognized him. "You've got some gall, showing up like this and asking me to sell you a horse. Look what you did to my hands." He held up two exposed hands, revealing scar tissue that

146

contracted the fingers. "If I could handle a pistol, I would shoot you dead where you stand." He reached for the shotgun leaning against his chair, but John Henry's left hand blocked the move. He lifted the pistol from under his jacket so the corral tender could see it. He next dropped the loads from the shotgun and returned it.

"I'm willing to pay up to seventy-five dollars for a good horse and used saddle."

"You're barking up the wrong tree, mister. Seeing that I own the only animals for sale in this miserable patch of windblown sand and feeling I would rather see you under six feet of dirt than standing before me, my price is a hundred and fifty dollars."

"I remind you, you miserable horse bandit, that I would be well within my rights to hang you for stealing my mount. Given that business, you owe me your life. Sell me a horse and saddle for seventy-five dollars or I will be traveling to your place to take them, and I will not be too particular about shooting you if you get in the way." John Henry counted out seventy-five dollars and waved it before the corral tender. Seeing sense in the exchange of words, the bearded man retrieved a brown-and-white spotted mustang from the corral. Taking one of three saddles he offered for sale, he saddled the mustang. John Henry paid him another dollar to corral the horse for the day. Crossing the path that ended in a dead end in front of the two saloons, Marge and John Henry returned to the tent.

Benny Benson watched them from the window of the larger saloon. He escaped the Apache stronghold in the Sangre de Cristos in the dead of night. Falling back on old habits, he rustled five heads of cattle and sold them to Broad-Butt Betty's kitchen so he could enjoy a night of debauchery. He now emerged from the saloon to confront John Henry. At first, John Henry did not recognize the Benson boy, now dressed like an Apache and wearing a scarf tied across his forehead, the preferred Apache flowered shirt hung over deerskin trousers; knee-high moccasins covered his feet. He cinched a holster holding a mother-of-pearl-handled Colt .45-caliber pistol to his waist.

"Why, if it isn't the bastard who jumped me in that dry wash as I tended to nature's call. I am most pleased to run into you, Summerfield." He pushed his hat back on his head. Seeing the red hair surprised John Henry, unprepared for a shootout. "How am I to repay you for burning down my family's ranch, kidnapping me and my family, and selling us off to the Apache? I've been beaten, tormented from sunup to sundown, and on a good day, staked out to bake under a blistering sun while my captors feasted on wild game and chanted wild, incomprehensible demon sounds." Benson drew his pistol and fired at John Henry, who stood about forty feet away; the bullet hit Marge in the chest. She fell immediately. John Henry knelt beside her to attend to her wound.

"Guess I won't be around to tend oranges with you, John Henry. Goodbye, my love." Marge's eyes went vacant, and he saw Benson's bullet killed her. John Henry saw death countless times, but witnessing Marge's death stunned him. He fought to regain his composure. No time existed to mourn her because death threatened him. An inexperienced gun hand, Benson continued to wildly fire at John Henry, bullets hitting the dirt and whistling around him and the woman he held in his arms. Forty feet was out of range for Marge's .32-caliber pistol. John Henry gently laid the woman he loved on the ground and closed the distance between the wild shooter and himself; Benson fired off all his loads and proceeded to reload. The bereaved man ran to within ten feet, took aim, and shot Benson three times through the heart. The young redheaded sibling of the two brothers who raped and murdered his daughter lay dead at his feet, the freckled face appearing innocent in death. There would be no more cattle rustling and hell-raising for the dead boy at Broad-Butt Betty's Wild Wind Hole. Summerfield removed Benson's pistol belt, taking his .45-caliber pistol, then carried Marge to their tent. A crowd of gamblers and beer drinkers witnessed the shootout in a place where shootouts were common and went unreported to the law.

*

At morning's first light, John Henry constructed a *travois* and placed Marge's blanket-wrapped body on it, then hitched the rig to his mule and headed to Las Vegas to bury the woman Benson cut down. He bought Benson's Winchester rifle from the Gila Monster Saloon barkeep; except for his derringer, he felt fully armed. He paid the mortician in Las Vegas to dress Marge in a respectable dress and ordered a tombstone with an engraving that read:

Marge Hillbrandt
Born Ohio
Died New Mexico Territory, 1885
Betrothed of JH Summerfield

With the word "betrothed," he gave Marge a measure of respect for her eternal rest that he failed to provide her in her mortal life. Only the mortician stood at his side at the burial site John Henry selected, next to his daughter's grave, as he eulogized the woman he grew to love:

"Marge Hillbrandt left an Ohio farm life of drudgery only to find a harder life on the western frontier. Despite being thrown into the frontier's harsh caprice, she kept her sweet voice, warm smile, and unselfish and giving nature. A hothead took her life between what I guess to be twenty-five to thirty years of age. I only knew her briefly, but she captured my heart. I will miss you, Marge."

Unsure whether or not the sheriff issued an arrest warrant against him for burning down four ranches, John Henry nonetheless made a distasteful visit to the Las Vegas sheriff's office. He needed more information on Francis Bolingbrook to flush him and his murderous gang out.

*

A rare cloudburst fell on John Henry as he stood near the Las Vegas plaza arch looking upon the one-story mud-brick structure that housed the sheriff's office. The dirt street quickly turned into a quagmire of mud puddles where wagon wheels rutted it. Behind him, saloons stretched out for a city block, the downpour forcing foot traffic inside. The young deputy Tommy McGrath, who befriended John Henry and attended his daughter's funeral, held his sentinel post on a porch sheltered from the rain, cradling a shotgun. John Henry did not immediately approach the deputy, standing in the rain and remembering the pistol-whipping the white-haired, mustachioed sheriff gave him and knowing he could suffer a similar beating. Deciding to undergo a beating if necessary, he stepped out of the rain onto the porch where the deputy sat.

"Good afternoon, Mister Summerfield. If you're here to see the sheriff, your timing is bad, as he once again enjoys his lunch hour, requesting not to be disturbed."

"Good afternoon, Deputy. From my experience, seeing your ill-tempered boss is never a good time. I need information on a marauding gunslinger named Francis Bolingbrook, so I'll take my chances with the sheriff."

"Once again, you cannot say I didn't warn you," the deputy replied, extending his boyish smile and opening the door for John Henry. Inside, he came upon the two smartly dressed deputies who, unable to toss horseshoes because of the rain, played checkers in the sheriff's office. As before, both deputies, wearing identical white shirts, black vests, and black trousers, were cleanshaven except for pencil mustaches. Both deputies slicked down their hair and wore straight-brimmed hats tilted back as if they prowled for female company. Both curiously eyed John Henry as he studied the sheriff sitting at his desk eating steak and washing it down with beer. The large Smith & Wesson single-action pistol hanging from his shoulder holster caught John Henry's eye. As before, a derby hat tilted back over his neatly parted white hair.

"I came to ask the sheriff about a man named Francis Bolingbrook. I know him to be the leader of the murderous gang that burned the Cardwell Ranch."

The sheriff pushed his half-finished steak to the side of his desk. With a grunt of disgust, he quaffed what was left in his glass of beer and approached the man who interrupted his lunch. "I heard some Texas boys killed you in Mexico. And here you are turning up like a bad penny, interrupting my lunch hour once again. Are you looking for another beating, Summerfield?"

"I've got my fill of beatings this year, Sheriff. I overlooked the last one you gave me, but if you have a second one in mind, consequences will fall on you."

"You don't say. Did you hear that, deputies? This man just threatened a legitimately elected sheriff of San Miguel County. I know you for the Fort Hays City scofflaw who shot seven Texas cowboys in two days."

"Not sure exactly what a scofflaw is, but if he is one you referenced, then you know I'm not a man to be fooled with." The hard glint in the sheriff's eyes flickered as if he believed the same.

"No one is fooling around here, Summerfield. I'm within my rights to pursue my duty as I see fit. Grab him, boys." The pair drew their mother-of-pearl-grip pistols and grasped John Henry by his arms; He felt two pistols pressing against his back. The Sheriff searched the restrained man for weapons and found none. "I ought to beat you to a pulp. Instead, I'll put the word out to the vigilante boys, who don't take kindly to a ranch burner."

John Henry realized that someone from the Miller or Apple family reported the destruction of their ranches to the sheriff—and yet it seemed the lawman would not arrest him. It was possible the sheriff felt no jury would convict him and that he, the Fort Hays City gunfighter, would later come after him.

"Your local mortician related to me that public opinion is on my side for taking revenge on the families of my daughter's murderers, so your vigilantes won't be stringing up a rope on the town windmill. I need you to identify the background of one last wrongdoer involved in the Cardwell murders and kidnapping. He goes by the name of Francis Bolingbrook and hails from Kansas. I came to see if you possess a wanted poster on this Bolingbrook."

"Even if I wanted to help you, which I don't, I am unfamiliar with Bolingbrook. Get the hell out of my office before I hurt you."

"It seems to me, Sheriff, that you are afraid of this Bolingbrook, given your reluctance to chase the gang that kidnapped the Cardwell females and now your refusal to turn over what information you acquired about Bolingbrook."

Throw him the hell out of here." The deputies roughly escorted John Henry to the office door. The sheriff caught him up and exclaimed, "The next time I see you, Summerfield, it will be to hang you. And that day will be when wanted posters on you show up." A slight smile formed on John Henry's lips—at that moment, he knew word of the shoot-out with Benny Benson failed to reach this hard-nosed sheriff, and even if it did, there was little he could do about it. The deputies pushed him off the porch into the rain. As the rain drenched him, John Henry noted the young deputy he knew as Tommy McGrath vacated his post.

The sky cleared once the cloudburst roared through the New Mexico town. Believing it untypical for the young deputy quit his post, John Henry suspected he probably found a reason to do so. He remembered that McGrath worshipped his daughter, Jane, for nurturing and feeding him during his school days and guessed the boy would appear at Jane's grave after he showed up in Las Vegas.

The grass began to grow over Jane's burial plot; freshly turned dirt, muddy from the recent downpour, covered Marge. During the greater part of the day, John Henry paid his respects to the two cherished women he buried. Under the post-rainfall sun, his wet clothes dried on his body. Gradually, the sun moved into the western sky, bringing on the evening hour.

"This newly filled-in grave belongs to someone dear to you, Mister Summerfield?" the young deputy asked, handing the older man a bouquet of wild desert sunflowers. John Henry guessed he left work early to pick the round-petaled yellow flowers for Jane's grave.

"The grave belongs to a woman with a golden heart who captured my heart. I am saddened to state that a gunman senselessly shot her dead." John Henry divided the wildflowers, placing bouquets of equal size on each grave.

"Did you seek justice for her death?"

"He was gunned down in his turn." John Henry saw that his answer satisfied the deputy.

I been tending your daughter Jane's grave, and it would be little trouble for me to tend to that of this golden-hearted woman as well."

"You are an honorable young man, and I am grateful for what attention you can give these graves," John Henry replied—well aware that short time remained of his life and his own time as a grave tender short. "The woman's name was Marge Hillbrandt."

"If you recall, Mister Summerfield, I told you I am an incorrigible eavesdropper. I overheard your conversation with the sheriff today. One of the duties he has assigned me is to file wanted posters. We received a wanted poster for Francis Bolingbrook after escaping the army's lockup at Leavenworth about a year ago. Sheriff wanted nothing to do with him, as he is a mad killer with a reputation as a fast draw and a deadly shooter. This Bolingbrook showed up in Las Vegas about six months ago before your daughter was kidnapped. Sheriff overlooked the holstered pistol he carried. Instead of arresting him, he asked him politely to put his pistol in his saddlebag. I believe they struck a deal wherein the sheriff would not attempt to enforce the order for Bolingbrook's arrest if the killer behaved himself while in Las Vegas. The sheriff has been reluctant to challenge gunfighters with notorious reputations such as follow you and Bolingbrook. I believe that's why he released you today without a pistol-whipping."

"I'm no gunfighter, Deputy. Just a man seeking revenge on behalf of his murdered daughter."

"I pulled this poster for you."

John Henry studied the poster, surprised to see it offered a reward of only $150; the prison-escapee-wanted posters he viewed over the years nearly always offered at least $1000. Given the low reward for Bolingbrook's capture, it became evident to John Henry that Bolingbrook knew powerful supporters, likely army men. The lithograph image showed a pock-faced man with two braided pigtails falling from his sideburns. The broadness of the head shot indicated a large man. Ice-cold eyes—blue, he guessed—gave the man a fearsome countenance.

Sheriff received a follow-up bulletin by mail indicating that this Bolingbrook if in Mexico, might travel through Las Vegas heading north to contact his parents, who operate a stagecoach station and boardinghouse somewhere west of Lawrence, Kansas on the Oregon/California Trail. Study that face, Mister Summerfield, because I must return the poster from where I took it."

*

Francis Bolingbrook left the Oklahoma Territory after discovering the woman's mutilated body removed from the desolate gully where she'd been hung, surmising that someone, maybe even a posse, was nosing about, but most probably that someone was the ranch-burner. He pulled his gang out of Mexico after selling the other woman into prostitution, because he heard a rumor that the government planned to dispatch a big navy payroll. The killer imagined a slow death for John Henry Summerfield. He visualized shooting him in both arms and legs until the man fell helplessly at his feet. Then he would put a bullet between his open eyes, giving him time to savor death. The Benson brothers, riders in Bolingbrook's gang, received word that Summerfield shot their younger brother. The ex-Rebel Alsop and the cousins Miller and Apple—relentlessly pestered Bolingbrook with demands to take revenge on the lone rider from Kansas who burned their ranches and sold off their family members to the Apache. The Mexican half-breed, Justo Trujillo, approached him just as fired up because the gunman invaded his home in Mexico. Clever and plotting by nature, Bolingbrook, the Plains Indian fighter and Union scout, possessed little liking for ex-Rebels and Mexicans; it would be no great loss to him if they found themselves shot dead after the planned payroll robbery.

By now, Francis Bolingbrook knew the ranch burner to be the shooter of seven cowboys in Fort Hays City and a veteran plainsman. But for now, this Summerfield would be spared death, as Bolingbrook planned bigger fish to fry. He and his gang planned to rob a heavily armed navy payroll being dispatched by railroad to San Diego from the U.S. Treasury at Tucson and stopping at Holton on the Alamo River, a fuel depot just east of the Imperial Valley in California. He knew the Pacific Squadron would be anchoring in San Diego Bay for annual repair and resupply by their store ships, out-of-date ships anchored in the bay to hold supplies. There, enlisted men and officers would receive back pay and shore leave. A loose-mouthed and salty navy man told him that the payroll would be as much as seventy-five to one hundred thousand U.S. dollars. He did not know the date and time the train would depart from Tucson. For that reason, Bolingbrook and his restless followers camped on the desert floor outside of Holton with supplies and two wagons. One wagon carried a Gatling gun stolen from the Mexican Army; the other wagon Bolingbrook intended to haul the stolen payroll, expecting a good portion of it to be in silver coin. He felt safe in California, knowing the army showed little interest in recapturing him. A year back in time, federal agents caught him after he robbed a train running through Julesburg, Colorado, and the court sent him to the Kansas federal prison manned by US Army personnel. Most personnel were veterans of the past Red Cloud and Sitting Bull Sioux wars. Bolingbrook's bravery in facing ferocious Sioux warriors and slaughtering them earned him respect among enlisted men and field officers. After only four months in prison, the guards included him in a trustees' detail, moving prison cattle from one grazing area to another. The sergeant in charge of the detail ordered him to bring back a stray steer that wandered off. Bolingbrook never returned, and the army did not report him missing until two days later.

Bolingbrook did not regret the killings and subsequent destruction at the Cardwell ranch. He sold off the two young girls for jewelry and money the Apache accumulated raiding ranches in the Southwest. But no matter how much positive spin he put on it,

155

the Cardwell raid turned out to be a miscalculation, as it put an experienced tracker and gunman on his tail. Bolingbrook felt the raid good fun, but slim pickings compared to what lawbreaking he now planned.

Chapter 11

John Henry terrorized the families of all six of the murderous gang, that murdered his daughter yet the gang would not come after him, even after he said he would face them in Las Vegas. He planned a strong proclamation to flush out Francis Bolingbrook and his gang, realizing that the headman would run out of options after he destroyed the senior Bolingbrook's stagecoach depot in Kansas. He visited a Las Vegas general store and bought six miners' dynamite sticks. Following the Santa Fe Trail toward St. Louis, riding his newly acquired brown-and-white mustang and desiring speed, he left the mule behind. He left the trail east of the Arkansas River, cutting north through Kansas.

Gone were the days of Bloody Kansas, when the murderous Border Ruffians fought the equally brutal Red Legs for the right to claim Kansas as a free or slave state. Lawrence, the place of William Quantrill's bloody raid, and Pottawatomie, the place of John Brown's murderous raid, were now law-abiding locales. The border war between Kansas and Missouri resided in history. The Indian Removal Act vanquished the Kansa, Osage, and Ottawa to occupying small plots of reservation land in the Oklahoma Territory. The Texas cattle drivers, such strongmen as James Knox Ulsterman, and the wild railroad towns where they sold their herds in Kansas and raised hell also resided in history. Endless wheat fields faced John Henry as he rode north through Kansas; he realized that farmers, having replaced gunslingers, prevailed in the state.

With the army's help, John Henry a reputed gunslinger following his shootout at Fort Hays City, fled Kansas ten years ago. The army still maintained the lonesome Fort Hays, perched on a windblown, rolling hill, but John Henry felt no desire to pay a visit there; his only desire was to attend to his business and leave the state as soon as possible. Having deserted Benevolence and his infant daughter to the sunbaked plains and the awful fate that awaited them made him uncomfortable in Kansas. He never calmed his guilt over abandoning his wife and child. Moreover, he felt pressed to move fast, because the Apache would not wait much longer for the rifles he promised them in exchange for the release of Benevolence's granddaughters.

The revenge seeker found that destroying ranches in New Mexico Territory went off without a hitch because he surprised the occupants. The element of surprise would be nonexistent this time; unbeknown to him, Francis Bolingbrook notified his parents by telegram to prepare themselves for an attack by Summerfield. Bolingbrook's parents, Richard and Elizabeth, were not the docile and overmatched ranchers along the Pecos River or the beaten Mexican family south of the border, who put up little resistance. Bolingbrook's parents were frontier fighters with a long history of fighting for Union causes and defending their stagecoach station against Southern sympathizers.

The New England Emigrant Aid Company recruited the parents from Vermont to settle around Lawrence to populate the territory so that it would become an anti-slavery state after the Kansas-Nebraska Act of 1854, authorizing open rangeland for settlement. After the Border Ruffians' attack on Lawrence, Richard Bolingbrook and his teenage son, Francis, joined Jennison's Jayhawkers to raid Southern sympathizers in Missouri, burning the sympathizers' homes and hanging their occupants. Later, the senior Bolingbrook joined the Seventh Kansas Cavalry to oppose the Rebel leader General 'Pappy Price,' who advanced the Rebel cause in Missouri. The Bolingbrooks fought in Kansas and Missouri pushing Price's volunteers back to Arkansas, leaving his wife and son to protect their holdings near the Oregon/California Trail. His wife, Elizabeth, needed little protection; she carried a

157

holstered pistol that she could shoot with skill. With the start of the Civil War, young Francis joined the army to fight rebels but was sent to the Wyoming frontier as a scout.

The senior Bolingbrooks were seasoned fighters and not about to be waylaid by a single raider; they hired Wade Ashman, a middle-aged, ex–deputy sheriff from Manhattan, west of Lawrence, to stand guard over their stagecoach station. Ashman lost his deputy job over a poker game at the Last Stop Saloon in which he thought the dealer cheated him. He subsequently robbed all three card players at gunpoint and, the town council fired him for his deed and exiled him from Lawrence town. The Bolingbrooks knew Summerfield's reputation as a coolheaded gunfighter unafraid of confrontation.

As the lone rider observed, Kansas was nothing like the mountainous New Mexico rangeland filled with canyons and dried gulches; it appeared flat and dry, and a rider rode exposed to any onlooker for miles. John Henry came upon the Bolingbrook stagecoach stop some fifty miles west of Lawrence, near the Missouri River, one of the first depots set up near where the Oregon and California Trails split. He spotted two identical two story mud-brick dwellings with open, narrow windows; one was for stabling horses, and the other housed the Bolingbrooks' depot and quarters. Both structures were worn and windblown and saw better days. The stable opened to a large corral. Inside the stable, John Henry spotted an old stagecoach and freight wagon; a team of six horses milled about in the stables in the early-morning hour. Because the railroad cut through Kansas on its journey to the West Coast, stagecoach business dwindled from long runs westward to much shorter local routes from Lawrence to Leavenworth, Manhattan, Atchison, and Fort Riley. A hand-lettered sign tacked over the depot's main door announced a weekly connection west to Denver. From the stage stop's appearance, the Bolingbrooks barely eked out a living; except for cook-fire smoke drifting from the chimney, the place looked deserted. A well-beaten road bent to the front of the depot, where at one time, a dining room and overnight boarding rooms buzzed with business. A foot-long bell on a six-foot-high tripod stood in front of the mud-brick dwelling to announce arrivals and departures. Little likelihood existed it would be rung this morning.

John Henry rode through the parched waist-high prairie grass, coming within a hundred yards of the stagecoach stop before a distant rifle cracked. A bullet tore into his left leg from whoever fired the shot. The round entered and departed John Henry's left hamstring, tearing muscle but missing bone, and struck his mount through the heart. The horse tumbled to the ground, pinning John Henry's right leg under it. Then rifle fire from both Bolingbrooks crouched behind their well, ripped into the prairie grass around John Henry, pinning him down; whoever fired the rifle shot that wounded him continued to fire while closing the distance between them. Fortunately, the dead horse shielded him from the attacker. No time existed for John Henry to free his leg before the ambusher and the Bolingbrooks closed in on him, nor could he free his Winchester rifle because of the horse's weight pressing upon it. Firing a pistol at such long range would be useless.

His inaction gave the elderly depot operators the courage to creep forward. The aging male appeared fence-post hard, wearing a flat-brimmed hat and a white homespun shirt tucked into coveralls that were, in turn, tucked into calf-high boots. The female wore an ankle-length, purple-flowered dress. A bonnet covered her head, unsuccessfully taming her wild gray hair.

John Henry pulled free the six dynamite sticks from his saddlebags. Even though the three ambushers were rapidly closing the gap, he took his time setting a fuse into a dynamite stick and securing it by wrapping and tying it off around the foot-long explosive stick. He lit a cigar he purchased to fire the dynamite. Both Bolingbrooks were unloading their rifles on him from fifty feet. John Henry waited until the lone ambusher, an overweight and aggressive mustachioed man reloading and firing his rifle, ran within thirty feet to finish off his prey, then lit the short fuse on the dynamite and threw it. The explosion went off within five feet of the ambusher, killing him instantly and flaring up a grass fire. The unexpected explosion spooked the senior Bolingbrooks, who thought they could kill the intruder, only to find they could also be killed. John Henry fused another stick of dynamite and tossed it in their direction, but it fell short as the Bolingbrooks retreated to the mud-brick depot.

With the grass fire now creeping toward him, John Henry used his bandanna to tie a tourniquet near his groin to stop the bleeding on his wounded leg; his other leg remained stuck under the dead horse. Long ago, he learned to deal with pain while functioning in a life-threatening situation. He managed to scoop out enough grass and prairie dirt to pull his leg out from under the saddle hitched to the horse's dead weight. Putting Francis Bolingbrook's parents on the run, he crawled toward their dwelling to press his advantage. The fire behind him crept forward, giving him a hellish backdrop. From behind thick mudbrick walls, the Bolingbrooks continued to fire upon him as he slithered through the tall prairie grass until he came within thirty feet of the two-story stable where the six sturdy horses were kept. He threw a third stick of dynamite and watched it bounce against the mud bricks, blowing away the entire front side of the structure and turning it into a blazing inferno. As did the spare stagecoach and freight wagon, the horses and livestock in the stables perished in flames.

The rifle fire from the Bolingbrooks ceased as they watched their life's work burn and then crumble. "Mister and Mistress Bolingbrook, lay down your arms and show yourselves, hands above your head in surrender, or else I will not hesitate to blow your place of business to kingdom come. When I do that, there is little likelihood you both won't be burned alive." The three previous dynamite explosions spoke volumes to the trapped occupants of the stagecoach depot. Two rifles and a pistol were tossed through the open front window, and within a few seconds, Richard and Elizabeth Bolingbrook appeared, holding their hands above their heads. The senior Bolingbrook, a tall, physical man,, hardened by prairie life, as his large, knurled hands and weather-beaten face indicated. His wife, her gun belt still cinched to her waist, also displayed a weather-beaten face and rock-hard body. Her gray hair hung disheveled about her bonnet-covered head. He collected the two rifles and pistol.

"Your son, Francis, unleashed a pack of murderers on the ranch of my ex-wife's daughters, murdering my daughter and selling off two young, innocent girls to the Apache in New Mexico Territory. I expect you know all that, given he figured I would show up here, alerting you so you could lie in ambush for me. You both look like hardworking, God-fearing parents, innocent of the foul deed perpetrated on the Cardwell ranch, but an example has to be made today. Be good enough to distance yourself from your stage stop." When the Bolingbrooks did as instructed, moving to the well, John Henry ordered, "Protect yourselves." He then lit a fourth stick of dynamite, threw it inside the old hotel and eating place, and then backed off some fifty feet. The explosion turned the dwelling into an inferno. After the flying debris settled, John Henry approached the parents, ordering them to face him. "Your son forced Claude Cardwell into a lopsided shootout that he could not win. He did this while the man's family looked on. I intend to force you into a shootout Mister Bolingbrook, with your wife looking on."

His wife let loose a hysterical shriek and screamed, "He cannot face off with you, Summerfield, as his hand is crippled with arthritis." John Henry raised his right hand, displaying only three fingers. He then pulled a strip of rawhide from his coat and cut it into half lengths. With one strip, he fixed his single-action Colt to his hand. He picked up the discarded Bolingbrook pistol, a .44caliber Remington, and walked to Mistress Bolingbrook. "Be good enough to hold out your hand." When she did as ordered, he emptied five cartridges into her hand. "Please extend your other hand." He handed her the Remington pistol and strip of rawhide and instructed her, "Load the pistol and tie it to your husband's hand as I tied my pistol."

"Richard is no match for a gunslinger like you."

161

"Your husband, rode and shot down rebels with the Jayhawkers and certainly would get a better chance against me than the innocent Claude Cardwell got against a seasoned killer like your son." Elizabeth loaded the .44- caliber pistol and placed her husband's index finger on the trigger. After delivering his deadly challenge, John Henry held his pistol by his side. His left leg throbbed, and he desperately wanted to loosen the tourniquet to relieve the pressure, but no time existed. "Your play, Mister Bolingbrook. I give you first draw."

For Richard Bolingbrook, a courageous Civil War fighter, taking the coward's way out never occurred to him. He raised the pistol and fired a second before John Henry fired his pistol. John Henry could not cock the single-action pistol with his three-fingered hand, so he pulled back the hammer with his left hand before taking aim and squeezing the trigger; the extra second taken to cock the pistol allowed Bolingbrook to fire first. But his awkwardness with a handgun because of arthritis deforming his hand caused his fired round to whiz by his attacker's head. John Henry's two-handed shot struck the stagecoach operator squarely in the forehead, killing him.

The victorious gunman felt no exhilaration, only the relief of completing the final act necessary to force the Bolingbrooks' son into a shootout. "I will spare you if you inform me of your son's whereabouts," he said to the overwrought female.

"Go to hell, you murdering bastard."

He might could torment the weather-beaten woman to get information, but John Henry owned no stomach for mistreating a woman. "Inform your son of today's events. If he wants revenge for today, tell him I wait him and his gang of murderers in Las Vegas, New Mexico Territory."

John Henry discovered two ranch horses and saddles inside a small shed thirty yards behind the destroyed stagecoach stop. Before the grass fire reached the small shed, he saddled one horse and mounted it despite the racking pain in his left leg. He led the other horse to where his saddle, saddlebags, and rifle remained attached to the Mustang shot dead by his attacker. Managing to free his saddle and gear, he saddled the fitter of the two animals he confiscated and shot the lesser horse.

In his mind, he threw the final dice when destroying the Bolingbrook ranch and rolled a six, the number of murderers he intended to kill before facing Francis Bolingbrook. By now, a half-mile-wide prairie fire raged behind him as he rode south to New Mexico Territory, where he hoped to find treatment for his wounded leg. John Henry set his mind on killing the men responsible for his daughter's death and fulfilling his promise to Benevolence. However, he did not intend to shoot down the Benson boy; the face-off with the senior Bolingbrooks took place without intent.

*

John Henry rode into Las Vegas in the dead of night to avoid attention from the hard-nosed sheriff who disliked him and found the shingle for a doctor's office hanging in front of a freshly whitewashed building. He waited in the seclusion of an adjacent alley for daylight when the physician would appear.

The physician, a rotund and white-whiskered man in his sixties, admitted John Henry to his office and ordered him to drop his trousers. He subsequently poured whiskey on the bullet's entrance and departure wounds to sanitize them, and then, using needle and thread, he sutured the wounds. For this painful treatment, the old physician charged John Henry two dollars. Limping noticeably, John Henry visited the graves of Marge and his daughter, Jane—two precious women lost to him. The young deputy who befriended him maintained the gravesites; two small bouquets of tiny purple desert wildflowers decorating the headstones gave proof of the deputy's attendance. John Henry became mindful that Jane was the daughter he never knew, the infant he deserted to fight a civil war, the prepubescent girl raised by Benevolence's four husbands. Standing over Marge's grave, he became mindful that he if did not give the revenge-minded boy,

163

Benny Benson, to the Apache, the goodhearted prostitute would still be alive.

He next rode to the stables where he left his mule, the only purchase left after the Salt Lake City stagecoach robbery. He intended to buy a tent and camp outside of Las Vegas to wait for the murderer Francis Bolingbrook and his six marauders to appear.

The noon hour fell on the town as John Henry approached the Las Vegas stables, a wood-planked, two-story structure displaying a large barn door that stood open for business. A fresh coat of red paint covered the street-side front. As John Henry tied off his horse and limped through the entrance, the stench of animal manure assaulted his nostrils. Each of the stable's ten stalls housed a horse. The extremely tall stable owner, thin as a rail and displaying black mutton-chop sideburns growing from a bald head, greeted him. The man wore wide suspenders over crusty underwear; his dark wool trousers appeared stained and unwashed for months.

"I came to collect my mule and pay you for your past attendance to him."

"Got him all snug down in that far-end stall on the right." The middle-aged owner tugged on one side of his muttonchops and then wiped the beads of sweat that formed on his forehead on his underwear sleeve. Usually, the owner would keep John Henry's mule, an animal he considered inferior to horses, in the outside corral attached to the back of the stables, not in the comfort of a stall alongside superior horseflesh.

"Very considerate of you to stable my mule outside in the sun, especially if you're charging me the stable fee." The stable owner shuffled his feet and rocked back and forth, his right hand rubbing his bald head, his left hand scratching his dirty underwear top. "You seem to be jumpy. Any reason for that?" John Henry inquired, suspecting something out of the norm but not knowing what.

"I got a busy afternoon ahead of me and can't be standing around jawing with you. Follow me, and I'll get your dang mule."

John Henry followed the lanky owner to the end stall. When he attempted to open the door to fetch his mule, the nervous stable owner held the door closed. "You stand right there by that opposite stall, and I'll bring your mule out to you."

John Henry swung the shotgun free of his shoulder, suspecting the stable owner planned some ruse. He heard shuffling behind him, but before he could turn his head felt like it exploded. His surroundings went black.

When John Henry regained consciousness, he sat upright on a bench constructed on a freight wagon bed to transport prisoners, finding himself chained hand and foot to the wagon's floor planks. He felt woozy, owing to what he suspected to be a pistol blow from behind. He glanced at the white-mustachioed, nattily dressed Las Vegas sheriff, who stood outside the wagon smiling his satisfaction.. Behind John Henry, a big, burly, mustachioed man wearing a holstered pistol with a shotgun leaning against his leg sat on the driver's bench. He looked like a lawman. John Henry stared at two additional mounted men, both heavily armed, wearing large, dark mustaches and dressed in expensive city suits and also bearing the look of lawmen. He figured the big men were bounty hunters or Pinkerton agents.

"Breaking the skull of a lowdown stagecoach robber like you gave me great satisfaction," the sheriff declared to John Henry. "I suspect you committed other crimes, like gunning down the young Benson boy, and I hope you will hang for them. In the meantime, I am handing you over to these Pinkerton men. This is something to remember me by." He drove his fist into the chained man's throat, leaving him slumped over on the bench and gasping for breath.

The older mounted man nudged his horse forward until it stopped beside John Henry. Blurred as he appeared to John Henry, the balding man with a sizable handlebar mustache appeared the same as he did in Grand Junction, wearing a heavy sweater over his wool shirt. A .38-caliber Smith & Wesson hung from his shoulder holster; A Colt single-action .45 long-barrel rested on the man's right hip. A bowie knife tucked into his calf-high boots.

"Did you think leaving an IOU for six hundred dollars would be fine and dandy with Wells Fargo? I'm here to tell you that is not so." He took a crumbled piece of paper, the one on which John Henry long ago scribbled an IOU, from his coat pocket and stuffed it into the prisoner's mouth.

Even as woozy as he was, John Henry spat out the IOU. "It seems you think that note is as worthless as I do. I am Milton Youngster, a representative of the Pinkerton Detective Agency out of Denver, Colorado. I am also the man you back shot and laid up for three months. These are my two associates, Jim Rankle and Barney Hantrel, both seasoned detectives and expert gun hands." John Henry felt the two men's cold and condemning eyes focus on him. "I ask you to keep their expertise in mind should you think about trying anything underhanded. We are taking you back to Salt Lake City to stand trial for robbing the Wells Fargo Overland stagecoach and stealing its property, namely six hundred dollars and two lead horses. You will be treated decently on your journey there, but should you give us any guff, the sheriff's punch will seem like a spoonful of elixir compared to what we will do to you." After Youngster delivered his warning, the driver slapped the reigns across the backsides of his mules, and the wagon lurched forward. Seeing double, John Henry noted that his mule and saddled horse were tied to the wagon's rear.

*

The three Pinkerton agents pushed the mules hard toward Salt Lake City; the crude wagon suspension, unable to absorb the road's ridges and potholes, bounced John Henry roughly about in his chained confinement. The constant jarring of the wagon kept John Henry in agony, his head splitting, his stomach retching, the wrist and leg irons cutting into his flesh. He was given water only once daily, and the New Mexico sun soon dehydrated him, causing him to develop dry heaves. His vision remained blurred, enough so that he saw two of everything. When they camped at night, the agents left John Henry chained to the hard wagon bench, with only a thin wool blanket to ward off the cold desert night air. A plate of beans in the morning was his only nourishment.

On the third day out, John Henry recognized the Sangre de Cristo mountain range, where he once befriended two Apache warriors on foot. Within the next hour, the wagon found where John Henry frequently left horses and captives for the Apache. He recognized the clump of brush and the adjacent gully where he once sequestered his horse and mule and subsequently walked into the Apache camp; there, he promised to obtain rifles for the Chiricahua Apache sheltered by the Jicarilla. Suffering a concussion and feeling nauseated as he did, his chances of getting the rifles to trade for Benevolence's granddaughters' release from the Navajo appeared remote.

Suddenly he heard an agonizing moan behind him, turned, and saw where an Apache arrow penetrated the Pinkerton driver's chest, driving the arrow point through his back. Blood stained his suit jacket front and back. Within seconds, a rifle bullet struck the rider Jim Rankle in the throat, and he tumbled from his saddle. Milton Youngster momentarily reined in his horse to make a stand and then, having second thoughts, spurred the animal, galloping across the open range, leaving his captive defenseless against the attackers. For his part, John Henry remained helpless to stop the mules from pulling the wagon along the road. He watched a band of Apache warriors, half on horseback and half on foot, pursue Youngster.

Within a few minutes, a warrior on foot halted the runaway mules and the wagon hauling the captive. Seeing John Henry chained hand and foot, he stripped the dying driver, Barney Hantrel, slumped over the forward bench of his clothing and boots. After searching the man's pockets, the Apache held a set of keys, one of which he used to unlock the groggy captive's irons. Two warriors then tossed John Henry to the ground, where he remained semi-conscious. Landing on a leg recently sutured added a knifing pain to John Henry's splitting headache.

An hour later, the band of Apache returned dragging Youngster, his wrists bound by rope so that he ran behind a warrior who was sat astride a trotting horse. stripped naked, Youngster' arms and legs revealed deep cuts by Apache knives. John Henry recognized the horses ridden by the Chiricahua as being among the ones he left as a gift to secure Apache cooperation weeks back. He counted seventeen warriors in the band, the same Apache that needed rifles to join Geronimo. As threatening as they looked, faces stained red and yellow ocher; their long black hair tied back by strips of cloth around their foreheads; they wore flowered shirts cinched at the waist by cartridge belts. The blood-thirsty Chiricahua did not harm John Henry.

A half-hour later, the freed, although battered, John Henry recognized the warrior now leading six riders toward him as the Jicarilla leader, Nantan Lupan. He rode up to the distraught Pinkerton agent—whose arms were bent behind him, forcing his face into the sand—inspected him, approving of his mistreatment, and then dismounted. Even as dizzy as he felt, John Henry figured the Chiricahua and Jicarilla rode in separate groups because the Chiricahua were renegade outlaws soon to join Geronimo in Mexico, whereas the Jicarilla, by following thirty minutes behind, could remain innocent of the attack on the Pinkerton agents, thus preventing an army attack on their camp. Innocence would be their explanation to the federal Indian agent, who would be backed by the U.S. Army.

The Chiricahua Apache intended to kill Milton Youngster and the wounded Barney Hantrel, but first, they would delight in torturing them, a pastime in which few savage nations could surpass them. John Henry surmised the Apache warriors spared him because they expected him to deliver the rifles. The warriors gathered two small piles of brush and fashioned two tall stakes on which they intended to burn the prisoners slowly. They lit a third pile of brush from which warriors took burning sticks and seared the naked bodies of the captives; other warriors cut off a small finger from each man. The arrow-speared Hantrel could not stand up to the torture and died bound to a stake. Thereafter, the Chiricahua Apache began to set fire to the brush around Youngster, grabbing his penis to cut it off, causing him to scream for mercy. Still dazed from the blow the Las Vegas Sheriff inflicted upon him, John Henry approached Nantan Lupan, whose bronze face resembled leather.

"I ask you to spare this white man."

"He is a captive of the Chiricahua. Not my captive. They feel much angry at you because you take too long to bring rifles."

"Ask them what they want to spare this white man's life." John Henry noted Youngster's feet and lower legs were beginning to blister from the brush fire set around him. He purposely wounded rather than kill the man at Grand Junction and now felt obligated to keep the Pinkerton agent alive. He waited for what seemed an eternity while Nantan Lupan conferred with the Chiricahua.

When the Jicarilla leader returned, he spoke: "They say one hundred rounds of ammunition for each rifle." John Henry figured the seventeen Chiricahua warriors would not accept the rifles without ammunition, so he instructed Smoker to acquire fifty rounds for each weapon; obtaining an additional fifty rounds per weapon would not be difficult in Santa Fe. Bringing more ammunition to renegade Chiricahua could not exacerbate the punishment, already a hanging offense, for arming Apache—he was already a hung man if connected to the crime.

"Tell them I agree if they will pull the white man from the fire." Nantan Lupan, reluctant to see Youngster spared, nonetheless signaled the Chiricahua by waving his hand across his chest, and two warriors cut the rope that bound the battered Pinkerton agent to the stake. In great pain from his burned legs, the captive collapsed on the desert floor, subsequently being kicked senseless by four warriors. "I will bring the rifles within one moon's cycle. Hold the white man until I return and can decide his fate. He is not to be further tortured."

"It will be done as you say. Chiricahua beat slaves, not torture them."

The Apache leader returned John Henry's weapons, horse, and mule. Nantan Lupan then fired a round from a single-shot derringer taken off the deceased Pinkerton agent, Rankle. The warriors, to a man, laughed at the tiny pistol. "I give you this child's weapon."

John Henry inspected the single shot manufactured as a Derringer Philadel pistol, a .43- caliber percussion cap weapon with a three-inch barrel, an outdated but serviceable weapon. He tucked it in his right inside coat pocket, a familiar place. Now fully armed with a single-action Colt revolver, shotgun, rifle, and derringer, John Henry mounted his horse. But he soon realized that he was in no condition to make the long ride to Santa Fe because of his concussion. Five miles distant from where he left the Apache, he dismounted and gathered enough branches, sticks, and brush to build a wickiup. He spread out his bedroll inside the crude shelter and fell asleep, partially protected from the howling evening wind. He slept the next forty-eight hours without interruption, waking to find that his head still ached, but his double vision disappeared. His mule and unsaddled horse grazed where he left them hobbled.

Chapter 12

The time to reap a small fortune arrived for the mounted man wearing two braided pigtails falling from his temples and uncut hair to his shoulder blades. The distinctive black shirt and red vest he wore, along with buckskin trousers, gave him a cavalier bearing. He and his heavily armed followers sat in their saddles, prepared for an imminent attack upon the Southern Pacific train pulling a coal car, two passenger cars, a freight car, and a caboose that now slowed to a stop at a tiny farming settlement named Holton, situated on the Alamo River just east of the Imperial Valley in California. Here the Southern Pacific train usually took on coal and water. The seven men observed a detail of navy police carrying rifles and twelve men standing by three wagons. One wagon looked like a freight hauler, and the other two appeared to be used to haul navy personnel.

For the moment, the leader of the robbers stirred in the saddle, shocked by the appearance of the navy personnel and their three wagons to collect the payroll. His informer, a disillusioned boatswain, a navy warrant officer, led him to believe the train would continue on to San Diego, but now he realized the tracks curved northwest toward Los Angeles. Francis Bolingbrook deduced by the movement he observed that the train, after making a coal and water refueling stop, would travel to Los Angeles, where a spur line took passengers and freight to San Diego; the railroad considered the small settlement secondary to an expanding Los Angeles.

Bolingbrook traced the boatswain assigned to distributing navy supplies from one of the store ships anchored in the San Diego Bay. These storage ships captured foreign prizes or decommissioned U.S. naval vessels, were used to supply the Pacific Squadron, as the navy had yet to install a naval base at San Diego Bay. The navy, undergoing a period of personnel cutbacks, denied the boatswain reenlistment. Angered by the forced retirement, the man became an easy target for Bolingbrook to corrupt. He bribed the boatswain with two hundred dollars to inform him of the departure of the large navy payroll, with the promise of another five hundred dollars after Bolingbrook successfully robbed the train. The boatswain had told him that the payroll would be sent from the U.S. Treasury located in the Arizona territorial capital of Tucson, destined for two newly commissioned ships of the line, both sail and steam-driven, scheduled to anchor within twenty-four hours in the bay. Each ship carried a marine platoon aboard. Accompanying these seventy-two-cannon gunships were a forty-eight-gun sloop of war and two frigates, each carrying twenty-eight cannons and two squads of marines. The naval force aboard the five ships totaled 365 enlisted men and officers and 220 Marines.

The pox-scarred man overcame his surprise at seeing the payroll transferred at Holton, subsequently seeing the unexpected exchange as an advantage rather than a setback. The robbers set the dynamite to blow the engine car off the tracks, crippling the train so that he and his men could thereafter sack the freight car and blow up the car carrying the troops. No necessity for that strategy existed now: both the marine and navy armed guard would move unprotected and unaware, transferring the payroll outside the train.

Bolingbrook watched two squads of marines —approximately twenty rifle-armed men— dispatched to Tucson to accompany the payroll to Holton disembark from the train and transfer the payroll to the waiting freight wagon. He saw no problem killing sailors or marines, who were no more than a special naval unit used for amphibious assaults. Tough fighters that they were rumored to be, the Marines were not part of the U.S. Army, whose men Bolingbrook held in special regard and would never ambush. With his wide-brimmed, floppy hat, he signaled the Benson brothers to move the wagon carrying the Gatling gun into position fast enough to take the navy and marine attachments by surprise. He earlier assigned Apple and Miller to the far side of the tracks to attack the military's rear and prevent retreat while he and Trujillo attacked from the front; he assigned Alsop to the empty wagon needed to escape with the payroll. Nearby were seven extra mounted horses and two mules Bolingbrook thought necessary for the gang's escape into Mexico. Within minutes, the Gatling gun's rat-a-tat, rat-a-tat—up to six hundred rounds per minute—sounded, and great puffs of sulfuric smoke encased the wagon and Benson brothers.

The Gatling gun cut down three-fourths of the navy and marine attachments caught in the open away from the train, ripping them to pieces—some two dozen guards, Bolingbrook noted with satisfaction. Apple and Miller attacked the crippled force seeking protection behind the wagons from the rear, while Bolingbrook and Trujillo made a frontal attack, catching the military attachment in their crossfire. The marine riflemen found no opportunity to take an accurate aim at the attackers as they scurried to find protection from the hail of bullets. Bolingbrook, fearless before the guards' return fire, dismounted and ran to the locomotive. He lit the thirty-second fuse on the dynamite, remounted, and rode back to where Trujillo had positioned himself. As anticipated, the dynamite charge blew the engine car off the tracks and onto its side. Flying fiery debris ignited the military wagons, forcing the marines and navy fighters to find whatever shelter they could behind the last troop-carrying wagon; there, they were pinned down by the Gatling gun. Under fire from marine rifles, Bolingbrook rushed to where the payroll wagon burned within fifteen feet of those he attacked. He saved eighty percent of the payroll by scattering burning currency over the ground and stomping on the paper money; the coins remained undamaged.

Alsop, evaluating the situation from higher up on a ridge, drove the wagon to where he and Bolingbrook, under weak fire from the pinned-down marines, could load the payroll upon their wagon. Once they removed the payroll from the fiery wreck, Bolingbrook, angered by the loss of some of the paper currency, concentrated on destroying what remained of the marine and navy details even though no good reason existed to do so; the gang successfully stolen the navy payroll and crippled the military attachment to the extent that no pursuit of them would be possible. He ordered the Benson brothers to concentrate the Gatling gun's .58- caliber bullets on the caboose, where a few sailors and marines found refuge. Then Bolingbrook, acting alone, set a dynamite charge underneath the caboose and subsequently blew it to smithereens.

The explosion also ignited the two passenger cars, prompting women, children, and men to flee the inferno. Bolingbrook dislodged Bradford Benson from the Gatling gun and then trained it upon the fleeing passengers. The large-caliber bullets ripped through fleeing civilians like hot embers through cheesecloth. Bolingbrook felt the same satisfaction, an addictive one, he decimating Sioux and Cheyenne villages on the northern plains. Bodies were scattered everywhere; if counted the number, it would be around fifty-six passengers shot down in cold blood, plus the detachments of dead marines and sailors. A few passengers remained in the burning cars. No qualms existed for Francis Bolingbrook, who, once he spilled blood, could not stop until there was no more blood to spill. In a killing frenzy, he set two more dynamite charges under the burning cars and ignited the fuses. Moving off to a distance and feeling a morbid exhilaration, he observed the passenger cars explode into burning wood missiles. Only five marines and one sailor remained alive under a burning transport wagon. Bolingbrook, desiring more mayhem, ordered the more aggressive Benson brother, Bryce, to blow the wagon to pieces with the Gatling gun until nothing but dust stirred.

Walking among the burning debris with a .45 revolver in each hand, the ex-Kansas Red Leg, who decimated Southern sympathizers with relish, nudged bodies with his boot, discharging a bullet into the head of any man, woman, or child that stirred. Even his bloodthirsty followers could not come to grips with such senseless murder. They rode off to a distance from death's smoky panorama and waited for their maniacal leader to finish his business, knowing every lawman in California and Arizona would soon be searching for them.

Chapter 13

News of the Southern Pacific massacre reached Santa Fe by the time John Henry collected the rifles Smoker purchased for the Apache. He figured Francis Bolingbrook led the navy payroll robbers and probably escaped into Mexico. He figured that because of the size of the payroll robbery and the number of massacred victims, including dead Navy and Marine personnel—somewhere in the seventies—every lawman in the territories, along with the army, navy, and marine patrols, would be on their trail. He discerned that the robbery at Holton stood as the reason Bolingbrook and his followers, well aware that he burned their home places and given members of their families to the Apache, did not try to track him down and kill him. He wondered what the odds were that Bolingbrook and his followers would chance leaving Mexico to kill him. He gave all seven men enough reason to risk capture for the opportunity to reap revenge upon him; he doubted Bolingbrook could swallow his father's death in a forced shootout and put aside the wanton destruction of his home place. He believed time would tell whether he would fulfill his vow to Benevolence.

The evening wind kicked up across the sandy, sagebrush-covered prairie as a western sun touched the Sangre de Cristo mountain peaks west of Las Vegas. Streams of spring runoff that flowed from low, rolling summits were drying up in the mountains turning brown from lack of rain. John Henry stood at the same spot where he left hostages and horses for the Apache, probably the exact spot where Francis Bolingbrook and his six murdering accomplices traded Clara Cardwell's young daughters to the Apache in exchange for valuables plundered from white settlers.

The injured man, suffering a leg wound and a concussion, nevertheless rode to Santa Fe and collected the rifles that Smoker stored in his hog-smoking warehouse. Still handicapped by the leg wound and bothered by headaches from the concussion, he dug deeply into his resolve to deliver the rifles to the Apache. Clara, wearing a black dress and fully recovered from her alcohol and laudanum addictions, once again a concerned mother, insisted on accompanying him to the Apache camp to collect her daughters; he saw no reason not to grant her the opportunity to receive her girls. Smoker, who grew attached to Benevolence's daughter with an avuncular affection, accompanied the party, driving the freight wagon with Clara at his side. John Henry knew Smoker not to be a coward, but being a fighter did not fit his character, because of his "storms in the head." As promised, John Henry delivered twenty brand new and illegal Winchester rifles to the Chiricahua, along with a hundred rounds of ammunition for each one; one rifle he presented to Nantan Lupan, the Jicarilla leader known as Gray Wolf, for calming Chiricahua warriors angry at the delay; a further two rifles were to be presented to the two powerful Navajo chiefs in whose custody Clara's girls found themselves.

John Henry felt uneasy, knowing these unpredictable Chiricahua would be riding past white settlers on the way to Mexico and would find it difficult not to attack them. If they chose to travel by Apache Pass, hopefully, the army would confront them, but that was a long shot. Smoker, already jumpy that the army might discover them delivering rifles to the Apache, approached him, eyes blinking, his vision blurred. He appeared extremely unsettled watching the Chiricahua warriors celebrating the delivery of the rifles, getting drunk and belligerent. Driven mad with pent-up hate at being subdued by whites, the Chiricahua rode wildly back and forth on horseback, shooting the Winchester rifles into the air and singing a war song. Nantan Lupan's Jicarilla followers, observing, repeated their death threats, an Apache version of a Greek chorus. The hard-looking Chiricahua and Jicarilla women beat sticks on rocks, ratcheting up the frenzy and chanting the same war song in an Athabaskan language fearful to the civilized ear.

"John, these heathens will kill us in the worst way if we don't depart now," Smoker whispered through lips that smacked as frequently as a clock's ticking."

"I agree. The situation is getting testy," John Henry responded. "We will conclude our business and be on our way." John Henry spoke offhandedly, artificially demonstrating control of the situation to settle Smoker's jitters.

Clara, on the other hand, operating under the false impression that her daughters would be given to her today, showed no such fear. She confronted the Jicarilla leader standing with Ben

Apple's pint-sized beside him. "We delivered the rifles, and you failed to deliver my children, Penny and Pauline. I suspect a heathen savage like you traded off my girls to the Navajo, and now you failed to get them back as you told this man, John Henry Summerfield, you would. I got a good mind to take one of those rifles and shoot you where you stand." John Henry stood uneasy at her side while she confronted Nantan Lupan. The Apache leader appeared chagrined by the confrontation but checked himself from knocking the black-clad widow to the ground. It pleased Nantan Lupan that the Chiricahua Apache obtained rifles, because he supported the warriors about to ride south across the desert plains to join Geronimo and fight their enemies with honor, so he did not want to create a distraction that would delay the Chiricahua from leaving. John Henry suspected the Jicarilla leader would be glad to be rid of the Chiricahua, thus avoiding being attacked by the army if the troop commander learned that the Chiricahua had been armed.

Ben Apple's undersized son naturally understood English and, now a complete Apache product with the given name of Little Man Yapping Big Talk withdrew his knife upon a person he considered a lowly female enemy with murderous intent.

"Hold your foul tongue, white woman. What I do and how I do it is not for you to speak," Nantan Lupan warned Grace in an authoritative manner that would not be challenged. The pint-sized boy, Nantan Lupan's adopted son, stepped forward and shouted in a child's squeaky voice, "You insulted my father. For that, you must die!" He lunged forward, brandishing his knife. Nantan Lupan, although pleased with the boy's aggressiveness, grabbed his shoulder, restraining him. Two Jicarilla warriors standing at Nantan Lupan's side, though not understanding their leader's English, saw his displeasure and seemed on the verge of dragging Clara off to some unpleasant treatment.

John Henry intervened, leading Grace away from Nantan Lupan and cautioning the distraught mother. "You are not helping the situation. These seventeen half-starved and angry Apache, wild with the notion that they will soon be joining Geronimo in Mexico, got no qualms about slaughtering us on the spot—that is, after torturing us until we beg to be killed. We are from the same white race they believe drove them from their hunting land. The only thing stopping them from killing us now is the Jicarilla leader you just screamed at. We have no choice but to accept that Nantan Lupan will deliver your children, as he has promised."

He positioned Clara in the wagon, his words of caution settling her anger, and then told Smoker to restrain her. John Henry saw another reason to calm Clara: The Pinkerton agent Milton Youngster, battered and traumatized, sat confused, with a rope around his neck periodically being yanked by an old Apache woman. John Henry understood the man still did not know whether he would live or die. The man's release presented a dilemma for John Henry, because if he let him ride to the nearest Pinkerton office he might return with a posse before John Henry had a chance to face off with Bolingbrook and the six men who destroyed the Cardwell ranch. The only other option was to return him to the Apache and certain death. So for the moment, he accepted possession of the docile captive, rope around his neck and hands bound behind him, uncertain about his intentions for the man. Suppressing a sigh of relief that neither Clara nor Smoker lost their lives, he led his party away from the Apache.

*

John Henry stirred from a restless sleep at the crack of dawn and found one of the new Winchester rifles pressed against his heart. "No kill Bad Hand. He friend to Chiricahua," an Apache shouted to his two cohorts. The captured man looked up to see the dark, sunburned face of the Chiricahua warrior whom he knew as Cracked Rock, an Apache who escaped from the San Carlos reservation in Arizona Territory. The warrior stood over him, hard and fit and in his early forties, his face greatly disfigured by an old bullet wound—the bullet entered his mouth and exited through his jawbone. John Henry quickly surmised that three Chiricahua

178

warriors crept undetected into their camp before dawn, guessing that Clara fell asleep on her watch. He figured she became so upset over not securing her two girls from the Apache that she spent a sleepless night and, physically drained, drifted into sleep while on watch.

After securing the Pinkerton agent's release, they moved toward Santa Fe, Smoker and Clara sitting on the wagon's bench with the Pinkerton agent lying in the wagon bed. He rode behind, intending to escort them within a few miles of Santa Fe and then detour toward Las Vegas. But darkness had consumed the prairie long before that departure, forcing the party of four to make camp. Smoker, Clara, and John Henry lay uncovered on the ground, suffering the cold desert night as best they could, with Youngster not faring any better in the wagon bed. The ex-frontiersman assigned Smoker the first watch, and he took the second, leaving the final watch for Clara—which, as it turned out, was a mistake.

Unable to intervene because of the rifle pressed against his chest, he watched the Chiricahua tear off her dress and drag her off to a clump of brush after binding her hand and foot. It appeared that raping a white woman will be delayed, because that warrior left Clara and rejoined his cohort, and the two of them grabbed the Pinkerton agent, Milton Youngster, and bound him to a wagon wheel. Smoker, too paralyzed by the Apache's sudden appearance to move, sat frozen on the ground. Gathering his thoughts as best as he could, John Henry guessed the seventeen Chiricahua that he armed with new Winchesters split into small groups to slip by army patrols undetected on their trek to Mexico. This small renegade group holding them captive could not resist the temptation, it seemed, to wreak death upon the first whites they came upon.

The two other warriors, not wanting to linger in one place too long because of the threat of discovery, quickly sliced off the Pinkerton agent's ears and then his nose. When Youngster screamed piteously for mercy, they cut out his tongue. Cracked Rock shouted a warning to them in Apache. Deprived of the time to adequately torture Youngster, one of the Apache gutted him from groin to breast bone. John Henry watched the innocent victim slump forward, his bloody intestines pouring onto the ground—a ghastly sight. They next stripped Smoker naked and appeared on the verge of tying him to another wagon wheel. This manhandling was too much for the small, nonviolent businessman. An epileptic fit began to overtake his hunched, arthritic body.

A dazed look appeared on Smoker's face; his eyes blinked, and his lips smacked uncontrollably. Drool seeped from the corners of his mouth. The two fierce Chiricahua warriors relaxed their grip on him as if seeing his body bent by arthritis for the first time. They appeared mesmerized by the sudden change in his demeanor. Exhaling a huge gasp, Smoker arched his back to what seemed beyond human endurance, his hands scraping the sand behind him. Next, his teeth began to chatter, provoking the Chiricahua to release him. Smoker spun in circles, his trembling arms outstretched, performing a demonic spinning dance but struggling to breathe properly.

John Henry spoke to a distracted Cracked Rock. "Storms in the head possess him." Cracked Rock did not respond. Smoker's actions froze his thoughts and thawed his superstition. John Henry and the three Chiricahua warriors looked on as Smoker stopped spinning, picked up hands full of small rocks, and tossed them overhead. Then, as if seeing skyrockets explode in the sky above, he crouched under the imaginary blasts and then threw himself prone into the prairie dirt, repeating the process in a strange choreography that went on for a good five minutes. After a dozen such devilish dances, he stood upright, seemingly composed. But then his naked skin flushed crimson, and then his body turned blue because he stopped breathing. As he faced the two Chiricahua warriors who meant to torture him, his eyes rolled back so that only the whites were visible. His mouth overflowed with a milky foam that splattered the two Chiricahua men and he collapsed at the dumbfounded warriors' feet. Feeling morbidly bound, they cringed backward. Smoker's body, lying supine on the ground, vibrated violently.

Cracked Rock jumped to his feet, his rifle pointed away from John Henry. "Evil spirit come upon us. We must flee this place before we become like him," he yelled to his cohorts, unhinged by what he witnessed. The Chiricahua tossed John Henry's weapons into the distance, riding off without plundering their stores or raping Clara. John Henry quickly searched Smoker's clothing, putting a leather-wrapped pig bone in his mouth to save his teeth from shattering. Smoker's storms in the head, although a curse issued to the small, goodhearted man, became a godsend to John Henry and Clara.

John Henry scooped out a man-size hole in the prairie sand and buried Milton Youngster, the Pinkerton agent, fully aware that he alone bore the responsibility for an innocent man's death. Had John Henry not robbed a stagecoach of six hundred dollars outside of Salt Lake City and subsequently shot-gunned the legs of the agent who pursued him, Youngster would still be alive. Milton Youngster's death became a blight on his conscience, one he must live with. On a happier note, Smoker regained consciousness in a few hours, confused and extremely fatigued. Concerned about Clara's well-being, Smoker went to her and found a woman who escaped rape and possible death at Apache's hands. An intrepid spirit prevailed in her, as she, a true frontier woman, overcame frontier fears.

*

Bursting with success, Bolingbrook and his slaughtering gang rode their mounts into frothing sweats crossing into Mexico as the sun set at their backs and traveled southeast of the border seeking sanctuary. They pushed the mules until they could barely walk, pulling the freight wagon loaded with U.S.-minted twenty dollar coins and a large security box filled with currency. To a man, they rode their first mounts until the horses staggered and then saddled their extra horses and pushed them to exhaustion. The gang took no time to count their loot, although they knew they possessed fifteen heavy bags of twenty-dollar silver pieces and one eighteen by eighteen by fourteen-inch security box with U.S. fifty-

and one-hundred-dollar denominations. The robbers' objective was to put as much distance between Holton, California and themselves as possible; accordingly, they stayed in the saddle throughout the night, gratified they saw no posse following them.

By midmorning, the robbers came upon Sonoyta de la Rio, a tiny village of some two hundred occupants situated five miles downstream from the headwaters of the Yaqui River. The river flowed at an ankle-deep level through desert terrain, frothing here and there over exposed boulders. Standing in the water, a dozen old women and a few prepubescent girls laundered clothing; they dressed in homespun sleeveless blouses and coarse although colorful skirts,. The gang slowed their weary horses to a walk, examining the small village. The brown-skinned villagers, if alarmed over seven weary and dusty, heavily armed *americanos* appearing out of nowhere, mostly remained stoic and did their best to fulfill their morning routines.

Charles Miller drove the wagon loaded with the navy payroll to a remote spot along the river where he found shade. Bolingbrook noted the village's water well, an impressive three-foot-high, circular stone structure that supplied plentiful water; there, women queued up with empty buckets.

In the village's tiny market square, where the road widened, a tenacious sun beat down on a cluster of one-story adobe dwellings wherein residents established a solitary cantina, a shabby ten-room hotel, and an eatery. A more majestic two-story church with a bell tower dominated the cluster of buildings. Within the open eatery, a barefooted man and woman dressed plainly in white homespun shirts and baggy pantaloons browned tortillas and cooked chilies and strips of meat on a metal plate over an open wood fire. The three-sided open eatery hosted one old man bent over a tortilla, dripping beans onto his lap. One-room adobe dwellings were scattered around the outskirts of the village, where meager gardens were maintained. Very few dwellings showed doors or blankets hung over entrances; in all cases, what windows the adobe huts afforded stood unprotected against the elements.

Barefooted women wore white blouses and full skirts dyed in red, blue, and yellow patterns, and the men wore white cotton shirts and baggy pantaloons that fell short of their ankles.

Villagers moved about the dirt street shopping for essentials; men led burros laden with firewood and hay for sale; women carried baskets of wet laundry; boys herded goats through the humble settlement to areas of uneaten sagebrush. Similarly poorly-dressed, barefooted children, some in threadbare hand-me-downs, meandered behind the adults. Other village dwellers crouched in the buildings' shade, watching the activity. A few prosperous occupants wore crude sandals. The young women appeared quite fetching to the robbers, their long black hair falling around dark porcelain faces. Similarly, complexioned men, except for the young, wore large mustaches and dark hair falling to shoulder length. Bolingbrook observed that the occupants appeared backward, but most important, they appeared docile and would give him no trouble.

His eyes scanned the three-hundred-foot-long street, seeing no *pistoleros* or Mexican lawmen or no armed Mexicans to obstruct his movements. He kept his restless men in the wilderness outside of Holton, California for six weeks until they successfully pulled off one of the biggest train robberies in the territories and prevailed in a fierce gunfight against trained military men. Consequently, the men expected at least a fortnight's reward comprised of drinking, whoring, and being tended upon like newly rich men.

Bolingbrook realized he risked everything returning to the United States because law authorities would be searching for him and his six followers. Therefore he did not want to provoke an incident in Mexico. He waited until his followers tied off their mounts in front of the cantina and stood at the bar inside; he meant to mitigate his and his men's presence in Sonoyta de la Rio. First, he sent a bucket of beer and a bottle of Mexican liquor to Miller, guarding the stolen payroll so the man would not wander to the cantina. He spoke enough Spanish to inquire of a teenage boy watering his three goats at the river where the village headman resided. The boy informed him that the village mayor was one Ramón Ramirez, who operated a general store out of the front of his *casa* next to the church.

Inside the *casa*, a large adobe dwelling built with window panes and a door, he found the mayor, well-groomed and well dressed in a matching, tight-fitting blue jacket and trousers with a long white, red, and green sash wrapped around his waist. The thirty-year-old mayor served customers and stood next to his very attractive raven-haired sister—a young woman barely twenty years old, if that, equally well dressed in a beige riding jacket and green ankle-length skirt with a white sash wrapped around her waist. Both siblings wore leather boots that distinguished them from the poorly dressed villagers. Moving about behind a small counter in front of shelves stocked with food products, they seemed to own a thriving business, as their customers sought sacks of corn and flour and an occasional slab of fatback. Canned products were available, although few villagers could afford to pay their price. Some poverty-stricken patrons traded freshly laid eggs and freshly made tortillas for beans and flour.

Bolingbrook's impressive stature and unique outfit—red vest over a black shirt and two mother-of-pearl-handled revolvers—startled the brother and sister. Removing his wide, floppy hat, the outlaw flashed his warmest smile and extended a heartfelt greeting in hesitant Spanish: "*Buenos dias,* Señor and Señorita Ramirez." He knew he could never fulfill the description of "ladies' man," but nonetheless saw he provoked an animalistic curiosity in the young woman, Reza.

"You may address me as 'Señora,' as I am a married woman," the sister corrected.

Bolingbrook dipped his head in a gesture of apology. "Allow me to introduce myself. I am Francis Baker." He explained, "My boys and I just herded cattle to Villahermosa and need some rest and recreation. I want to rent your village for two weeks and am willing to pay two hundred Yankee dollars for the opportunity. My men will patronize the cantina and the brothel on the outskirts of town. For those privileges, I will give an extra two hundred dollars to be split between the two establishments." The payroll robber's offer was extravagant, given that a silver Yankee dollar equaled ninety pesos. He felt confident his offer would be accepted.

Ramirez once recovered from his initial shock at Bolingbrook's flamboyant appearance and lavish offer, seemed overjoyed. He and his sister conversed in Spanish, of which Bolingbrook picked up enough words to understand the gist of the exchange. Ramón Ramirez convinced his sister, who was initially opposed to having *norte americanos* in their midst, by stating, "Two hundred US dollars would buy every member of the village, children and infants included, three months' supply of food or enough money for a family to buy a goat or pig. Two hundred more Yankee dollars circulating in our village will guarantee a decent life for this year." He added, "We been blessed with a godsend that cannot be refused, because no offer like it will appear again." Even as skeptical as she felt, Reza gave in to her older brother's argument.

"We agreed to your offer, señor, if you give us your word, you or your men will inflict no violence on our people, and that our young ones will be left unmolested."

"We are in agreement, Señor Ramirez."

Bolingbrook satisfied the arrangement would buy him two weeks' safe haven, warned his men not to cause trouble with the locals, ignoring the warning, his six followers liquored up in the short time he spent with the Ramirez brother and sister. Bolingbrook rarely drank more than one beer at any opportunity. Even as thirsty as he felt, he denied himself a beer, choosing instead to find a room and a bath and then one of the attractive young women occupying the village—he felt he would rather seduce an innocent young woman than pay for a prostitute thrashing atop a bed soiled by grimy customers. His original plan called for him to travel deeper into the Mexican interior and split up the shares of the navy payroll, with him taking the lion's share. He would then buy a *rancho*, settle down and live like a Mexican oligarch. All this would have be possible if not for the obsessed fanatic Summerfield, who burned down five of his gang members' home places, plus his own in Kansas, and then trading their relatives to the Apache, in addition to killing the Benson kid and shooting down his dad. He surmised that Summerfield asked for no bounty from the Apache for the horses and whites he gave them because he attempted to recover the Cardwell girls that he and his men traded away to the Apache. He could not live with himself if he did not pursue Summerfield and kill him in the manner in which the man shot down his dad while his mom looked on. He saw the irony that his dad's death echoed the shootout he forced upon Claude Cardwell, but this irony could not mitigate the rage he felt toward Summerfield.

Bolingbrook realized he faced a most formidable foe in the ex-army scout and Plains Indian fighter, a Union soldier who fought loathsome Johnny Rebs precisely like he did as a young man. This Summerfield once eked out a living on the same desolate Kansas plains he and his parents survived on. An unnatural similarity existed in their makeup, and he wondered if he, a notorious gunslinger, could display the same kind of bravado as Summerfield, who now waited in Las Vegas to face seven expert gunmen, knowing the odds were heavily against him—a foolhardy undertaking. He concluded that Summerfield possessed no fear. Now, circumstances demanded that he, probably the most wanted man in the Southwest, risk capture in United States territory to kill the fanatic who stalked him and his men. If his men died in the pursuit of Summerfield's death, it would be a boon to him, because there would be less payroll to share.

His mind tossed about the knowledge that Winston Williams recruited a motley group of petty crooks and murderers, training them to be bank and stagecoach robbers. As a Rebel officer, Williams enlisted fellow Rebels Bradford, Bryce Benson, and Wade Alsop. Having ridden with the gang before he pushed Williams out, he knew the carrot-topped Brad Benson to be a gambler, a whiskey drinker, and a killer of drunken cowboys and prospectors he taunted into barroom brawls. Benson's much mellower brother, the equally red-haired, older Bryce, once burglarized a showgirl's hotel room and was caught red-handed, subsequently serving three years in a Santa Fe prison. Once out of prison, he and his brother took up with a whore who doped clients, allowing the brothers to rob them and on occasion murder them. Another rebel Bolingbrook couldn't accept was Wade Alsop, bad in the blood, a pickpocket and throat slitter dedicated to emptying men's pockets before he joined Williams.

Charles Miller became a well-known petty thief, a waylayer of drunks in alleys, and a backstabber when displeased at a perceived offense against his person. The fancy dresser Ben Apple never stooped to such lowlife endeavors except for rape, which he thought a man's right; he always fancied himself a gunslinger who couldn't be killed. Bolingbrook thought him half-crazy, a dangerous and unpredictable man.

If Summerfield knew Apple perpetrated the torture inflicted upon his daughter when she refused to pleasure him in the manner he desired, his attention would first be drawn to that psychopath. Apple strung up his daughter to a dead tree in that desolate canyon in the Oklahoma Territory and sliced her body with his knife. But it was the gringo hater and treacherous killer Justo Trujillo who gutted Summerfield's daughter for the pleasure of seeing a white woman suffer a lingering death. Bolingbrook watched Summerfield's daughter's torture and subsequent gutting from a distance and did nothing to stop it. He disliked Mexicans and savages as much as he disliked Rebels, and both bad bloodlines resided in Trujillo.

*

Four days passed without incident since Bolingbrook's gang entered Sonoyta de la Rio. But trouble's ugly head would not remain submerged in a tiny village where drunken killers roamed

187

and thought themselves superior to the brown-skinned Mexican peasants.

Reza Ramirez Zenata's nineteen-year-old husband, Juan Peña Zenata, as handsome as his wife was beautiful, decided he would not be denied his right to frequent the village cantina because a bunch of *gringos* occupied it. Like most teenagers, he felt invincible, and more so because he was one of the more privileged villagers since he married the sister of the wealthy man who became mayor of his village. Zenata came from a well-to-do ranching family in Sonora, his father and Ramón Ramirez arranged the marriage to Reza when he turned fifteen. Therefore, superiority coated his demeanor as he entered the cantina, a dark and musty rectangular room choked with cigar smoke and with only one small window admitting light. To demonstrate his manhood to the two *gringos* standing at the bar, he ordered a beer and a shot of tequila, exactly the combination they were drinking. Two Bolingbrook gang members—Charles Miller, relieved from guarding the payroll, and Brad Benson—eyed the young Mexican maliciously. They examined his store-bought red velvet jacket and black metal-studded pants buttoned down over hand-tooled riding boots. The boy appeared to be Benson's size—the redheaded killer fingered the white lacy shirt, picturing himself in the youth's attire. Unperturbed by Benson's ill manner, Zenata pushed his large sombrero up on his forehead, fingered the ends of a still-growing mustache, and, showing perfectly white and well-formed teeth, smiled elfishly as he spoke:

"*Buenas tardes, señores.* Since we welcome you as guests in my village, allow me to buy you your next drink." In his peculiar and arrogant manner, he stressed the word 'we.'

"It's not in our nature to lower ourselves to accepting drinks from degenerate bean-eaters," Brad Benson, the killer of barroom drunks, replied, mindful disregarding Bolingbrook's not to stir up trouble with the locals.

"As you can see, señor, I carry no pistol." Despite this omission, a bowie knife resided on Zenata's left hip. "But I can address your insult with my fists if you dare to step into the street with me." Miller saw Benson's hand drop to his holstered revolver. Taking his cohort by the shoulder, he led him to a table away from the escalating confrontation; Benson, leery of Bolingbrook's retaliation if he tangled with the Mexican boy, did not resist.

Puzzled at the gringos' retreat but encouraged by his prowess, Zenata observed three other gringos engaged in a Yankee poker game, playing for U.S. dollars. The game provoked his curiosity. He just made two gringos back off and wondered how the three at the table would react to him joining them. He believed the three men—Ben Apple, Wade Alsop, and Justo Trujillo—to be cattle-driving gringos, and not the deadly murderers that they were. Showing the arrogance privileged Mexicans display, he walked to the card table and sat on the vacant chair. The action immediately provoked an angry response from Alsop, who jumped up and drew his pistol. Ben Apple smiled menacingly but laid a restraining hand on the pistol, lowering it to Alsop's holster. Trujillo, half-Mexican, showed no emotion, curious about the Mexican youth's intent.

Apple saw an opportunity to humble the high-born Mexican. "If you want to join this poker game, show us your money, Señor Fuzzy Face," he declared, aware that this youngster was a brother-in-law to Ramón Ramirez but, to him, still an inferior Mexican. His cohorts exhibited condescending smiles at Apple's insult. Juan Zenata, keeping his composure, placed two thousand pesos on the table, equaling approximately twenty-two U.S. dollars.

"That is Mexican money, not worth a piss in a pot," Alsop remarked.

"It will spend well enough in this village. Let him play," Trujillo ordered. Neither Alsop nor Apple desired a dispute with the dangerous half-breed, so they accepted the Mexican and his pesos.

"Now that we have four players, I say it's time for a fresh deck of cards." Alsop scooped up the playing cards from the table and replaced them with a deck he took from his shirt pocket. Neither of his cohorts objected, and the Mexican youth looked on, too inexperienced to recognize the *gringo's* ploy. They played Draw Poker, which mandated that Apple deal five cards to each player. Then the four men leaned back in their chairs or hunched over their cards, deciding strategies. After the opening bet of one silver dollar, Alsop and Trujillo folded their cards. They knew not to bet because Apple nicked the edges of the aces and those of the kings twice. The slick-dealing man believed he dealt the Mexican youth two kings and knew he dealt himself two aces, exchanging dealt cards for new ones. He took one card and the boy three. If the Mexican drew two kings to a Full House, Apple slid another ace from his sleeve into his playing hand, giving him three aces and two fours.

Apple and the Mexican youth raised the stakes until the young aristocrat bet all his pesos. Confident that he would take the pot, Apple displayed his three aces and two fours and waited for the Mexican to show his cards. Zenata grimaced, hesitating, as he stared at Apple's three aces. Triumphant, he laid his cards on the table, revealing two tens, two aces, and no kings. Apple, irked by an error caused by consuming too much liquor, saw that he mishandled the notched cards, dealing the Mexican aces instead of kings. Glaring at him, the teenager fingered the ace of hearts, a duplicate of the ace in Apple's hand.

"It seems, señor, that your deck of cards has five aces—one too many for a fair game. I will not call you a card cheater, merely a fast-fingered scoundrel who lost count of his aces. Your carelessness caused you to default this pot to me, so I will take the money and consider my honor upheld." The Mexican youth stood and then scooped the pesos and Yankee coins into his sombrero. Apple smiled a sort of agreement to the overconfident teenager. Curiosity over Apple's rare congeniality fixated his two cohorts, who observed, unsure what to expect from him. Juan Zenata turned to exit the cantina.

"Draw your weapon, you Mexican bastard," Apple screamed, and when the youth turned to him, he shot the boy. The brother-in-law to the mayor fell to the floor, his body briefly twitching before he expired. The dimly lit cantina fell silent except for the desert wind blowing through the village. It sent sand through cracks in the floorboards, leaving the dead Mexican's body covered in grime. Apple's cigar trailed smoke off the table's edge. The three American desperados resumed their card game, and Brad Benson and Charles Miller continued drinking beer and tequila after ordering the bartender to drag the mayor's young brother-in-law into the street.

*

Francis Bolingbrook sat in a hard-backed chair on the dirt sidewalk outside the run-down hotel, watching a girl smooth the sidewalk's dirt with a broom. In the distance behind her, he saw Ramón Ramirez approaching him, walking stiffly and angrily, followed by four men. Ramirez wore no weapons but clenched his hands into fists. His followers carried machetes, tools of their trade, as their weapons. Bolingbrook stood up to greet the group but mainly to get at his pistols if necessary. The sweeping girl, noting the mayor's unhappy demeanor, sought safety inside the hotel. Ramirez did not remove his sombrero, custom when greeting a generous patron such as Bolingbrook. Instead, he barked his words, a combination of broken English and fluent Spanish:

"Your sweet-selling gunman shot down *el marido de mi hermana* in cold blood and left his body in the street like that of a dead cur for my villagers to view. He cowardly gunned down my brother-in-law as he was leaving the cantina! Señor Baker, my young sister is now a widow with three little ones to care for, the oldest being four. Her bed has no *esposo* to fill it. The *ninos* have no papa to put food on their plates. I left my bereaved sister crying hysterically and pulling out her hair over the loss of her husband."

Hearing that Ben Apple gunned down a Mexican from a highly placed family became Bolingbrook's worst news. He decided not to reply before hearing Ramirez's accounting. "When a shooting takes place in our village—especially one that is highly questionable, as was the death of *el marido de mi hermana*, Juan Peña Zenata—our law dictates that the shooter stand trial and be judged by seven of our villagers. This judgment must take place tomorrow morning. If the sweet-smelling *americano* is found guilty, we must hang him."

Bolingbrook gritted his teeth. Ben Apple would not accord the description 'Sweet-smelling little man' to Apple; "*Goddamned troublemaking psychopath*" would be more apt, he thought. Apple, with one stupid move, shattered his sanctuary. Bolingbrook could not give a fiddler's damn about a dead Mexican, and under most circumstances, the easiest thing to do would be to shoot the Mexican mayor and the four peasants who stood behind him. But killing a Mexican official would provoke the Mexican authorities to pursue him, and consequently, his plans for settling in Mexico would be finished before they began.

The killer looked away and scrutinized the street to the right and left of him. The street traffic seemed routine, with villagers going about their business. Viewing nothing threatening, he took a calming breath, maintaining a friendly manner.

"Señor Ramirez, I am saddened and shocked to learn of your brother-in-law's death at the hands of one of my men. Unfortunately, my other men will not stand for Mexicanos judging their *compañero*, let alone hang him. Therefore, no village judgment can take place." Ramirez stiffened, shuffling his weight from foot to foot. Bolingbrook felt tight in his stomach, figuring that his village sanctuary would abruptly end if the Mexican stomped away to summon other villagers. Bolingbrook added some persuasion: "My men would rather die in a gun battle with your villagers than see one of their own hanged." He doubted one gang member would turn sideways if they hanged Apple. "My men may die in battle, but not before killing most of your villagers. That would be bad for all concerned. I propose this solution: I will personally express my sympathy to your beautiful sister and her little ones. The sweet-smelling man will also apologize to her and then present her with one thousand dollars in U.S. silver coins so that her children's mourning will be less painful. If this is agreeable to you and your sister, we can save much bloodshed in the village."

Ramirez realized a thousand Yankee dollars was a fortune, more than his sister would likely see in a lifetime. She and her children could live like royalty, with servants in a big house—they could even live on Avenida de la Gran in Mexico City. For himself, the huge cash offering would relieve him of the responsibility of feeding and caring for his sister's children. "I will speak to my sister to ask if your offer will soften her pain. And then I must speak to the village men to determine if your offer is as honorable as passing judgment on the sweet-smelling gunman."

*

The following Sunday morning, Bolingbrook met with his men next to the payroll wagon by the river. All seven men brought their horses to water; hobbled, the animals drank from an ankle-deep stream. A cooling breeze blowing off the water refreshed the air. The murderers' leader sat on the wagon's tailgate, his men sitting on saddles or crouching on their haunches. They smoked cigars and drank tequila straight from the bottle even at this early hour.

"If we don't pay off the Mexican widow that one trigger-happy dumb ass shot down, the villagers will rise against us. We can kill them all, but where would that leave us? Hunted down by the authorities here in Mexico and United States territory. We have no choice but to pay the widow one thousand U.S. dollars. Our choice is who will pay the widow—be it the seven of us sharing the amount equally, or shall Mister Ben Apple pay it because of his dumb-ass act?" Apple's five cohorts, lean and lanky grizzly men, more plainly dressed in range clothes than their shorter cohort in his new store-bought duds, reeking of cologne, to a man stated, "The dumb ass should pay the woman, as it is his mess to clean up."

"Go to hell, you bunch of selfish bastards. I ain't paying no thousand dollars." Apple drew his .38-caliber revolver. "We can have it out now, and I'll kill you all because a bullet has not been made to kill me," he declared, insane with rage facing the five outlaws who betrayed him. But losing his temper would be rash, causing the small killer to lose track of the gang's deadliest member—Bolingbrook. The long-haired and much larger Bolingbrook pressed his .45-caliber revolver against Apple's temple.

"This will be your best chance to find out whether or not my bullet can kill you. Holster your pistol, or I'll send you back to hell from whence you came." Bolingbrook pulled the hammer back on his six-inch-barreled weapon, which sounded a morbid, metallic click. Apple stood there for over a minute, fuming. Feeling Bolingbrook's heavy bore pressed against his head, he decided not to risk the chance he could be killed and holstered his weapon. "Now you have a choice, Ben Apple—you can pay these brown-skinned Mexicans, or I can let them hang you. Which will it be?"

"I will pay the bitch." Apple stomped off to groom his horse.

The men prepared to return to the village and go about their drinking, gambling, and whoring when the mayor emerged, this time wearing a holstered pistol over his fancy waist sash, a large-caliber and bulky weapon of Mexican manufacture. Ten armed villagers followed him; their weapons ranged from flintlock rifles to single-shot carbines, unwieldy shotguns, and outdated Confederate percussion revolvers showing disuse. The mayor's followers spread out behind him. Bolingbrook saw that he faced an explosive confrontation if he did not cool the situation.

"Señor Baker, my sister, although heartbroken, will accept remuneration for her husband shot down in cold blood. But the men and women of the village remain dissatisfied with your offer. They feel you insulted their honor by seeing a dead villager thrown so callously into the street and must be compensated. In my village, forty-two families, twenty-three widows, eleven older men, and five orphans are cared for by our most holy father, the priest who speaks God's word at the Church of the Merciful Virgin Mother. You and your men must pay twenty Yankee dollars to each of them, including our priest, a total of two hundred and fifty villagers."

"I'm surprised you forgot to include your burros, goats, and pigs," Bolingbrook responded. He figured that the mayor's demand totaled five thousand dollars. He looked to the unpredictable psychopath, Apple, and saw that he also calculated the amount. *It seems*, he thought, *Stupidity surrounds me, first Apple's and now the mayor's.*

"We are prepared to apprehend your man for trial if the village's demand cannot be satisfied." Bolingbrook's men stirred, fingering the restraining throngs on their pistols, their eyes locked on the armed Mexican peasants. Showing no emotion but feeling turmoil in his gut, Bolingbrook thought *this must be the worst time to demand so much money, as the gang were liquored up, heavily armed, and outraged by the Mexican's demand.*

Bolingbrook counted the navy payroll, and the amount fell far short of the hundred thousand dollars he hoped to take; the cash in the wagon bed totaled only sixty-three thousand dollars. Split seven ways, that amount totaled approximately nine thousand dollars for each man. But Bolingbrook figured to take a thousand from each of the six men, giving him fifteen thousand and leaving them eight thousand each.

Apple was not stupid—a thousand to the widow and five thousand to the villagers would leave him with only two thousand dollars, far short of the gain the others realized. Bolingbrook stood up from the wagon's tailgate, intending to reason with Ramirez.

The armed peasants behind the mayor appeared stone-faced and stoic as if the situation seemed as routine as clearing a planting field of rocks. If Bolingbrook couldn't dissuade the mayor from his outrageous demand, he would have to shoot him. As far as the ten armed peasants, he doubted they could inflict much damage before he and his men shot them down. "Señor Ramirez, we are cattle drivers, not train robbers. Where are we to get that kind of money?"

"Your wagon, señor. I looked under the tarp when your man dozed. You have so much Yankee money that what the villagers ask for is. . . ." The mayor did not finish his argument because Ben Apple stepped from behind Bolingbrook's large frame and shot him through the forehead. The mayor collapsed against Bolingbrook, protecting him from Ramirez's followers, who opened fire from a short distance. At the same time, Bolingbrook's followers, much better armed and more accurate, opened fire; some crouched, some lay belly down. Under a blaze of bullets, the gunmen shot the peasants; ten bullet-ridden bodies in homespun shirts and pantaloons crumbled to the ground, coating it with blood.

Feeling the mayor collapse against his thighs, Bolingbrook kicked him onto the dirt. The mayor's head wound stained his boot, and he used the Mexican's fancy south-of-the-border blue jacket to wipe the blood from his boot. *What is done is done*, he thought, without so much as a grimace. His exercised men milled about the bodies, empty weapons in their hands. Except for Ramirez, the pickings from the dead turned out to be miserly; later, he knew, the men would draw cards to see who got the pesos, the silver pocket watch, and the fancy sash taken from Ramirez. There would be no gain in stripping Ramirez of his clothing because a hunted man in Mexico could not visit a general store.

Apple held a smoking mother-of-pearl-handled .45-caliber single-action Colt revolver; the two Bensons carried Henry Rimfire repeating .44-caliber rifles and Colt Frontier .45-caliber side arms hot to the touch; Alsop preferred a single-action Smith

& Wesson Schofield army revolver with a four-and-three-quarter-inch barrel and a deadly revolving-cylinder shotgun, and both barrels now seeped sulfuric smoke. Miller reloaded his Remington .44-caliber single-action revolver and maneuverable Sharps carbine rifle. Trujillo, preferring the lighter-weight Remington .38-caliber pistol, pushed the still-smoking weapon into his holster; he also wiped a bowie knife's blade clean of blood, having retrieved it from the chest of a peasant twenty feet from where he stood. The deadliest killer shot only two villagers; the other outgunned peasants fell before he could kill more. The professional killers fired seventy to a hundred bullets during rifle and shotgun blasts. The peasants fired forty inaccurate rounds at most; some weapons jammed, and more than a few cartridges failed to ignite.

Bolingbrook, as quick a thinker as a fast draw, swallowed his exasperation at their sanctuary being so stupidly interrupted. When his men saddled their horses, mounted, and Miller sat behind the reins of the mules hitched to the wagon loaded with the stolen payroll, he rallied them. "Events did not turn out as expected, so we must make the most of a bad situation. Any thought of a good life in Mexico is lost. We will split up and make our way to Canada, a cold land but one with few lawmen, and where they won't give a damn about dead Mexicans." He figured the Mounties would give more than a damn about dead the U.S. Navy and Marine personnel and any dead Canadian who rode the payroll train, but now was not the time to mention it; he would deal with that problem when he faced it. "Canada is far away, and traveling alone will be the smartest way. But before we begin that journey, I want to remind you that a three-fingered rabid wolf named John Henry Summerfield cools his heels, waiting for us to show our faces in Las Vegas, New Mexico Territory. Let us not disappoint him. I remind you, Benson brothers, that this three-fingered killer burned your family home, shot the livestock, threatened to hang your dad, and left your sister, her baby, and her boychild for the Apache to mistreat. He undertook these dastardly deeds before he shot down your young brother, Benny, near that sinful sinkhole, Broad-Butt Betty's brothel."

Outrage scraped the redheaded brothers, who felt thwarted in their attempts kill the demon Bolingbrook described. "And you, Wade Alsop, he gave your four sisters to the Apache to rape and bear savage hellcats.

"You, Charles Miller, must remember that he also burned down your home place and sold off the horses your parents worked a lifetime to own." Miller and Alsop exchanged hateful glares, reaffirming a mutual thirst to kill Summerfield.

"And you, Ben Apple, your home place and family fared no better. Rumors state your tiny son has been brainwashed into thinking he is a wild heathen warrior, son to an Apache chief and lost forever to being white." Apple half smiled, indicating that killing the man who terrorized his family would be a pleasure.

"You, Justo Trujillo—your parents, wife, and lame daughter, terrorized by Summerfield as they were, suffered great humiliation. Are you a man to accept such injury to your honor, or will you seek revenge?" The Mexican/Comanche blood mix appeared stoic, but his cohorts knew his emotionless expression covered a cold-blooded determination to shoot down Summerfield.

"This Summerfield burned my home place, shot my old dad, his hands crippled with arthritis, and left my gray-haired mom alone and half-crazy with grief. I would rather die in the streets of Las Vegas than flee to Canada without killing Summerfield. I say we ride now and kill this three-fingered rabid bastard who harmed our families and then make our way to Canada." Bolingbrook, a gruff and burly man with a voice roused by pent-up malice filled with a hot outrage. He saw that they, wild on adrenaline after killing eleven Mexicans, would ignore the risk of capture in New Mexico Territory to wreak revenge.

Bolingbrook reasoned that it would be necessary to cut his losses and neutralize the villagers before they learned of the mayor's death—once armed, they would pursue him and the stolen navy payroll. Accordingly, he and his men dynamited the church during Sunday Mass, killing most adult males in the village. Bolingbrook figured the dead women and children were no more than collateral damage. He and his men left Mexico before the *federales* picked up their trail.

The stolen navy payroll presented a problem for Bolingbrook, planning as he did to kill Summerfield in Las Vegas: He could not trust one of the gang members to guard it because, as devious as they were, the guard would likely flee with it. A string of abandoned mines existed in the foothills northeast of Las Vegas that no longer produced gold. Finding no other choice, the gang leader allowed his followers to witness him hide the navy payroll fifty yards back in a deserted, crudely cut-out tunnel. Whoever survived the shootout with Summerfield would race back to collect the money; he figured that someone would be him.

*

After stabling his horse and mule at a horse ranch a few miles out of Las Vegas, John Henry used the better part of his dwindling funds to rent a second-floor room at El Porvenir Hotel. The room he chose overlooked the Gallinas River Bridge, a seventy-five-foot-long iron structure with wood planking placed underfoot to accommodate traffic; the bridge existed as the main entrance to Las Vegas, emptying onto Bridge Street, which fed into the town plaza. John Henry surveyed the plaza with the infamous hanging windmill situated dead center in a seventy-five by forty-yard neatly-maintained dirt expanse; a perimeter white picket fence distinguished the plaza. The Atchison, Topeka, and Santa Fe railroad tracks ran parallel to the plaza's southern boundary, exiting west from the depot and heading toward Santa Fe.

The windmill, a thirty-foot, three-tiered wood-frame structure, pumped water to a nearby public drinking fountain of impressive stone construction for the town's residents and the businesses flanking the plaza's northern, eastern, and western sides. The windmill displayed three tiers—the bottom tier buit

199

twenty-five feet wide by eighteen feet deep; the second tier fifteen feet by nine feet deep; and the upper tier, holding the windmill, ten feet by seven feet deep. Maintenance ladders were staggered across the three levels to gain access to the windmill at the top.
Past public hangings, as near as John Henry could tell, took place on the second level, where a hangman's noose left by town officials dangled in the wind—a warning to would-be criminals.

On the plaza's northern end, the main business section, split by Bridge Street leading into it, a string of eateries and haberdashery shops stood. The shops specialized in hats, dresses, leather goods, and various merchandise in popular demand. The coral-colored Plaza Hotel reigned as the grandest building on the plaza, a five-story structure displaying oversized windows and balconies overlooking the expanse below. Appearing second in dominance over the plaza, the Nuestra Señora de la Dolores Catholic Church held sway at one end, the bells in its double belfries tolling hourly for the town.

Hinderstrandt's Gunsmith Shop, Goldman's Saddle Shop, and a general store named Gross and Blackwell maintained occupancy between the hotel and the church. All the shops and eateries rimming the Plaza shared a wall, forming a frontage that blocked entrance and exit except for the main entrance off Bridge Street. Las Vegas politicians constructed wooded sidewalks under a long veranda to shield patrons from the hot New Mexico sun and unpredictable incumbent weather.

During the second day's surveillance, John Henry noticed heavily armed men trickling one at a time over the bridge, their horses' hooves sounding a click-clack on the wood planking. They drifted into the plaza, where he imagined they took rooms at one of the four hotels. The infamous Francis Bolingbrook delayed his appearance, although when a redheaded rider, evidently one of the Benson brothers, rode underneath his window, he knew the time arrived to seek revenge. His first challenge would be to subdue the hard-nosed sheriff and his deputies. Checking his nondescript appearance in a foggy mirror, he saw a middle-aged man weathered by a precarious life, wearing a worn suit jacket and creaseless wool trousers that covered the tops of his scuffed boots. Summerfield suffered considerably since leaving Los Angeles on the road to this day. Now his quest would soon end. He thought the image looking back at him might be the last reflection he would ever observe. He collected his weapons—the single-action Colt .45, the Winchester rifle, muzzle down and slung over his right shoulder, the small Philadel Derringer secured in his suit jacket's right breast pocket, and the charred although recently cleaned Navy Colt percussion pistol tucked into the back of his trousers. He clutched the double-barreled shotgun in his right hand. The gunman sawed the barrels to half size during this last wait, anticipating a short-range confrontation. Waiting until the lunch hour arrived, he placed a beaten, flat crown cowboy's wide brim range hat on his head and crossed Bridge Street diagonally to the sheriff's office. He ignored the foot traffic. As expected, the young deputy Tommy McGrath, who befriended him numerous times, sat on the porch cradling a shotgun.

Alarmed at the heavily armed man approaching him, the young deputy sprang to his feet but did not level the shotgun at John Henry. His voice surged with alarm as he warned, "I can't let you go in there armed as you are. The sheriff will shoot you at first sight."

"Deputy, we both know the sheriff is a mean, cowardly bastard whose comeuppance is long overdue. You did me good service in the past, and I'm obliged to do you no harm. Do not put me in a position where I must subdue you. You best leave your post and find some business out of town." To give force to his words, John Henry brought his shotgun to the level of the deputy's chest. The young man appeared psychologically injured at being threatened by the man he admired and considered a friend.

"You aim to kill the sheriff?"

"No, I mean to lock him up for a spell until I can attend to some long overdue business."

John Henry waited until the young deputy rode his horse toward the Gallinas River Bridge that would take him out of town. Then he crept through the empty sheriff's office, housing two vacant cells, to the rear door leading to the backyard and cracked open the door. The spacious yard sprawled directly behind the Plaza Hotel. Exactly as on the first visit he paid to the sheriff, John Henry noted that the man's two smartly dressed deputies pitched horseshoes in the yard. This time they placed their holstered pistols on pegs attached to the outside wall of the sheriff's office. The white-haired, mustachioed sheriff who pistol-whipped him out of meanness and later cold-cocked him from behind in the service of the Pinkerton agents now cut away at a sizable beefsteak on a small table before him, careful not to spill the contents of a beer glass filled to the rim. Lunchtime seemed a ritual for the compact, middle-aged man and his deputies. Duplicating John Henry's first visit, the law officer's derby hat tilted back over the thinning hair through which the man spent considerable time perfecting a part down the middle. His gold watch dangled on a gold chain over his vest. The large Smith & Wesson single-action pistol he favored hung from his shoulder holster.

John Henry waited until the Sheriff seated ten feet away, dabbed a napkin at his white, oversized mustache and then leaned back in his chair to light his customary cigar. The deputies, wearing identical pencil mustaches, noted the sheriff's action, believing they still owned another fifteen minutes to pitch horseshoes and concentrated on their game. When the sheriff struck the match to light his cigar, John Henry kicked open the rear door to the office and moved upon the man who inflicted so much injury on him. With one hand holding a cigar and the other a lit match, John Henry's quick appearance hand-tied the sheriff.

"You lousy bastard. I will see you swinging from the windmill within the hour!" the sheriff cried.

With one quick maneuver, John Henry swung the butt of his shotgun diagonally upward, smacking the sheriff across the jaw. The two-hundred-pound man collapsed across the table, scattering his steak plate, beer glass, and eating utensils over the yard. The commotion immediately caught the deputies' attention, but John Henry stood between them and their pistols, his short-barreled shotgun trained on them.

"I have no qualms about blowing your legs out from under you should you try something stupid." The deputies, dropping their defiant bearing, took his warning to heart and raised their hands, indicating they would not confront him. John Henry removed the unconscious sheriff's Smith & Wesson pistol from his shoulder holster, unloaded it, and ordered one deputy to toss it down the outhouse waste hole.

He then ordered them to drag the sheriff into an empty jail cell and, once there, shackled him hand and foot. Next, John Henry ordered them to gag the sheriff with his bandanna and tie it off with a strip of rawhide he carried. He then ordered one deputy to shackle and gag the other. Finally, he shackled and gagged the second deputy. The sheriff regained consciousness; he could not speak, and his face looked like it would explode. Remembering the unnecessary concussion he received from the malicious sheriff in the Las Vegas stable, he struck the man in the mouth with the barrel of the shotgun, a slashing downward blow. He watched blood soak the man's gag. He then locked the cell and the office's front and rear entrance doors.

John Henry stood on the front porch of the sheriff's office, deciding upon his next move. He figured that the entire Bolingbrook gang rode into town by this time. Once they found lodging and attended to their horses, the three-fingered gunslinger surmised they would first search for him in the saloons; fully-armed, deadly killers that they were, they would not disarm over an insignificant sheriff's posted law forbidding firearms. He also figured Bolingbrook too savvy to allow his men to collect in one spot; he would separate them to find the man who terrorized their families. Directly across Bridge Street and before the plaza entrance, the Buffalo Hall Saloon, the largest and most active among a string of saloons lining First Street, did a bristling business judging by the din of voices and piano music caressing the street.

Good fortune stayed with John Henry as he noticed two armed men enter the Buffalo Hall Saloon. Always reluctant to enter a saloon where trouble lay thick and heavy, especially now he that carried two shoulder arms and pistols, he, depending upon a nondescript appearance, took a seat at a far-end table near a thirty-foot-long bar. No one inside the bar gave him as much as a second glance. He cradled his shotgun under the table, focusing on a small man standing at the bar.

The Buffalo Hall Saloon conducted business grandiosely: A dapper man wearing a bow tie and sleeve garters dexterously fingered a piano filling the expanse with music near a dark stage at the far end of the large room. Two saloon women hummed "Carve Dat Possum" while prancing to the minstrel music. The room showed twenty tables and sets of chairs, along with three poker tables and a roulette table. It being the noon hour, patrons delayed filling the saloon; three men sat at one poker table, and a half dozen wagered at the roulette table. Saloon women—some attractive, some past attractiveness—were dressed provocatively, in low-cut tops and short-skirted dresses. Showing a lot of chest and leg, faces powdered, and lips colored red, they sat at empty tables or meandered around the barroom.

John Henry's eyes trained upon a small man, a mere five feet, three inches tall and reeking of cologne, who stood alone at one end of the bar, sipping a flat beer, seemingly more interested in what he mumbled to himself than getting drunk. He wore a lavender rosebud-embroidered silk vest over a mint green ruffled shirt. Looking every bit the dandy, he pushed his gray derby hat back over slicked-down, sandy hair. John Henry thought the small man would be laughable if not for his frosty, bottomless blue eyes, so protruding that they seemed about to pop out of his head, and the old bullet wounds scarring his left cheek and wrist. A mother-of-pearl-handled, silver-plated Colt revolver hung off his right hip;

a Remington breech-loading rifle lay on the bar next to the man's beer. John Henry thought the prominent display of weapons in a town forbidding guns kept patrons away from the man's end of the bar.

The other gunman gambled at the roulette table. He appeared much older than the small gunman at the bar; blond hair over a high wrinkled forehead stood out as his most prominent feature. The outlaw wore an eastern style short-brimmed hat and loose necktie over a dusty, striped shirt. A battered face held deep, narrow-set, red-rimmed eyes and a nose bent to the left side. John Henry guessed him to be Charles Miller, the waylayer of drunks.

Ben Apple focused on two prostitutes at the bar's far end while delivering his mumbled soliloquy. Simmering with an acidic mixture of guilt and vengeance, and knowing that, outnumbered as he found himself, he must act quickly. John Henry carried his shotgun in one hand, moving to the bar unnoticed, and placed both his shoulder pistols on the counter's surface. He moved within three feet of the small man's back and listened to his rambling:

"These are hard-looking whores I am staring at, and I'm telling you, I don't want any lovin' demanding pay. A good-looking, sweet-smelling, and fancy-dressed fellow like me prefers a woman who can be seduced by my charm. I'm mindful that some highbred females resist a gent. Such resistance gives a fellow a hot rush, and I welcome it. Sometimes women resist too much, which sets a determined fellow like me on a different path.

"After they absorb a few belly punches, a fellow must force his affection upon them. Usually, that will complete the task at hand. But sometimes, it doesn't, as in the case of that tall, shapely schoolmarm-looking woman up in the Oklahoma Territory. We snatched her, as delicious-looking as a fresh-baked cherry pie, along with her sister outside of Las Vegas. Belly punches failed to gain her cooperation, so I sliced her up so she would come around to pleasure me the way I like. Why would she not cooperate like her sister, who, after a few belt lashings across her bare behind, pleasured those of us who sought her company; this puzzles me."

John Henry now felt certain this little man, Ben Apple, strung up his daughter, Jane, and after torturing her, left her naked, degraded, and dangling from the limb of a gnarled mesquite tree in a barren land, starved for water. If he could salvage anything out of the savage death his daughter suffered, he felt she kept her respect right to her end, refusing to submit to those filthy beasts.

"I wasn't but half finished with her when that maniac half breed slit her from her privates to her titties. The brown bastard laughed while her guts poured out on the ground. Trujillo did me wrong that day." Apple's words stunned John Henry; he did not suspect the half-breed Trujillo, whose family he spared, so brutally gutted his daughter. The two heathens left Jane to rot or, worse yet, be eaten piecemeal by wild animals. He recalled the coyotes he witnessed stripping flesh from his daughter's legs, the vultures circling overhead, waiting to feast on what human flesh remained on that infamous Black Mesa.

Simmering in a caustic stew of guilt and revenge, John Henry withdrew the single shot Philadel Derringer with his left hand. Pulling the weapon's hammer back under his coat to muffle the metallic sound, he placed it within a few inches of the fancy-dressed killer's head and spoke: "Ben Apple?"

The small psychopath turned at the sound of his name, and John Henry squeezed the trigger. The large .43-caliber bullet blew a hole in Apple's forehead. The man who thought he could not be killed fell onto the bar and then slid onto the sawdust-covered floor, dead in a heartbeat's flicker. John Henry realized he murdered someone. Heretofore, he never ever thought of shooting a defenseless man, even someone as vile as Ben Apple, and no time existed for self-recrimination.

John Henry quickly turned his attention to Apple's armed cohort standing by the roulette table. The man stared at Apple, crumbed on the floor, his blood soaking the barroom's sawdust. John Henry dropped the derringer; once fired, it was useless until reloaded. The older gunman, distracted by the spinning roulette wheel, carelessly held a glass of beer in his gun hand. Instead of dropping the glass, he took extra seconds to place it on the roulette table. He then drew his pistol, but in his haste, it caught the hem of his coat, causing his response to come late. John Henry's left hand pulled the single-action Colt .45 from the holster across his chest, gripping the weapon with his three-fingered right hand, and aimed.

It took him an extra second to pull back the Colt's hammer with his left hand, but still, he fired his pistol sooner than the opposing gunman. Just as John Henry riddled the shirt while practicing his aim in that Colorado ravine a long time back, his two shots struck the outlaw's chest, dropping Charles Miller in a bloody heap over the roulette table, the tiny metal ball still bouncing across spinning numbers. In a saloon where patrons and their panderers seldom heard gunfire, they froze long enough for the gunfighter to grab his shotgun and rifle and run onto Bridge Street, knowing the gunfire would alert Bolingbrook and his gang.

Curious saloon patrons rushed onto First and Bridge Streets and watched him approach the plaza. A passenger-heavy streetcar resembling a train's passenger car, pulled by a mule, traveled down Bridge Street into the plaza. John Henry hopped aboard the slow-moving transport crossing under the plaza arch, disembarking among passengers at the public drinking fountain where a thirsty crowd gathered. He hoped to blend in until he could assess his situation. Benevolence's ex-husband killed two of the murderers; five remained. In a few minutes, he spotted two redheaded men mounted on horses coming from the direction of the railroad tracks, galloping across the plaza toward the Buffalo Hall Saloon. Thirty feet behind and spurring his gelding at an angle to the Benson brothers, a big man with icy-blue eyes and pigtails bouncing from the sides of his head under a black range hat caught John Henry's eye. He wore a red vest over a black shirt; the rider could be none other than Francis Bolingbrook.

John Henry stepped away from the water fountain and focused on the redheaded Benson brothers, who were almost upon him. The older Bryce Benson, his hat hanging by a loop around the neck and bouncing on his back, rode five feet ahead of his brother, pistol in hand. The man received a recent haircut and shave. He, neatly dressed in a dark suit, could be a ladies' man instead of a killer with his clean-cut, well-proportioned features. His younger brother, opposite in appearance, allowed his curly hair to grow wild; his freckled baby face, pug nose, and round cheeks seemed incongruent with the faces of the murderous gang he rode with. He slapped his horse's flank with his pistol-bearing hand.

John Henry cocked the hammers on the shotgun and moved toward the men, making his appearance noticeable. As it did in Fort Hays City ten years ago, circumstance favored him: The horses could be spooked, and their riders' pistol aim hampered by unsteady mounts. When the Benson horses galloped to within twenty paces, John Henry fired a shotgun load at their legs. Their legs hit by scattering pellets, both animals reared and jerked about, the riders struggling to control them. John Henry moved closer and fired his shotgun point-blank into Bryce Benson before he could get off a shot. Blood quickly stained Benson's neat jacket and white shirt. The older brother slumped in the saddle, and his injured horse galloped from the fray.

Brad Benson fired two wild shots and tried to turn his panic-stricken horse, but the horse remained uncontrollable, bucking one way and another, with the surviving brother barely staying in the saddle. The unmanageable horse gave John Henry time to insert a new shotgun shell into an empty chamber. He chased the redheaded murderer and, on the run, fired his shotgun. The twelve-gauge blast hit the spooked horse in the rear haunches and Benson in the small of his back. Bolingbrook drew his pistol but could not get off a clean shot because Benson's wounded horse rampaged before him. Benson's horse, crazy with pain, bucked and reared several times until it collided with Bolingbrook's horse. Both horses tangled and crashed onto the dirt, causing Benson and his horse to roll over Bolingbrook. In a tangle and thrashing about, one horse's hoof struck the gang leader in the temple, stunning him. Brad Benson lay unconscious a few feet away.

Dropping his empty shotgun and taking advantage of his good fortune, John Henry swung his rifle into a firing position and rushed forward to kill Bolingbrook. He came within a few feet of the felled man, close enough to see that his menacing cobalt eyes were dazed. The instigator of his daughter's death gazed at the rifle trained on him, believing he reached his end. John Henry levered a bullet into the rifle's chamber and held the muzzle over the dazed man, but before he could squeeze the trigger, a salvo of gunfire struck the dirt around him, close enough to indicate he could be killed at any second; one round struck the rifle's magazine, splintering the wood stock, blowing it from his hands, stinging his left hand so severely his fingers went numb. The lucky shot destroyed the rifle. Trujillo and Alsop dismounted from their horses and fired their handguns while moving toward him, less than twenty yards distant.

Believing bullets would soon riddle him, John Henry lunged for Bolingbrook's spooked horse and grabbed the head harness. Using the large animal as a shield, he hung on the creature's neck, directing it to gallop toward the Plaza Hotel, where he hoped to find shelter from the barrage of bullets. The toes of his boots plowed into the plaza dirt, and he barely held on to the horse dragging him.

The frightened animal dragged him ninety feet to the hotel's veranda. The bullets of both outlaws tore into the large gelding, slowing it to a stumbling walk. As if oblivious to the hail of bullets, spectators occupied the wooden sidewalk in front of the hotel; John Henry forced the horse to stagger past them. Even as close to death as he felt himself to be, their fascinated faces intrigued him. Death as a spectacle remained a nineteenth-century priority, enough so for spectators to risk their lives. The exhausted horse dropped dead in front of a saddle shop. John Henry's attackers now moved to the plaza drinking fountain, inserting cartridges into their weapons' chambers and firing upon him as fast as their hands could move. Their gunfire scattered drinking-fountain visitors in both directions toward the plaza fence. John

Henry returned fire from behind the dead horse, slowing his pursuers long enough for him to run past the saddle shop and into Hinderstrandt's Gunsmith Shop. He viewed his pursuers: Wade Alsop wore a leather vest over a collarless shirt buttoned to the neck and a full cartridge belt buckled over leather chaps. A mustache and short chin beard under emotionless eyes decorated his face. Trujillo allowed his hair to grow long and unruly so that it furled from under a low-crowned, flat Mexican hat. Like in the portrait John Henry viewed hanging on the wall of the Trujillo shanty, the Mexican dressed immaculately in a vaquero outfit, this time decorating his midriff with a red and green sash tied off in a bow on his left side. To his surprise, the outgunned Summerfield also saw a wounded Brad Benson hobbling behind the two killers, dragging his left leg and firing his pistol continuously. A hail of bullets riddled the gun shop as John Henry's pursuers crept forward and took shelter on both sides of its doorway.

Being a gunfighter, John Henry wanted his holster to rest comfortably on his hip, so he carried only six pistol reloads in his holster belt. He now saw only three loaded cartridges remained in his pistol. He dropped the empty two-barrel shotgun in the street. The Navy Colt he once handled so expertly felt clumsy in his hand, as he only practiced firing it twice since leaving Los Angeles.

He needed ammunition to hold off the three men firing into the gun shop. He ordered the gun shop owner, Hinderstrandt, to give him a box of .45-caliber cartridges, but the extremely tall man, standing somewhere around six feet, four inches in height and carrying a belly the size of a pot stove, became too frightened to comply. He cried out, "If those bullets hit my sacks of gunpowder, we both will be blown into the kingdom to come!"

"Gunpowder?" John Henry repeated, crouched behind the display counter. He gazed at a half dozen bowling-ball-sized canvas sacks tied off with heavy string under the counter. "Fire up the kerosene lantern and hand it to me," he ordered Hinderstrandt, who appeared close to bawling, his big jowly face a mask of fear. John Henry placed his pistol against the man's balding head.

Hinderstrandt did as told and then desperately tried to find shelter away from the remaining gunpowder sacks.

The three gang members pursuing John Henry, the killer of their cohorts, adopted a strategy where they alternated shots, one firing at him from the doorway while the others reloaded so that a constant barrage of bullets kept him pinned down. Immediately after Alsop emptied his pistol, John Henry untied the strings of two sacks of gunpowder and tossed them into the doorway; the contents spilled out onto the wooden sidewalk.

He tossed the lit kerosene lamp, hearing it shatter on the floor. The fiery kerosene ignited the gunpowder, the flames crawling up Alsop's trousers and then consuming his torso. The man, a flaming pillar, stumbled onto the plaza and rolled about in the dirt, trying to extinguish the flames. Witnessing their cohort becoming a human torch and hearing his flesh crackling confounded Trujillo and Benson, allowing John Henry to stand and shoot the suffering man. His act snapped the killers from their fixation on their flaming cohort, and they once again opened fire on John Henry.

The long-legged, potbellied gun store owner resembling a freakish cricket crawled out the back door, heading toward the rear of the Plaza Hotel, where he hoped sanity still existed. Seeing an escape route for himself, John Henry tossed another sack of gunpowder into the flames. The subsequent flare-up consumed the front of the gun shop, and he used the blazing effect to grab a box of cartridges before he escaped through the backdoor. John Henry reminded himself that only the wounded Benson brother and the mixed-blood Trujillo pursued him—four men were dead, and three remained, the most dangerous one injured. He needed to somehow get past the two gunmen and back to the plaza to kill the stunned Bolingbrook. Pausing at the gun shop's rear door, he assessed whether or not the fire stopped the gunmen. A volley of gunfire smacked into the back door's casement, close enough to his head that wood fragments stung his face; the gunfire indicated the two men were hot on his heels.

John Henry, less fearing for his life than desiring to get at Bolingbrook, ran down an alley barely large enough to accommodate a horse. He pulled at locked shop doors, anxious to find an entrance to the plaza; he saw no unlocked doors until he reached the church. Exhausted after clinging to the horse and running a good sixty feet down the alley, he grasped his knees and gasped for oxygen, not knowing if the outlaws followed him. Breathing heavily, he found the side service door to the church unlocked, and once inside the rear hallway, found the priest's sacristy and kitchen doors open and both areas deserted; everyone inside the church rushed onto the plaza to view the gunfight. Returning to the plaza where he last saw the unconscious outlaw leader and killing him obsessed John Henry, but he realized the injured Brad Benson and dangerous Justo Trujillo stood between him and Bolingbrook.

The breathless man approached the nave of the Nuestra Señora de la Dolores church from the priest's rear entrance. He saw the nave soared three stories high; light poured in through color-stained glass windows, depicting Jesus Christ and his disciples in various biblical scenarios. The Señora of past years spent a fortune on the church's construction—an oak-beam ceiling held crystal chandeliers sparkling in multicolored reflections from the glass windows. However, no worshiping benches covered the nave's marble floor. The gunfighter figured worshipers must stand or kneel on cold marble to enter heaven above. The Señora, it seemed to John Henry, purchased her way to heaven.

He crept upon the ceremonial platform rising three feet above the worshipers' floor. He scanned the altar with its red velvet, lavish gold-trimmed armchair placed prominently off to one side and a heavy solid wood lectern from which priests gave sermons. Finally, his eyes settled on the marble altar table, covered by a white tablecloth touching the floor; a tall, thick candle, a wine decanter, a chalice, and a Roman missal were ceremoniously placed on the altar for the priest to perform his ceremony. John Henry hid under the altar tablecloth that draped to the floor. He saw the heavy double wooden entrance doors at the front of the church were left open by the priest and his staff in their rush to witness the gunfire.

The two men pursuing him anticipated his escape route and now crouched before the church's stone front, too far for an accurate pistol shot. John Henry watched Trujillo retreat from the open doors, spectators scattering from his path. The killer's curious action indicated to the hidden man that the gunman would not fire his weapons upon or inside a Catholic church; he guessed the man who gutted his daughter did not want to endanger his soul by shooting up the house of God. The wounded Brad Benson, however, possessed no such scruples. He stepped through the open doors, moved past the holy-water font, and took shelter behind one of the eight large marble pillars supporting the ornate ceiling. The milk-white marble pillars were positioned two abreast across the forty-foot width of the nave and four in line along the eighty-foot depth of the cavernous room. Benson moved from pillar to pillar until he came within a few feet of the priest's pulpit. Once positioned behind the heavy wood lectern, he, on a hunch, fired two shots into the tablecloth dangling from the altar table.

The pistol fire barely missed John Henry, who crouched under the far side of the alter table. He fired three return shots at the wood lectern Benson crouched behind, splintering wood and blowing marble chips across the floor. He emptied his Colt pistol and then reached in his pocket for the box of cartridges to reload. Immediately upon taking a cartridge, he realized that in his haste to escape the gun shop riddled with gunfire, he grabbed the wrong box of cartridges; the shells were .44 caliber and made for a rifle, too small in diameter and too long to fit in the chamber of his .45-caliber pistol. He holstered the useless pistol, grabbed the Navy Colt tucked under his belt, and strapped it to his three-fingered right hand with a strip of rawhide he carried.

He flattened his body, prone, under the marble altar while the redheaded murderer shot the tablecloth to pieces, destroying candle, wine decanter, chalice, and missal, and then confidently began reloading his pistol. John Henry rolled out from under the table, across the dais and down three steps onto the marble floor. He fingered the six-and-a-half-inch barrel of the Navy Colt pistol that survived the fire intended to bake his brains in Mexico. Although aesthetically streamlined, compared to the newer Colt revolver, it felt clumsy in his hand. The weapon took five percussion caps that ignited gunpowder behind lead .36-caliber balls and cotton pads tamped into the cylinders. Because the weapon demanded a time-consuming effort to reload, John Henry carried no reloads.

Benson fired a volley of gunshots in his direction, but the bullets were errant, destroying the red velvet gold-trimmed chair. Sheltered by the three-foot-high dais rising above the nave floor, John Henry raised his decades-old pistol and fired a ball at Benson's exposed body. His shot went delinquent, hitting the man in the heel of his foot. Benson yelped in pain. And then, for some unlikely reason, he crawled back to the closest pillar. John Henry fired a second shot at him, and again the bullet struck low, hitting the marble floor and sending chips into Benson's face. The retreating man slumped into a sitting position behind the first pillar in his path, his extended legs exposed.

John Henry possessed only three loaded chambers in the revolver strapped to his hand and did not want to spend them wounding his attacker's legs. Benson did not move, so he counted off what he thought to be three minutes. Benson still did not move his legs. Keeping his pistol trained on the outlaw, John Henry crawled to get a better look at him. When he moved to where he could view the motionless man, Summerfield saw that Benson held his pistol in his lap but seemed unable or unwilling to use it. John Henry noticed that his foot bled and his face trickled blood from the marble chips embedded there, but these wounds failed to hinder a ruthless man like Benson.

"The buckshot you back-shot me with caused my legs to crumble under me. My spine has lost feeling, and my arms are wobbly. I believe you put me a step away from my grave.

Summerfield, it does not suit me to lie here and feel life drain from me, so I ask you to put a bullet through my heart."

John Henry took Benson's pistol from his motionless hand. "I don't think you're worth a bullet, but then again, I cannot risk you will recover from your wounds." The younger Benson took part in destroying the Cardwell ranch and probably raped Jane and her half-sister. John Henry felt no compassion for him. He placed Benson's revolver over his heart and squeezed the trigger—five men dead, and two left to be killed.

He found the cartridges in Benson's Colt Frontier .45 pistol spent. John Henry quickly checked the dead man's gun belt for additional cartridges. The leather ringlets were empty, so he tossed the useless pistol by the corpse. The gunfighter noted he and Benson destroyed the church's ceremonial altar. But he gave the destruction no second thought because the church stood as a Catholic worshipping place, and if he pursued a religion, it would not be Catholic.

John Henry crept from pillar to pillar until he reached the church's open entrance doors. He could not spot Trujillo. After a few minutes wait, the veteran gunslinger chanced rolling out onto the wooden sidewalk, prepared to be shot at. He lay exposed for a time that seemed an eternity; no gunfire followed his movement. He guessed Trujillo, mindful that he killed five of his cohorts within the last hour, wanted no part of him. He assumed the Mexican/Comanche decided to seek out Bolingbrook rather than face a proficient killer alone; he could have felt that only Bolingbrook could handle his gun handling. The Mexican fled on foot, leaving his horse, saddle, and empty rifle scabbard. Trujillo carried his seldom-used rifle with him. John Henry mounted Trujillo's horse and rode about the plaza searching for the south-of-the-border killer. He did not know Trujillo, unable to find Bolingbrook at the spot where he lay injured, became spooked. He first thought to run away but, being too proud to run, fled to the only shelter he felt suitable: the top landing of the windmill.

John Henry saw Bryce Benson's corpse lying by a distant fence and guessed that his horse dislodged its dead rider and jumped the fence, probably chasing his brother's wounded horse, for it, also disappeared. Desperate for ammunition, the gunman rode to where Benson's body lay and discovered that his rifle and gun belt were missing.

A crowd formed around Alsop's smoldering corpse by the burning gun shop. John Henry saw that the town's fire brigade stopped at the plaza's entrance, leery of becoming exposed to the running gunfight. John Henry rode to the edge of the crowd watching the gun shop burn, his appearance scattering them, but not before he overheard the town people wondering why the sheriff failed to make an appearance after they called to him to halt the violence overwhelming the plaza. John Henry expected someone would eventually free the Sheriff from his locked cell, so time became a third enemy.

He checked Bolingbrook's dead horse for weapons and ammunition, but looters stripped the saddle, saddlebags, reins, and harness from the horse. Turning his attention to where he dropped his shotgun at the plaza entrance, he saw it also picked up. He next studied where he last saw Bolingbrook fall to the ground. Only a patch of disturbed dirt remained where Benson and his horse rolled over Bolingbrook; the gang leader must have picked himself up and retrieved the shoulder arm and ammunition off the older Benson's dead body. Pieces of John Henry's shattered Winchester rifle stuck in the dirt, but souvenir hunters picked up the stock and barrel. The pistol Bryce Benson dropped also disappeared, probably picked up by a spectator. A large crowd gathered at the plaza entrance, some climbing the two-story arch for a better view of the shootout, preventing John Henry from retracing his steps to the Buffalo Hall Saloon and collect Apple and Miller's weapons.

The information he collected on Bolingbrook informed John Henry that the gunfighter would never desist from trying to kill him. Before he could root out the gang leader, he must eliminate the other surviving marauder. Except for the crowds gathered by the plaza entrance and the burning gun shop, the vast dirt expanse rimmed by a white picket fence appeared empty. He saw that the fire brigade, pressured by a hysterical Hinderstrandt, began to form a water-bucket line from the drinking fountain to his burning shop. A good chance loomed that the entire gun shop would explode, but that became the least of his concerns.

John Henry studied the windmill and could see something amiss. Dismounting and using Trujillo's horse as a shield, he approached the windmill. Summerfield saw someone removed the ladders leading to the windmill's top, so it followed that Trujillo climbed to the top to take shelter, taking the ladders with him. John Henry in a quandary about how to get at the half-breed outlaw with only three loaded cylinders in the Navy Colt strapped to his three-fingered hand. Taking shelter behind Trujillo's horse, the pursuer noticed the gunman did not take his saddlebags. Searching the saddlebags for a firearm, he saw that Trujillo carried two sticks of dynamite wrapped in a shirt; a roll of fuse and a pocket-sized case of stogies accompanied the dynamite, but no extra pistol.

John Henry fired a round, hitting the windmill blade, to verify that the killer hid underneath. A return rifle shot struck the horse in the head, collapsing him and exposing the attacker below. Trujillo then peppered the horse with rifle fire, trying to kill the exposed man. The heavy rifle fire prompted John Henry to roll under the windmill's lower platform. Down to his last two pistol loads, he saw no alternative but to set off a charge of dynamite to drive his prey from his refuge. He realized that such an explosion might bring the vigilantes—every frontier town organized vigilantes, and Las Vegas was no exception. He set the fuse in a dynamite stick and lit one of Trujillo's stogies. John Henry then took shelter behind an eight-by-eight-inch vertical post at the far end of the windmill platform, fired the fuse, and tossed the dynamite stick as far as he could pass the platform's far end. The blast violently rocked all three platforms, shaking the windmill where Trujillo sought refuge on top.

Shouting at the top of his voice, he warned, "That is just a taste of what is in store for you, Justo Trujillo." He pulled himself up onto the lower platform. "You can't see me because I am right under you. Remember the hangman's noose town officials left hanging to warn people like you and me not to stir up trouble? I am now tightening that noose around the stick of dynamite you left in your saddlebags, which I intend to elevate and position directly under you so that it will blow you into bloody patches. Suppose the explosion did not separate your head from your body. In that case, you will certainly fall into a bonfire of destroyed timbers and die the agonizing death you witnessed Alsop suffer." In truth, John Henry did not intent to destroy the windmill, as he planned a particular death for the killer who gutted his daughter. "You climb down out of there, and I will see you die a more humane death."

"You mean to give me a bullet in the gut," the trapped man called back in surprisingly well-spoken English. John Henry heard no panic in Trujillo's voice.

"I mean to give you a chance."

"And what would that be?"

"Leave all your weapons behind except for your pistol or the knife you are so handy with, and then climb down, and we can go at each other. You don't have much time to mull over a decision because town vigilantes are probably gathering as I speak, and you know what they do to our kind. There will be no executioner to check our weight against the length of the hangman's rope. Slow strangulation or our heads pulled off, will be our fate." His last words took effect, and John Henry saw a ladder drop down to the windmill's middle platform. Trujillo, his gun in hand, trained it on what he could see of the platform below. When the Mexican/Comanche began his descent to the lower platform, his stalker saw that his knife still hung in the scabbard over the neat bow of his red and green sash.

"I will shoot you right here if you don't discard one of your weapons. If you recall, my condition called for only one weapon."

"How do I know you won't shoot me before I have a chance to face off with you?"

"The only choice you have is to choose your weapon. I could shoot you right here and now if I thought so." Trujillo pointed his pistol skyward until he descended the ladder and faced John Henry. Seeing his south-of-the-border, fancy-dressed foe's pistol pointed at the sky, the avenger waited until he tossed the pistol to the plaza dirt below. The description Damsel Dunbar gave John Henry in the Sangre de Cristo mountain range months back held true: Trujillo, being a less-than-deadly pistol shot, preferred to kill with his knife, a skill in which he saw no equals.

"I see you strapped your pistol to your hand. It seems only fair, señor, that I hold my knife at my side like you position your weapon."

John Henry nodded his assent and waited until the man held the knife at his side. "Count off to three; on that last number, do your best."

"*Uno, dos . . .*" Trujillo, moving before finishing the full count, quickly fingered the bowie knife blade. Holding the unwieldy Navy Colt, John Henry knew the Mexican killer would be quicker, so he anticipated his move and lunged to his left side, ramming into a pillar. The thrown blade penetrated his upper left thigh opposite his groin, severing three inches of skin and muscle but leaving his leg functional. He did not shoot the devious killer, having another death in mind for him. Sensing he was a dead man, Trujillo stood frozen upon the platform.

The pain in John Henry's upper stayed bearable, although he could see blood drenching his trousers. He pulled a strip of leather from his coat pocket and ordered the Mexican to tie a tourniquet to his wounded leg. He held the pistol to the man's head while he performed the task. Because of his lunge to the side, the blade embedded into his leg at an angle; the wound looked non-life threatening. Tapping his prisoner's head with the pistol to remind him not to try anything underhanded, John Henry, taking a big chance, told him to pull the knife blade from his flesh.

The withdrawal felt intentionally jerky and slow and brought tears to his eyes, but John Henry's perseverance prevailed. Relieving Trujillo of the knife, he ordered the unarmed man to undo his gun belt and sash and turn around so that his back faced him. The revenge seeker tied a strip of rawhide to the killer's left wrist and another to his right. He then knotted the rawhides' loose ends, tightly binding both wrists. Taking the long, colorful sash that fancy-dressed Mexicans preferred to wrap two or three times around their waist and let dangle off their side to their boot tops, tying one end in the form of a noose to Trujillo's neck and the other end he tossed over the upper beam of the windmill's second level, especially nailed in place for the town's infamous hangings.

Not having enough sash left to tie off the end to the windmill frame, he wrapped the loose end around his left wrist three times and gripped the sash tightly with his hand. He pushed the man who gutted his daughter to the edge of the windmill platform and shoved him over it. The man jerked violently, dropping three feet off the ground, pulling John Henry upright by his left arm. It took all his strength, his arm feeling like it would be pulled from its socket as he held onto the loose end while the man thrashed about, legs kicking at space.

"I hope there is a hell for degenerates like you." John Henry gave the killer a suitable epitaph.

Hanging never became a pleasant sight: a victim's face turned crimson, and his eyes bulged. Frontier hanging materialized in slow strangulation, heinous in execution. John Henry rationalized that enough justification existed to avenge his daughter's appalling death. Five minutes later, when John Henry's left arm felt paralyzed, and his wounded leg throbbed like the beasts of hell chewed on it, the hung man stopped writhing, his tongue protruding from his mouth, his trousers' front soiled. Feeling no time existed for delighting in revenge, John Henry released the sash, and Trujillo's body fell onto the dirt below. He dropped, exhausted, against a vertical post supporting the windmill's upper platform. Taking the time to catch his breath, he thought, *Six dead, one left to kill.*

Descending to the ground, he picked up Trujillo's .38-caliber pistol from the dirt, intending to use it. But before John Henry could undo the leather throng lashing the Colt pistol to his hand and holster Trujillo's pistol, he saw Bolingbrook facing him, pistol in hand; the killer wore no hat, and the left side of his bloody head swelled profusely from the horse's kick. The big man appeared to stagger when he walked. "You won't need the half-breed's pistol, seeing that you already have one lashed to your hand. Be good enough to return Trujillo's pistol to his corpse." Bolingbrook smiled, knowing he possessed the upper hand.

Francis Bolingbrook found himself temporarily incapacitated by the horse's freak kick to the head. When he regained consciousness, he found shelter inside a café named Rosaria's on the plaza's west side, but not before he noted Alsop's charred carcass, the burning gun shop, and Bryce Benson's body lying by the white picket fence. Apple and Miller were nowhere to be seen, so he concluded Summerfield dispatched them to hell. He then staggered to Benson, lying dead at the plaza periphery, and removed his weapons, figuring Summerfield would come close to exhausting his ammunition. From where he sat inside the café before an untouched plate of refried beans and corn tortillas, he kept a watch on the plaza. Gun in hand, the killer warned Rosaria and her half dozen patrons not to leave the café. He watched Trujillo hide at the top of the windmill and Summerfield pursuing him. Injured, his head throbbing, Bolingbrook decided to let the Mexican face Summerfield alone, not risking his person until it became necessary.

"I will hand it to you, Summerfield. There aren't many men alive who could put six gunmen in their graves to get at me. You did me a favor killing off those men, as there will be no payroll money sharing."

"That is assuming you live to collect the money. I aim to collect your life for what you did to the Cardwell Ranch and my daughter."

"You don't stand a chance facing me in a shootout. But I will give you a chance. Hold your pistol at your side, as my mother wrote me you did when you gunned down my dad." Bolingbrook's usually cold and calculating demeanor stiffened after he spoke; John Henry realized the only affection this killer possessed centered on his parents. "All you have to do is raise and cock your pistol," Bolingbrook suggested, confident of his superiority. John Henry dropped his pistol to his side, using whatever advantage given him. Bolingbrook holstered his pistol. "You and I have faced death so often that death lost its chill." John Henry heard Bolingbrook theorize before he raised his pistol and pulled back the hammer. Knowing the pistol fired low, he aimed six inches over Bolingbrook's head. But he never got a chance to squeeze the trigger because two bullets hit him dead center in the chest. The pain shooting through his body was excruciating. He tried to raise his arms to steady the pistol and get off a shot, only his arms would not move.

The realization the murderer bested him, shooting him dead, became a black shawl enveloping his being. He never imagined death would drain him so thoroughly. He dropped to his knees, helpless to stop the ruthless gunfighter from slowly inching forward and placing the muzzle of his Colt .45 against his forehead. He scanned the plaza, surreal to him as it appeared without motion; the tardy vigilantes, if any, would not save him. Yet John Henry felt no remorse, knowing he did his best to seek revenge.

What the revenge seeker visualized but could not witness at this moment saw his ex-wife's two young, Navajo-dressed granddaughters holding hands and walking across the New Mexico plains toward Santa Fe, freed by the Apache.

He heard a firearm's explosion and dropped face-down in the dirt, wondering why he felt no impact. Through blurry eyes, he saw Francis Bolingbrook plunged face down beside him. The killer lay motionless.

"Mister Summerfield, you and that outlaw gang sure made a mess of our plaza." The dying man saw the knee of Tommy McGrath pressed into the dirt before the deputy rolled him to his side. The boyish deputy sheriff held a shotgun, smoke seeping from the barrel. "I know you told me to stay away, but as I told you, curiosity always gets the best of me. And you sure gave me a lot to be curious about today."

John Henry tried to speak, but his tongue felt leaden. Knowing death would take him at any second, he mustered his body's last scrap of resolve and spat out words as if they were poison. "Prop . . . me up . . . over this mon . . . monster's body." Tommy raised him over Bolingbrook, holding him upright on lifeless legs. Summerfield saw Tommy shot-gunned the murderer from close range, blowing a sizable hole through his back.

It took him some seconds to articulate his last words. The road to his shootout turned out successful, so he spoke to the dead man with uncanny clarity:

"Benevolence Summerfield sends her regards."

THE END

www.ingramcontent.com/pod-product-compliance
Lightning Source LLC
Chambersburg PA
CBHW050356030726
47503CB00006B/1884